"You think

"Yes."

A tiny smirk of satisfaction curled her kissable lips. The slender rim of fur at her wrists taunted him and made him remember all the naughty things he'd imagined doing with her over the years.

Yes, he'd had a few dreams.

Ridge averted his gaze. Though he felt sure the sex had been great, it was only a hopeful memory. He was a fool to believe it had been anything more than a stupid night of drunken folly. Damn that vodka!

He tugged out the papers from his coat and waved them before her.

"Okay, okay!" She paced before the counter, twirling a finger around the end of a luscious twist of black hair. "You want something from me? First you have to give something to me."

He had not expected this visit to be easy.

"What's your price, witch?"

Books by Michele Hauf

MICHELE HAUF

has been writing romance, action-adventure and fantasy stories for more than twenty years. Her first published novel was *Dark Rapture*. France, musketeers, vampires and faeries populate her stories. And if she followed the adage "write what you know," all her stories would have snow in them. Fortunately, she steps beyond her comfort zone and writes about countries she has never visited and creatures she has never seen.

Michele can be found on Facebook and Twitter and michelehauf.com. You can also write to Michele at: P.O. Box 23, Anoka, MN 55303.

THE WEREWOLF'S WIFE

MICHELE HAUF

TORONTO NEW YORK LONDON
AMSTERDAM PARIS SYDNEY HAMBURG
STOCKHOLM ATHENS TOKYO MILAN MADRID
PRAGUE WARSAW BUDAPEST AUCKLAND

Recycling programs
for this product may
not exist in your area.

ISBN-13: 978-0-373-61880-4

THE WEREWOLF'S WIFE

Copyright © 2012 by Michele Hauf

Dear Reader,

I confess I display pictures on my computer monitor of my hero as I'm writing a story. Many times that hero will resemble a favorite actor. I like casting my stories that way, and it's helpful to have a visual as I'm writing. When I'm reading another author's story, I always cast the characters. It's a natural thing to do, and I suspect many of you do it, as well. I also know that not everyone imagines the character the same, and for that reason it's probably not wise to reveal who inspired my hero's physical looks, just in case you don't necessarily find that particular actor as sexy as I do.

Alas, I cannot resist with this book. Ridge Addison is one of my favorite heroes, both in physicality, rugged good looks and emotion. And staring at a picture of Jason Statham every day for the months I was working on this story made the job that much easier. ;-)

Who do you like to imagine your heroes and heroines to look like? Stop by my blog or Facebook page, and let me know!

Michele

This one is for all my Twitter followers.
You tweeple are swell.

Chapter 1

Ridge Addison swung an ax, chipping out wood at the base of a dead pine tree he wanted to lay flat for firewood. He and a friend had been working all afternoon under a steady snowfall, and dark was beginning to layer the sky. One last chop...

The pine tree creaked. The trunk split at the base and the thirty-foot tree toppled onto the frozen forest grounds outside the Northern pack's compound, situated thirty miles northeast of the Twin Cities.

Fellow pack member Jason Crews called, "Timber!" but they were the only two on the private land.

The men stood back, waiting for stray branches to finish falling from nearby trees before Jason picked up the chain saw in preparation to remove the branches.

"Wait," Ridge said.

Jason paused, chain saw held at the ready.

Ridge glanced up. The half-moon was already bright. The sky was gray and a perfect snow fell. Perfect meaning huge, downy flakes fell straight down, slowly, softly, without a sound.

"Just wanted to enjoy it a moment," he said, and then signaled Jason to go for it.

The chain saw snarled. The man ripped into the tree, making quick work and leaving a cleanly stripped trunk. This winter they were clearing out the dead and diseased trees. Ridge had plans to start a horse logging company that traveled from forest to forest, wherever the landowners wanted them to go, clearing and cutting back deadwood. A necessary service to keep forests healthy while also respecting nature. It was ecological and used no trucks, only horsepower, thereby leaving the forest in as good condition as when they arrived.

Jason shut off the chain saw and slapped the sawdust from his overalls. Both men had been bundled against the shrill January cold this morning, but over the course of the day they'd stripped to half overalls, flannel shirts and heavy-duty leather gloves as they'd worked up a good sweat.

Ridge was considering making Jason pack scion, since they were sorely in need of structure after the recent events that saw him become the new pack leader.

But then, how to structure a measly four wolves? The pack was dwindling daily. When yet another wolf packed his things and told Ridge he was leaving for a rival pack because he needed family, well, there was no argument to be served to match the werewolf's innate and instinctual need for family.

He and Jason had surveyed the land before Christmas—the pack owned well over five hundred acres, seventy percent of it forested land. As the new pack principal, Ridge was responsible for the pack and for the members' living quarters, if they chose to live at the compound. Only two remained at the compound—he and Jason. The other two lived with their families in the Twin Cities suburbs.

A pitiful pack, but he wasn't willing to give up on building a healthy group that considered itself family.

"I say we call it a day," Ridge suggested, and received a confirming nod from Jason.

They packed the equipment into cases and duffels. Tomorrow, they'd lead out the draft horse from the stable, hook chains to the fallen tree and drag it back to the compound for cutting into lumber and firewood. More backbreaking labor that felt so good to complete.

"It feels good out here," he said, drawing in the brisk, sawdust-scented air. "Most of the bad karma doesn't cling to this sight."

Because the bad karma had all been invoked elsewhere.

Ridge had been principal almost four months. Formerly, he'd been the right-hand man to his predecessor, principal Masterson, though not the second-in-command scion. That was until Amandus Masterson had been revealed to be plotting against a local vampire tribe, Nava, in an attempt to stage an all-out war. There had been casualties, Masterson being one of them—at Ridge's talons.

He did not for one moment regret killing the pack leader. It had to be done. At the time, all of the pack had stood beside him, showing their accord. Ridge had been protecting the leader's daughter, Blu, and the vampire tribe leader, Creed Saint-Pierre. And he'd been defending all werewolves against the heinous label of vampire killers. The Northern pack had been involved in the blood sport—a wicked game that pitted blood-starved vampires against one another to the death—that had left a bloody mar upon their familial image.

He'd do the same again if necessary. Ridge was not a man to jump into the fray without cause, but rather thought through every move, and never regretted those moves. Ever. He stood for what he believed just. Let no man challenge him without due strength and strong morals.

Whipping a stone across the open field edging the forest, he winced as the scar along his torso tugged. He regretted nothing—except one incident over a decade ago that had left him with the scar. Funny how it was never the war and strife that wounded a man deeply, rather the emotional and feminine.

He never would figure out female emotions. Did any man have that figured out?

"So when you going to make yourself official?" Jason asked as they paused at the edge of a cornfield abutting the pack's property. Crisp brown stalks jutted up through the blanket of snow.

"Official?" Ridge hefted the heavy chain saw case over his shoulder. "I thought I already was. That little ceremony performed by Severo a couple weeks ago didn't do the trick?"

Severo was the lone werewolf on the Council, a group of paranormals who oversaw the paranormal nations. Their attempt to bring the werewolves and vampires to a peaceable understanding last year had worked to some degree. The wolves and vampires populating the United States maintained a tentative cease-fire. Mostly.

"What I mean is," Jason continued, "pack leaders generally have a wife and family. It sets a good example for the rest of the pack."

"Right." That made sense. "The rest of the pack."

"If you want the last few to stay, you have to step up, Addison. Family equals leadership. You seem like a family man to me."

"I am. I would love to have a family."

But the scar stretching along his abdomen reminded him family was impossible due to the medical malady the deep wound had caused.

"Then you need to find yourself a wife," Jason said. "Get her pregnant. A lot. And start to rebuild the pack by example."

Ridge smirked and closed his eyes to fluffy snow-flakes that fell from above the bare-branched tree canopy. He chuffed out a laugh and his breath fogged before him. "Actually, I think I already have one of those."

"What?"

He smirked at Jason's utter surprise. "She's a witch," he said, feeling his jaw tighten. And, man, did his scar itch to think about her. "A very bad bit of witch, at that."

"Seriously? You're married? You don't seem very happy about it. Why didn't you ever tell anyone?"

"Because it was one of those drunken Las Vegas affairs I want to forget. Not that I can." He eased a palm over his hip, where the scar stretched down from his stomach. It had been so close to damaging the family jewels, but not quite. Yet the internal damage it had caused was monumental.

"So you're married to a witch, but you haven't talked to her since Vegas?"

"Exactly. Twelve, thirteen years ago, or thereabouts."

"Huh. Do you foresee a reunion any time soon?"

"Not particularly. Like I said, she's one bad bit of witch."

"Well, you need to ditch her if you want to start a real family. Not too many women would take to you having a wife. No dates without a clean slate."

"You've got a point. S'pose a trip to the city is in order. I've been putting it off for years."

"That horrible?"

"There's not a nastier bit of magic in the States, I'm sure. Think you can go on the computer and get me information on how to obtain divorce papers? I don't want to get any closer to the wicked witch of the Midwest than I have to. If I can email the papers to her, all the better."

*Twelve or thirteen years earlier,
outskirts of Las Vegas*

Raging, high blue flames were visible behind the ramshackle brown barn set half a mile off the road. Ridge had pulled off the highway outside of Las Vegas, feeling the urge for a dash across the desert on this night following the full moon. A wise wolf never disregarded the call of the moon. But the run would have to wait. He smelled danger.

He raced across the barren dirt yard and through the

garbage piled behind the barn scattered with old car parts, tires and scrap iron.

A woman screamed, and his heart clenched. Had she been trapped by the flames?

Arriving before the blaze behind the barn, he surprised a tall man in blue jeans and no shirt, bleeding from the forehead and wielding nothing more than his hand in a direct gesture toward a stacked pile of wood. Shouting a strange word Ridge didn't recognize, the man flicked his hand and flames shot toward the pyre—*from his hand.*

A damned fire witch, Ridge guessed. Speaking a spell in Latin. He hadn't thought they were common. Witches feared fire; it was the one thing that could kill them.

The strange blue flames suddenly flared higher and then parted to reveal, in the center of the vast pyre, a woman. Tied to a pole. Screaming as the flames threatened and crept closer to lick at her pant legs.

Ridge's heart choked up to his throat. How could anyone be so cruel?

He didn't give the horror another thought. Reacting to the angry growl inside his gut that abhorred violence toward women, Ridge ran toward the fire witch who directed the flames, and leaped. Soaring through the air, he landed the hard rubber sole of his boot on the man's jaw. Impact sent the startled pyromaniac flailing to the ground.

Without thought for his own safety, Ridge lunged for the woman tied to the pole in the center of the blazing pyre. His body hit hers. Like lava, her form felt molten and too hot. Thin and trembling as she was, her struggles were futile. Flames chewed at his jeans, but he wore heavy leather biker boots so didn't fear getting burned.

The woman's screams choked into sobs. Leaping, he held her to his body and they tumbled over the flames and to the ground. She screamed again, as the impact couldn't have been easy, and now he rolled with her on the ground to put out any fire that may have ignited clothing.

He spat gravel and clambered away from the fire. Dragging the pole with the woman still tied to it away from the pyre, he hastily worked at the ropes about her hands and ankles and was relieved when she tried to help him. "You okay? What's up with that bit of nasty?"

She coughed and heaved, likely from smoke inhalation. "Get me out of here."

"You burned?"

"Don't…think so."

He lifted her in his arms, a frail, broken bird, and she melted against him. Her pale hair and clothing were as hot as her flesh, but all he saw on her were dirt smudges, no telltale burns or red welts.

Striding past the man on the ground, who had roused and was on all fours, Ridge kicked him squarely in the jaw, dropping him flat.

"You want me to take care of him permanently?" he asked the woman shivering in his arms.

"No, just…take me away from here. Anywhere. I…" Her lashes fluttered and her head bobbled, nearing a faint. "Goddess, I need a drink."

Ridge found a cheesy bar on the older part of the Las Vegas strip decorated in more pink and purple neon than most of the skeevy dives he'd passed. The woman downed a vodka straight in the time it took for him to return from the men's room. She allowed him to wipe off the soot blackening her face with a wet paper towel, and then ordered another round.

Two hours later they were both so drunk, Ridge kept thinking he should have gotten her name when she had been sober enough to recall it. But when the question reached the tip of his tongue, she tilted another drink down his throat, and the two laughed over their horrible adventure escaping the flames.

"I love you," she slurred. "You big, hunky man, you. You saved my life."

"I did." He laid his head on her shoulder and toyed with the reddish-blond hair that smelled smoky and a little like coconuts. Burnt coconuts, actually. "You're soft."

"You're sexy."

"You're the prettiest girl I've ever met," he said on a contented sigh.

"Sexiest guy, hands down."

"Let's get married."

"By Elvis!"

She lifted what may have been her tenth—or thirteenth—vodka to salute, and Ridge swept his arm to clink his glass against hers, but missed, his arm swinging around and splashing the trio of strippers sitting in the next booth.

Half an hour later, Elvis pronounced Mr. and Mrs. Addison happily married. To the tune of Billy Idol's "White Wedding," the groom lifted his smoke-smudged bride into his arms and walked down the short red-carpeted aisle and right into the red-and-black-striped wall behind the electric organ.

As the couple tumbled about in a tangle of limbs and fits of giggles, Elvis—the rhinestone-spangled leisure suit version—bent over them and pointed out the cheap stained-glass window to the hotel across the street. "Because I'd hate to see either of you behind the wheel right now."

They saluted the King of Rock and staggered across the street. It took three tries to actually make it to the other side without ending up back at the Viva Las Vegas chapel.

Room 12 had probably seen some crazy things during the motel's sixty-year run, but this night it would see the weirdest.

Clothing was torn away. Laughter accompanied sensual moans and sudden giggles. They didn't kiss much. Too difficult to get the aim right with their blurry brains.

Ridge, while in his cups, couldn't stop touching his sexy new wife everywhere. Her skin felt softer than anything he'd known. Thank heavens, she hadn't been burned. Her hair, tangled and dirty, and smelling like a burnt coconut, appealed as no woman's ever had.

Despite his inebriation, something deep inside him growled in a knowing way. *Mine. Meant for me.*

He ignored the growl—to his detriment—and managed to find his way between her slender, smooth legs. Remarkably, his cock was hard, which only proved how much she turned him on, even two sheets to the wind. Her fingers grasping greedily at his thick, muscled arms, she let out a long, delicious moan as he fit himself inside her.

For one perfect moment, he grew sober and fell into the heavenly sanctuary of her body.

This is where you belong.

"Oh, Ridge," she moaned. He'd told her his name after Elvis had prompted him. What was hers? Something like Gail or Abby. "Yes!" Her body bucked beneath his, and he chased the climax that was so close to exploding in his loins.

That inner growl he had ignored? Well, now it turned into a real growl. He let out a low and wanting howl that vibrated in his bones. Even drunk, he knew this was Not A Good Thing.

Or rather, Just Plain Bad Timing.

Thrusting quickly, Ridge ignored the shift in his bones and the stretch of skin that prickled with fur. He was almost there. Just a few more thrusts…

Climax shuddered through his body—which was now halfway between man and beast.

He lost hold on the woman's narrow shoulders and his talons cut into the mattress. His shoulders stretched and the bones reshaped. Fur pushed through his pores. His torso lengthened. Paws slipped off the bed.

Bloodshot blue eyes flashed open and his pretty new wife gaped. That look was one hundred percent sober. Without pause, she scrambled onto her elbows, hauled up her leg and kicked Ridge's furred chest. He stumbled backward and off the creaky old bed, his paws slapping the wall.

He growled, revealing a maw of meat-tearing teeth.

"What the hell?" His wife huffed and gasped, clasping a hand to her bare and oh-so-gorgeous breasts. Then she angled those wicked blue eyes on him and pointed a finger. "Ignis!"

The rusted tin lamp on the nightstand flickered out. The electrical outlet, which was missing an outlet plate, sparked and smoked. The television shot out sparks from behind the tube, and the LED clock on the nightstand exploded in a stunning shower of white sparks.

Ridge's werewolf yowled as some kind of weird electricity hit him in the gut, burrowing deep through his skin and burning his very organs. All he could think was magic. He'd been struck by magic. The woman was a witch! Which went a long way in explaining why she'd been tied to a stake and surrounded by fire—the only way to kill a witch. She and the bastard flinging fire from his fingers were both witches. What had he interrupted?

The burn in his gut flared a sizzling path to his loins. The magic still cut through him. Ridge gripped his penis protectively. His muscles clenched and he let out a desperate howl that was abruptly cut off.

As his werewolf collapsed, his wolf-shaped head landing on the end of the bed, Ridge had one thought: werewolves should never mess with witches.

Chapter 2

Present, in Minneapolis

Abigail dusted the soccer ball on the floor next to the Powder Pro snowshoes, which sat next to the football and a tennis racket. This boy's room was classic, but it hadn't felt the thud of a basketball on its walls or heard loud rock music vibrate the artist's pens in the drawers for months.

Ryan was due back from Switzerland this evening. She wanted to put the finishing touches to the cleaning before leaving for the airport to pick him up. He'd been less than thrilled when she'd mentioned the Swiss prep school last spring, but since he'd arrived in the summer for admissions, she rarely got a phone call from him because he'd made so many friends, and "Mom, the skiing!"

A total boy, Ryan liked anything sporty, dirty and rough. Winter sports, especially. His hair had grown shaggy and he was wearing his jeans loose to reveal the waistband of his boxer shorts—a style she abhorred but "Mom, all the guys do it!" He'd yet to discover the mystical, wondrous attraction to girls, but she felt sure that was just around the corner, and actually looked forward to her son going girl crazy. Of course, no girl would be deserving of her boy.

He hadn't shown signs of developing magic yet, so she was thankful for that in ways she wasn't willing to admit to herself.

It wasn't common for male children of witches to be born with innate magic unless both his parents had mastered the same magics. With the combined genetic capabilities, then the possibility of gaining magic increased greatly, but as with most witches, they didn't come into their magic until puberty. Judging from her last phone conversation, as she'd kept a chuckle to herself to hear her son's voice crack and bellow, Ryan was toeing that change right now.

On the other hand, there was another warning sign she hoped would not rear up in her son's body. She actually prayed to a god she had never before worshipped that sign would never come to fruition.

And then sometimes she did wish it would show up. It would make Ryan's life more difficult, but it would appease her aching heart in ways she could never completely explain to her son.

Smoothing out the blue-and-black-striped bedspread, she eyed the box wrapped in sparkly red-and-green Christmas paper on the stand by the bed. They hadn't been able to share Christmas together, which they did celebrate, even though witches did not tend to observe the Christian holidays.

Ryan had never been bothered when other kids received gifts at the end of the year. He thought it materialistic, yet he didn't protest when she gave him one because any excuse to give a gift was always fun. He was going to flip when he opened the Nintendo game system. He'd wanted one for over a year, and though his birthday was in the spring, he deserved it for his straight-A report card.

Flipping off the lights in his room, Abigail strolled through the living room, patting Swell Cat on his big black head as she passed the pink velvet couch. He meowed a feline approval and stretched along the back of the couch, his tail curling tightly before it tucked along his plump body.

Life was about as perfect as a contented cat, she mused. Her reputation as one of the baddest witches in the States had taken a nosedive, but that was for the best considering she now had a son. Despite her fears over the years, nothing had come to harm her little family, thanks to the protection measures she had instituted. And she would remain vigilant on that front.

Wandering into her bedroom, she sorted through the dresses and tops in the walk-in closet without touching them. She stood in the center and with a flick of her finger, magically slid the hangers side to side. Citrus and clove tickled the air, wafting from the fresh orange balls she kept tucked here and there throughout the house. She stuck cloves into the orange peel and they lasted weeks, dispersing their fresh scent. It was a brutal eleven degrees below zero this fine January day, so she aimed for a sweater.

She'd come to Minnesota at the turn of the twentieth century. It had seemed a nice, quiet place after Europe, domestic and unassuming, yet hardy. Deeply grounded in their Scandinavian heritage, the people had been welcoming and had never suspected a witch had moved into their quaint Lake Harriet neighborhood.

She'd needed that anonymity. It was easy enough to get along when your neighbors didn't believe in all the silly nonsense mortal minds conjured when they thought the word *witch*. It was never accurate, and always involved the devil, black robes and dancing naked under the full moon. Ridiculous.

Well, the devil and robes part. There was nothing whatsoever wrong with dancing naked once in a while. Skyclad had been her preferred casual dress, until she'd become a mother.

And back then after her move, she'd been recruited to serve on the Witches' Greater Midwest Council, which had a base in Minneapolis, so living here had been a no-brainer. She no longer served on that council, made up exclusively of witches, but now instead served on *the* Council, which oversaw all the paranormal nations, except the sidhe.

Some days she wondered how long she could stick it out here in the Midwest, home of plaid shirts, gas-guzzling SUVs and tater tot hot dishes drenched in cream of mushroom soup. The bad girl inside her would never completely be put down. And Minnesota winters were enough to send her up a wall clambering for spring sunshine and fresh lilacs.

She was in the mood for Venice, perhaps even Mumbai. Someplace warm, and center of the city, tucked within the cosmopolitan and the haut couture. A place where, at the snap of a finger, she could buy fresh seafood and decadent five-star chocolate desserts. And that wasn't a magical finger snap. She wanted to go someplace where a man knew how to please a woman, and wouldn't stop until he got things right.

Wasn't easy getting dates when your tween-age inquisitive son always tagged along to the bookstores and coffee shops. She could conjure a love spell, but that was cheating. And besides, men under the influence of a spell were not true to themselves, and thus, could never be true to her, either.

Despite giving up on the need for a serious relationship over a decade ago, she did favor having a lover. No woman should be without a sexual partner for too long. And her attachment issues were improving, so really, she was ready. Bring on the sexy man with a foreign accent and a focused need to please her.

Slipping on a white cotton sweater over her pink camisole, she checked her side view in the mirror and winked. Soft pink rabbit fur rimmed the collar and sleeve hems. She loved the sensual brush of fur over her skin, though the sensory trill did remind her she was quite loverless at the moment. Guess it was time to go out and see what she could shovel up from the slim pickings. There were yet a few gems buried in the area's waist-high snow, she felt sure.

"You still got it, Abigail. Even after four and a half centuries."

One advantage to immortality was her never-aging appearance, and the wicked resistance to gaining weight no matter how many times she treated herself to triple chocolate cake. Go, immortality!

"Now to find a man who is strong enough to take on this witch…and her son."

Her smile dropped and she sighed. A man like that would truly be one in a million, but she was up for the hunt. So long as he didn't wear plaid, didn't mind she liked to play Mozart louder than Ryan played his heavy metal, liked to eat things such as foie gras and truffles, and oh yes, could please her in every way imaginable in the bedroom—and anywhere else the mood struck them.

Out in the kitchen, with a flick of her fingers, her purse and the Smart car keys floated into her grasp. She touched the garage doorknob, when the phone rang. Glancing over a shoulder to check the caller ID—because if it was anyone on the Council, she'd let it ring to message—she noted it was a foreign number.

"Switzerland?" She'd checked in with Ryan last night to make sure he was ready. "I wonder if the flight was delayed. Hello?"

A metallic click sounded, and then a voice, obviously altered because it sounded robotic, said, "Getting ready to pick up your son, Ms. Rowan?"

"Who is this?" She stared into the receiver, as if that would produce an image of the caller, but she had no such magic. "Tell me your name, or I'm hanging up right now."

"You hang up, your son will hate you for it."

"You're lying. What's going on?"

The voice buzzed metallically and Abigail heard someone crying in the background. That sound had *not* been mechanically altered.

"Ryan?" Her hands began to shake, and her heartbeats stuttered against her ribs. The scent of burning electronics pierced the air. She clenched the plastic receiver. "Ryan, is that you?"

"That was your son. A little jet lag, I'm sure, is the reason for the emotions. Now listen. I'll only say this once."

She nodded, her fingers growing white about the phone.

"Your son did get on the plane from Switzerland to Detroit this morning. We managed to get him an earlier flight, and notified his school and they were very cooperative getting him to the airport on time. One of my associates has picked him up at the Detroit airport, much to the little kicker's protests."

Ryan had struggled against his kidnappers? Abigail gasped and a mournful moan escaped. "Where is he?"

"He is in our custody in an undisclosed location somewhere in the United States. We are keeping him in protective custody, for his sake and yours."

"Protective? You've kidnapped him! Who are you?"

Her fingers clenched and she felt the heat burgeon in her palms until her fingertips turned red. The electrical outlet next to the oven began to glow.

"I can alleviate your concerns by telling you we are allied with the Light."

The Light was what the witches called themselves, though a few did practice dark magic. Witches had taken her son?

"I don't understand this. What do you want? Who are you? I can give you money."

"We don't want money, Ms. Rowan. And we don't want you running to the Council to tattle on us."

They knew about the Council? That confirmed the

caller must be from the paranormal nations. But it didn't confirm they were actually of the Light.

"Tell me what you want. I'll decide myself if it's something I should keep from the Council. You know I do sit on the Council, so in essence, they already know."

"You won't bring this to them if you want to see your son alive."

Abigail caught a gasp in her throat. She could barely hear over her pounding heart. Tears leaked from her eyes. She caught her hip against the kitchen counter and leaned against it for support. Sparks flashed from the outlet. She tucked her fingers under an arm to keep accidental magic from shooting out.

Her voice trembled when she said, "Go on."

"Listen carefully. Write down the name I am about to give you. If you don't find this vampire within forty-eight hours…well, then, we won't be able to protect your son."

"A vampire? What do witches want with a vampire?"

The pause on the line made her regret the outburst. Hell, she wanted answers. No one told her what to do. She told others what to do. But this was different. She had to do as they said, or at least make it appear as if she were playing along. Her son's life was on the line.

"What do witches usually do with vampires?" finally came the reply.

Once every century witches needed to consume a live, beating vampire heart to maintain their immortality. It was an odd request, since most witches had no problem obtaining a source, as the vampires were called.

"Can't you get your own source? My son is an innocent. There's no need to involve him—"

"As I've said, we are protecting him from forces beyond your control."

"Beyond my— You're speaking nonsense. I've protected him all his life."

"And look how easily we were able to apprehend him. Tut, tut, Ms. Rowan. Perhaps you need to review your protection procedures. Now, write down this address. We'll meet exactly forty-eight hours from now."

She scribbled down the address and the vampire's name on the notepad stuck to the refrigerator with a magnet. She recognized the location as north of the Twin Cities. "Let me speak to Ryan."

Click.

The drone of the disconnected receiver sliced through her heart. Abigail dropped it to the floor and followed by plunging to her knees and bowing her head into her hands.

Above her head, the electrical outlet exploded and the plastic cover shot across the room. Sparks showered the glass stove top but did not take to flame.

The only flames in the room were those inside Abigail's heart. Someone had taken her son. The bad witch she had once been raged to the surface and punched the cabinet, cracking the wood door in two.

Ridge rapped on the door to a Victorian house in the elite Lake Harriet neighborhood off Upton Avenue. A person had to be rich to live in one of these cozy and finely preserved houses a short walk from the lake where sailboats and personal watercraft dotted the water in the summer. He'd seen a kite-sailer skimming the frozen lake after he'd parked the pickup and got out. Crazy kids.

Despite the cottage look of the house and the quiet neighborhood, the area was too upscale for him. And the houses were packed together tighter than sardines in a tin. Made his skin prickle, and not in the good prickly way he was accustomed to. He preferred the country, with room to breathe in the fresh air and trees, lots and lots of trees.

The bright red front door swung open. A gorgeous blue-eyed witch dressed in sexy, body-hugging white took one look at him, chirped as if she'd seen a ghost, and slammed the door in his face.

At least she hadn't wielded the finger of pain at him. He counted himself lucky so far.

Ridge rapped again. "Abigail, we need to talk. And you know what about."

The glimpse of long dark hair curling over her shoulders, and those bright eyes, stirred an innate desire he'd thought he'd never feel for her again. She hadn't changed much, though she'd been a blonde when he'd seen her earlier this summer following the Creed wedding, and in Vegas, but women were always dying their hair for reasons beyond his comprehension. No matter, she looked…clearer than he recalled. And he knew why. He'd been sober since that crazy night in Vegas.

The door opened again and she stuck her head out. He caught the scent of coconuts and was instantly transported to that cheesy motel room amidst giggles and haphazard sex. "I don't have time for this, Ridge. I've an emergency."

The door slammed again, obliterating all images of that crazy night. For the better.

This time he leaned against the door, but as he thought to twist the fancy glass knob and walk right in, his manners—and his sense of self-preservation—reminded him he'd probably be safer on this side of the door. With a wince, he pondered how well the thin slab of wood would protect him against magic.

There wasn't much he feared. Vampires gave him no challenge. Faeries were amiable toward him. Demons just plain creeped him out. But a smart wolf never returned to a place—or person—of danger.

"Just a few minutes, please, Abigail?"

It was cold today, and no matter how many layers he wore, he still felt the wind tickle down his neck and ice over his shoulders. But he had to be here. Jason had said an actual signature was required. Email wouldn't cut it for a divorce.

"No, we don't need to talk," she called, opening the door a crack and gifting him with a flash of heat from inside. "It never happened. I've moved on. You've moved on. We're all good. Life goes on. Goodbye."

Ridge blocked the door with a fist. He pressed against the weight of the tiny witch trying her best to defeat his strength. "I happen to have a piece of paper that says it did happen."

"You what?"

"Signed by Elvis, even. It's a little wrinkled, but it's legal. Elvis was his middle name. The guy who married us was an actual ordained minister, can you believe that?"

"Well, tear it up!"

That would be the obvious action. But Jason had checked online and their nuptials had been recorded in the Clark County Marriage Bureau of Las Vegas. The receptionist, appropriately named Priscilla LisaMarie Jones, had signed as a witness. Richard Addison's marriage to Abigail Rowan was legal, whether or not he had the paper to prove it.

"Maybe I don't want to tear it up," he said, trying a new angle. It wouldn't serve his purpose to barge in and demand. And he didn't want to walk away with another scar. Kindness never hurt a man's position. "I did save your life."

"And I am very thankful for that," she said through the slightly opened door. He couldn't see her, but could feel her determination; she was putting all her weight against the door. Did she hate him so much she couldn't give him a few minutes? "Really, I am thankful for the rescue. I don't think I ever said it to you while sober."

"I don't need your thanks."

"But you need to keep me your wife? What's that about?"

"That is not what I want from you."

"Then tear the damn thing up and leave me alone."

"What if I want to convince you I'm worth a shot?" He winced. It was a means to get him inside, to talk rationally with her. He wasn't seriously considering keeping her as his wife. But he had to play the witch carefully.

And protect his balls against sudden blasts of magic.

"Please, Ridge, we don't even know one another. You know nothing about me."

"I know you like vodka."

"Used to like vodka. I haven't gone near a drop of that devil's brew since that night."

"That bad of a memory, eh?"

"Something like that."

"I had no idea I was responsible for such a horrible

memory." Then again, wolfing out on an unsuspecting woman was enough to scare anyone for life.

"It wasn't you, Ridge. Well, it was, but there was also the part where I was strapped to a stake and flames were whipping about my ankles. I'd say that was the worst memory."

"Thank God for that. I mean, that it was your worst memory. I'd hate it to be me that was your worst." Because memories never went away, and their haunting ability could fell a grown man to his knees. "I scared you. I'm sorry."

"I wasn't scared, I was…startled. I'm sorry, Ridge. This is not a good time to talk."

He maintained his position, keeping her from closing the door. "You scarred me, Abigail. To my core. And that scar has kept you in my mind."

"Then why didn't you come to me sooner? It's been thirteen years, and all of a sudden you want to start things with me again?"

"I didn't suggest that—"

"Does this have something to do with you taking over as principal of the Northern pack? Don't tell me you need a wifey to—"

"You already are my wife, Abigail. And it's not because of the pack."

He stopped, not wanting to lie to her. Of course it was for the pack. His life revolved around trying to rescue the pitiful remnants of a pack he held in his charge.

"Could we please talk face-to-face? It's below zero out here."

"I understand wolves handle the cold well."

They did, but that didn't mean he didn't prefer a

warm living room. Did the woman not have a compassionate bone in her body?

"Did you bring along divorce papers?"

He tapped his coat pocket. "If I came at a bad time—"

Silence crackled like the ice lining the rain gutters overhead, crisp and foreboding.

"Doesn't take more than a minute to sign some silly papers, does it?" She swung the door open. "Hurry. Get inside."

Sensing an odd urgency about her, Ridge crossed the threshold and stomped his boots on the rug to shake off the snow from the treads, but he kept his senses dialed on high alert. The house was indeed cozy and warm.

The black cat sitting on the back of a blatantly pink sofa took one look at him, hissed and darted out of the room.

"Didn't much care for you, either," he commented, and followed Abigail through to the kitchen, where she grabbed a black leather purse to mine for a pen. "That your familiar?"

"What? Swell Cat? I don't do familiars, nor do I summon demons. He's just a regular, unshifting mutt of a cat—who doesn't like dogs."

At the unsavory remark, his jaw tightened. Wolves did not like to be called dogs, or even hear finely veiled references. But he'd shackle his anger because he respected Abigail's power and knew it took but a gesture from her to put out some kind of magic he didn't know how to fight.

He scented a metallic, smoky flavor on the air and his eyes went straight to a blackened outlet that had soot streaks crawling out in all directions along the wall.

"Electrical problem?"

"Yes."

She wasn't in the mood to talk, rooting around in her purse to keep her eyes off him. Fine. He knew this wasn't easy for either of them.

She was as gorgeous as he remembered her. But behind the alluringly cool beauty and sexy figure lurked a wicked maelstrom of magic.

He remained by the wall, not about to step too close to the witch, who paced back and forth before the counter as if she were looking for something, or had forgotten to pack something. Electrical problem? Yeah, right. There was something about Abigail and electricity— but he wasn't sure how it worked.

"What is it?" he asked, sure her nervousness wasn't simply from him being here. "You look like the devil Himself is arriving for a visit."

"Don't invoke that bastard."

"Sorry." Say the devil's name three times, and—look out. "Something's wrong, Abigail, and I'm getting the feeling it has nothing to do with your long-forgotten husband showing up on your doorstep."

She flashed him a gaze that told him she would have never put such a label to him. Nor would he. Why had he said that? He shouldn't claim a title he'd never earned.

Something about standing in her presence was loosening his resolve to get the divorce papers signed and get out of Dodge. Something that he saw reflected as sadness in her gorgeous eyes. He'd forgotten her beauty. Her compelling presence. Those sexy bow lips. He was a real pushover for women in distress, and had the scars to prove it.

"Can you tell me about it?"

"Something is wrong." She pushed shaky fingers through the thick spill of hair that beamed blue within the black as the cruel winter sun shone through it. He'd not remembered its brilliance or that it looked so liquid, as if he could swim in it. "The worst wrong of all wrongs, that's all."

"Then this can wait." He tapped his coat where he'd tucked the divorce papers.

"No, I…" She stopped before him, arms crossed tightly over her chest, her eyes unwilling to meet his. Everything about her was tense and wrapped up and not the normal Abigail that he barely knew.

Every instinctual alert inside him screamed that the woman was in trouble.

Then suddenly she locked onto his gaze. Her eyes twinkled, and an eyebrow lifted, as if a devious plot had just hatched. "You're about the most honorable werewolf in the area. You're strong and smart."

"That remains to be seen. My pack is dwindling faster than you can howl at the moon. I wouldn't say that makes me the smartest pack leader around."

"You defended the vampires by taking out your own pack principal."

He looked down and aside, his eyes tracking the water puddles from his boots. He didn't need to be reminded of what he'd done to win his position, but no wolf in the area would let him forget it. Opinions on his honor and smartness varied wildly, from doing the right thing, to being a traitor to his breed.

He'd only done what was necessary.

"You're like some kind of chivalrous knight or something," she continued with the weird praise. "I've seen warriors like you in the sixteenth century. You ooze nobility and valor, Ridge. And damn, you are looking fine lately. You work out?"

The comments felt so wrong coming from a known sneaky witch who had taken joy in the painful act of shackling the magic of a vampire tribe leader not months ago. "What are you getting at?"

She pressed her fingers over his jacket. The papers beneath crinkled. Her pale pink lips parted. Sexy, thick lips that glinted with gloss. Had those delicious lips ever kissed him? His memory was a little fuzzy on all the details from Vegas.

Ridge hoped she couldn't hear the pound of his heart over the crinkling of the paper, because right now it beat a thunderous pace at her closeness. He was two parts fearful of her power and two parts ready to shove her against the wall and kiss her in a way he'd never gotten to kiss her in Vegas.

Why were the details so lacking?

"You want me to sign the divorce papers?" she asked with a forced tone of sweetness. Ridge's red alert prickled the hairs at the base of his neck. What was she playing at?

"That was my objective in setting foot on your property and risking further damage to my delicates."

"Your delicates?"

"You put a damned spell on me that night in Vegas, Abigail. Because of it, I am now unable to have kids."

She cast a wondering gaze over his face, not meeting his eyes. He wanted that connection, to look into her and read her sincerity, if it existed.

"I did no such thing. Not on purpose." She looked

aside, then as if an afterthought added, "Hell, I'm sorry. But you deserved it for freaking me like that."

"I deserved emasculation?"

"I did no such thing!"

"Close. So freaking close. I always knew you were a bad bit of witch, but that was just mean, Abigail."

"You think I'm bad?"

He rubbed his abdomen and nodded. "Yes."

A tiny smirk of satisfaction curled her kissable lips. She was pleased with his assessment of her, obviously.

Creased pink slacks sat low on her hips and her short sweater revealed a slice of taut belly. The slender rim of fur at her wrists taunted him with a tease of softness, promising passion-laden kisses and all the naughty things he'd imagined doing with her over the years.

Yes, he'd had a few dreams.

Ridge averted his gaze. He did not find the witch attractive. Though he felt sure the sex had been great, it was only a hopeful memory. He was a fool to believe it had been anything more than a stupid night of drunken folly. Damn that vodka!

He tugged out the papers from his coat and waved them before her.

"Okay, okay!" She paced before the counter, twirling a finger about the end of a luscious twist of black hair. "You want something from me? First you have to give something to me."

He had not expected this visit to be easy.

"What's your price, witch?"

Pressing her hands to the counter and tensing her jaw, she seemed to struggle for a moment with what she would next say, and then, "Your help. I need the help of a noble warrior."

He shook his head, chuckling at the ridiculous request. "You've been watching too many movies."

"I rarely watch television. I don't need to. I've seen the real thing. And you are the real thing, Ridge. I don't have time to explain, because the clock is ticking and forty-eight hours is now closer to forty-seven."

"Abigail, you're beginning to sound a little crazy."

"Am I?" Her vibrant blue eyes finally met his, and he noticed they were bloodshot, as if she'd been crying. That wasn't the truth he'd been hoping to see there.

"What's wrong, Abigail? Talk to me."

"I am talking to you. I'll sign the papers as soon as you help me locate a vampire who has been kidnapped for blood sport by a local pack."

He whistled and stepped back a few paces. Mention of the blood sport always brought up his defenses. "You are not serious."

"Deadly."

"That's right, you're the grand high poobah on the Council for werewolf and vampire relations. Since when does the Council take an active role in rescuing vampires from the blood sport? They normally observe and suggest. I can't imagine they'd step in to personally act on the behalf of one missing vampire."

"They won't, and wouldn't conceive of taking an active role. The Council can't know about this. Please, Ridge, I need your expertise. You're familiar with all the packs in the state. Which ones are involved in blood sport?"

None of them. He hoped.

"I...can't do this."

Were some still involved? He was no fool. And he wasn't stupid enough to believe all the packs had taken the Saint-Pierre wedding as a means to step back from their vicious sport. But he didn't want to—could not— dredge the Northern pack through that bit of bad press again.

"I didn't come here to stick my nose into other packs' business. I just wanted to unload a wife."

"Oh yeah? Well, this wife is going to start nagging in about ten seconds if you don't help her. And trust me, I don't have to open my mouth to nag. I'll let my spells do the talking."

She waggled a finger before her, and that night in the Las Vegas motel returned in horrid detail to Ridge. The pain of the infliction had felt like hundreds of thousands of volts of electricity shocking his entire nervous system.

He glanced at the burned outlet and felt the urge to protectively cover his crotch, but he remained staunch.

"No magic, please. Is there anything else you'd rather have from me? I stand firm on not associating the Northern pack with the foul blood sport again."

She shook her head, lifting a trembling chin. The baddest of the bad was desperate for his help, and she was trying to keep a stiff upper lip about it. Interesting. But he couldn't resist that soft, quivering lip. Would a kiss be inappropriate right now?

Probably so.

Why was it always the damsels who managed to pierce his steel armor and touch his heart? A pouty lip, a few tears. That's all it took. He was a pushover, and nothing but.

"Fine, I'll see what I can do to help, but you swear you'll sign these papers after we've located the vamp?"

"Yes, but let's hurry. I want to go to the closest pack, and then on to the next until we find the vampire."

He grabbed her by the arm before she could head out the side door. "Why the urgency? You said you had forty-eight hours."

Bowing her head, she nodded. "A man, who I suspect is a witch, contacted me about an hour ago."

"You suspect he's a witch, but don't know for sure?"

"He said he was allied with the Light. But he could be anyone, really. I'm not normally frightened by anyone, you must understand. Hell, I've stood against the meanest of the mean, the sickest of the sick, the vilest of the vile. And I'm no angel myself."

He was about to agree, but held his tongue.

"But I could read the seriousness in his threat. He means business, Ridge. I have to find this missing vampire and bring him to a designated meeting spot in forty-eight hours."

"Or what? What are they holding against you that would make you go against the Council, when I know such an act could be grounds for dismissal?"

Abigail lifted her chin and bravely met Ridge's eyes. "They have my son."

Chapter 3

When Abigail wanted to leave immediately, Ridge suggested they take his truck. She didn't give him any more information about her son. He had no idea the witch had a kid. But it wasn't as if he'd kept tabs on her over the years.

Only in your dreams.

"I want to drive," she said, and veered toward the garage, exhibiting the no-nonsense, listen-to-me-or-I'll-zap-you attitude he knew all too well. "You agreed to help me, so get on board with the plan, Addison."

"Plan? When did we come up with a plan?" When she dangled her keys and stepped into the garage, curiosity led him to follow. "Is there a plan?"

"The plan is to get moving. Fast."

The garage was no warmer than the inside of an icebox, he noted before the door rolled up to reveal the gray evening sky and the security light outside blinked on. Ridge nearly tripped over a toy.

He backed away from the horrendous red-and-black thing some joker in an R&D department had decided to call a vehicle. It was one of those foreign jobs that would get eaten alive by a semitruck on an icy freeway. Not designed for Minnesota winters, that was for sure.

"Oh no. I'm not getting into that death trap. I'm sure you have to be a clown to ride in one of these."

"Ridge." She fixed him with an exasperated stare, and he almost looked away for fear her eyes might beam another blast of magic that had very likely left the kitchen wall scarred and bruised near the outlet.

Almost. He leaned his elbows onto the miniature atrocity and looked across the car at the most gorgeous set of sky blue eyes he'd seen. He hadn't recalled them being so…fathomless. As if mysteries and secrets swirled around inside the iris, and somewhere in there a man might trip and spiral endlessly after.

He'd like to trip. Had never once tripped in his dating history.

"Please, we have to hurry," the witch pleaded with him.

He relented to the compelling pull of the damsel's distressed gaze. Ridge folded himself into the passenger seat, and after adjusting it as far back as it would go, his shoulders still rubbed the door and his knees the dashboard.

"You're right." Abigail turned off the ignition with a frustrated sigh. "This car doesn't fit you. I'm sorry. Let's take yours."

Pleased to be behind the wheel of his Ford 350—and in control—Ridge navigated the pickup truck around the perimeter of the Twin Cities on Interstate 35W. The snowstorm they'd had three days ago had left a sheen of ice along the shoulder, but the main drive was thankfully clear and dry.

Abigail had suggested they begin with the River pack, located closest to the Cities, which occupied land on the Minnesota side of the St. Croix River.

"You're tilting at windmills," he said as they cruised the freeway amidst a blur of red taillights heading home during evening rush hour.

Through rain, snow, hail or sleet, the Minnesota driver never backed down from the challenge of rush hour. Another reason he was thankful his job wasn't nine-to-five or in a business complex. Ridge liked to drive, but preferred the rough back roads and anywhere away from traffic.

"After Creed Saint-Pierre and Blu Masterson got married, all the packs and vampire tribes in the area agreed to the pact to cease warring against one another," he said, feeling it was necessary to state what the witch obviously had overlooked.

"Do you really believe that, Ridge?"

"You tell me if it's something to believe. *Did* they all agree to play nice with each other? Doesn't the Council know?"

"We always know. I'd say seventy-five percent of the opposing forces have stepped back and are now minding their own business. The Council is extremely pleased over that. The wedding was worth the effort, if you ask me. The Kila and Nava tribes have been exemplary, but then the Kila leader, Nikolaus Drake, does sit on the Council, as well. And I'm sure some of the packs are participating—"

"Some of them? You said the Council always knows. And yet, you have no idea which packs are involved in the cease-fire, if any are."

"That information has yet to be gathered."

"Uh-huh. Or did the Council throw a big party for the wedding, then leave the newlyweds to flounder in hopes their love would bring peace and happiness to the world?"

"You're the one who blindly believes all the packs have ceased participating in the blood sport."

He tightened his grip on the steering wheel. He didn't know that for sure. And yes, he did want to blindly believe everyone—vampires and werewolves— could get along. But he wasn't stupid. Hell, he'd grown up knowing vampires were nasty, longtooth blood-suckers and should be taken down if they looked at him cross-eyed.

Of course, he'd grown up knowing that it was every man for himself, and no one, not even your own breed, could be relied upon to stand with you or to even be civil to you, let alone treat you with kindness.

"I know little about the River pack," he said, "save where they could possibly hold blood sport. That is *if* they are involved in the heinous games. Their compound is on the other side of Marine on St. Croix. But I don't know what you expect to do. We can't rush them and rescue the vampire if they do have him."

"Why not?"

He flashed her a glance, but couldn't find a joking smirk on her face. "I thought you were centuries old."

"I was born in 1550."

"So shouldn't you know more? Like how one lone wolf and a trigger-happy witch could never stand against an entire pack. Especially if they are holding the blood sport. You have to know how the wolves get worked up during a match. The scent of vampire blood excites them and jacks up their adrenaline. They think with their beast brain as opposed to their *were* minds. They will tear any outsider limb from limb."

He slowed and Abigail leaned over to check the speedometer. "What are you doing? We're on the clock!"

"We need to think this through more. A plan is in order. I'm going to take the next exit."

"No! We don't have time to think. Forty-eight hours, Ridge. More like forty-six now with this damned traffic. My son is in danger."

"Did the caller indicate he was in danger?"

"He's been kidnapped. What part of kidnapped does not entail danger to you?"

"You said they were keeping him in protective custody. Sounds kind of…protective to me."

"I can't believe you're being this stupid."

Yeah, him, either. The boy was in danger if some unknown had taken him from his mother's care. But he needed facts, information—more than a wild goose chase—to better understand the situation and come up with a plan. He did not like reacting.

"Tell me about him." He resumed speed, catching up with traffic, thinking if he could get more information from her, she may begin to trust him more, and then he could talk her out of this insane mission, at least until a workable plan had been solidified. "I didn't know you had a son."

"His name is Ryan and he attends boarding school in Switzerland. That's all you need to know."

"Fine."

Boarding school? He'd never understood a mother who could send her child away for months at a time. It was wrong. Children needed parents to thrive. And for protection. But who was he to judge? His opinion had no bearing right now. Abigail was a lioness out to protect her stolen cub. He should not stand in her way.

"Does the Council know you have a kid?"

He caught her gaze and she quickly looked out the window. Well hell, he couldn't prevent curiosity. She was known to have a wicked reputation. Motherly and protective were the last two words that came to his mind.

"I think Ravin Crosse—one of the witches on the Council—is aware," she offered, "but no one else knows. It's no one's business but my own. If I want to protect my family by keeping it a secret, that's my right. You know it isn't easy surviving in a world meant more for mortals than us."

"Is he a witch?"

"It's rare that magic is passed on to a son. That's something I won't know until he hits puberty."

"Which is when?"

She huffed and gave him her silence.

"Sorry. I won't ask about him again. Kids are miracles. You're lucky to be a mother."

It changed his mind a bit about Abigail to know she was a mother, and further, to know she so fiercely protected her own. He'd heard the rumors about her, that she was quick to judgment and the first in line to administer punishment at the Council's beckon. Rumor told she'd had a crazy love thing going with a vampire once, too, but he wasn't clear on that. What mattered was now she was clearly putting her child's interests in front of her own.

He'd do the same in her position. If he had a son, and someone threatened him, Ridge would show no mercy and take no prisoners. Forget the plan, he'd react without remorse. Let the bloody kidnappers beware his paternal wrath.

"So I'm surprised you didn't come to me sooner," she suddenly said. The cool darkness of the truck was intermittently lit from the glow of red taillights passing by. "It's been a long time. Figured you'd had a blackout and totally erased all memory of Vegas from your brain."

"Close." But he had never forgotten her sweet coconut scent or the softness of her skin. Never.

"So why now? It's been over a decade. You haven't found someone you wanted to marry until now?"

"What makes you think there's someone I want to marry?"

"Why else would you bother with a divorce from a marriage you'd forgotten, and so quickly?"

"Just want to clear away a past indiscretion and smooth the path for when the time does arrive that I want to marry. And I've never forgotten this marriage, just…tucked it away into a dark little corner of my mind."

"Yeah, a dark place," she said absently. Then, seeming to lift from the mysterious dark place, she asked, "So you don't have a girlfriend?"

"Not at the moment."

"You'll marry a werewolf," she stated.

He clenched his fingers about the steering wheel.

She had the aggravating manner of assuming her opinion was right.

He wasn't sure who or what breed he'd marry. Just because he was a wolf didn't mean he had to marry one. Though, a female wolf would be his ultimate match. Only a wolf could understand another wolf. There weren't a lot of females in the area, due to rampant hunting of werewolves by vampires in the mid-twentieth century, but their numbers were slowly increasing thanks to the packs' fierce protection of the valued females. Yet still, to find a female wolf *and* fall in love was like laying claim to a treasure that must be hoarded and prized. Lottery odds, that. He'd dated a werewolf once—unsuccessfully.

Last year when Amandus Masterson had still been the pack principal, he'd offered his daughter Blu's hand to Ridge in marriage as a means to forgo her marrying the vampire Creed Saint-Pierre. Ridge had been honored for but the moment it had taken him to hate the principal even more. He'd been shocked the father could so easily pawn off his daughter on the first wolf he'd hoped would serve to his advantage. Ridge had refused, and Amandus had then offered Blu to the next wolf to walk near him, an idiot underling.

Fortunately Blu, at the Council's insistence, had married Creed, and the match had surprisingly turned into the proverbial heaven-made pairing. The werewolf princess and the ancient warrior vampire, Creed Saint-Pierre, had quickly fallen in love, and Ridge could see the glow of love on Blu's face every time she visited the compound.

He was glad Blu still visited. He regarded her as a friend, and she him. It had been difficult for her, grow-

ing up in the pack compound without her mother. Persia
Masterson had suffered greatly at her husband's hand.
Blu had always believed her mother had run away when
she was young, never to be seen again.

Ridge had done his best to protect Persia, but he'd
been young as well, and a wolf could take only so many
beatings. Blu knew it had been his talon that had mur-
dered her father, and she did not hold him responsible
for committing an act she had later told him was just
and necessary.

There were days he blamed himself. *It was your
fault.* At the time, he'd taken out the one man who had
meant to bring down the pack by continuing to partake
in the blood sport and wage war against the local vampires. But if he'd been more sensible, probably he could
have found a less violent way to take care of Amandus
Masterson.

Probably not. The old wolf had possessed a mean
streak a mile deep. No one knew that better than his
deceased wife, Persia. Masterson had treated her worse
than a dog, and he'd tormented Ridge all his life. And
he'd thought nothing of creating the largest blood sport
complex in the state. The old man had been bad to the
bone.

"You're suddenly quiet," Abigail commented. "Thinking about the werewolf you hope to someday marry?"

If only his thoughts could touch something so light
and hopeful.

"I will marry for love, not because she's my breed."

"So you would marry a mortal?"

"I didn't say that."

A mortal and a werewolf presented a sticky situation.
Because the only way to bond with his mate involved

him having sex with her under the full moon—in were-wolf form—and mortals generally freaked whenever he wolfed out and proudly wore fur, talons and a toothy maw.

"Severo and Belladonna are making it work," she commented.

"Yes, but she wasn't mortal for long. She's vampire now."

"Right. Severo has developed an insatiable blood hunger now, too, because she bit him."

Ridge winced. The idea of craving blood, such as vampires did, twisted his gut into knots. Wolves did not consume blood or attack humans. Ever. They did not need humans to survive. They existed among the mortal breed, but kept their distance. Unfortunately, man would always reign supreme over the beasts.

"What about you?" he prompted. "I haven't had a knock on my door from you over the years. No boy-friend? No marriage plans? Or just happy to be my absent wife?"

"Please. I forgot all about that silly marriage days after the trip."

Ouch. That hurt. Because he had never forgotten.

"And I don't have time for a boyfriend."

"Yikes."

She shifted on the passenger seat to face him. "I mean…I don't know. I just…I don't handle relation-ships well. I have a tendency to become…"

"Too attached?"

She sighed heavily. "Obsessive."

"Ah."

Dare he ask? Hell, why not. The worst she could do was blast him, and probably she'd keep her magic holstered in a small space like this. "I think I once heard something about you and a vampire."

"Oh please, not the Truvin Stone thing. I will never live that one down."

"You don't have to tell me if you don't want to."

Her soft chuckle and shake of head spoke volumes. She'd apparently suffered countless rumors over the years, yet he did believe that one because it was the one he'd heard more than a few times.

"Like I said," she offered, "I fall in love too damn easy, and then I go straight on into obsession. I loved Truvin, and well, he was the first guy to show me real kindness. That was in the eighteenth century when witches were extremely unpopular. So what if he was a vampire? I had more power over him because back then the Protection still made witch's blood poisonous to vampires."

"You like to have control in a relationship?"

"Yes," she answered quickly. Then, with a shrug of her shoulder and an uncomfortable shift on the seat, she answered more softly. "It's hard to shuck off. The need for control. It's my protection."

He could understand that. A woman who was a witch had two marks against her in this patriarchal society.

"Anyway," she continued, "Truvin spurned me. And I don't blame him, because I got carried away with my adoration. We didn't see each other for centuries, and then we suddenly did a few decades ago. Let's say I had to give it one last go, and he wasn't pleased to see me. Hell, the things that follow a girl through the centuries. Sometimes I wish I was a familiar, because at least they don't remember their actions from one life to the next."

"When you know better you do better," Ridge said.

Her sigh pressed against his heart and he reached

across and clasped her hand. She tugged initially, then relaxed and gave his a squeeze. Her heartbeat warmed his palm.

"Thanks for telling me that. It makes me think you can trust me."

"I do trust you as far as being the rescuing knight and having a valorous code of honor you'll adhere to. I guess I spilled that embarrassing relationship stuff because I need you to know that if you have the slightest notion that we could become an actual *we,* you should give up now. I've learned to not be so clingy and in control. Mostly. I don't need to be in a relationship with a man anymore."

"So you're playing for your own team now?" He hitched a sneaky look her way.

"What? You think I'm a— No, I still like men. Lovers suit me, but a boyfriend? Not on my radar."

"I'm sorry about that. I think being in a relationship would be the best thing for a person's heart and soul. The soul needs love."

"The soul also requires freedom," she responded.

Her soft tropical scent filled his senses, and he was the one to break contact and put his hand on the wheel. They were opposites when it came to ideals for love.

And yet her scent had gotten into his senses and refused to leave. She would prove a distraction he'd once already fallen victim to. And if she wasn't interested, then he should listen to her warning and keep his focus on helping her, and not on her soft, kissable mouth.

Abigail turned to her side and yawned. She didn't want Ridge to see. Exhaustion tugged at her shoulder and neck muscles, but she couldn't afford to sleep. Ryan had to be freaking out. If witches held him, there was no telling what her son was thinking. He'd grown up knowing his mother was a witch, had witnessed her casual usage of magic in their daily lives, and she'd taught him that he existed in a realm populated by all breeds and creatures. As well, that this mortal realm was not the only one out there. Many, including Faery and Daemonia, and dozens others, existed alongside this one.

She had explained to Ryan he would come into his magic when puberty hit. Or not. She knew a daughter born of two fire witches was likely to also be a fire witch—and as a result, would drain her parents of that magic when she came into her own. But the males were hit and miss. Rarely did a boy gain magic from his mother if his father was mortal or another breed. But it could happen when both parents were witches, so she'd wanted to prepare him for that possibility.

Truth was, Ryan could gain magic—or something else all together. It was the something else that disturbed her now.

To keep her thoughts from dire scenarios, she let her gaze glide along Ridge's profile. The light from passing cars frequently glanced off his square jaw. He was a solidly built man with a thick, muscled neck that alluded to much physical labor, thanks to him being a lumberjack, or so she'd heard. His masculine yet crooked nose made her wonder if it had been redesigned once or twice in his lifetime due to brawls. His hard jaw was set and determined, and he wore stubble as a moustache and along his jaw. The hair on his scalp wasn't much longer than the stubble on his face. Dark brows furrowed over deep brown eyes that always startled her when they met gazes. He was so intense. Nothing ever appeared casual about him, and everything seemed as if it was the Most Important Thing to him.

And that everything growled power and strength. Don't mess with me, you'll regret it. It also screamed dangerous and wild. He was a beast, a man who possessed an animal side that must be released every full moon. A beast that could barge out if it wanted at any time of the month.

Like that night in Vegas.

She wasn't afraid of werewolves. Certainly she'd known her share through the centuries, and she was on good terms with Severo, who occasionally served the Council.

Werewolves were at times playful among their pack, and she knew they were devoted and protective of those they loved. But the man-beast werewolf form they shifted into did give her caution. A seven-foot man-wolf with razor-sharp talons and a maw full of teeth made for grinding and tearing wasn't something Abigail wanted to mess with or invite over for a cozy dinner over sauvignon blanc.

And yet, despite what she'd told him after he'd pounded on her front door, she *had* thought of Ridge over the years. Often. She didn't want him to know that seeing a television commercial for Las Vegas could rocket her memories back to that weird night of fire, vodka and crazy, drunken sex. And then on to dreams of what might have been with the sexy man who had selflessly saved her from the killing flames.

And she would never reveal that sometimes her dreams had her twisting between the sheets and moaning for the missing touch from the one man who had not only startled her but had also awakened her to new wants. He'd changed her in ways she was only beginning to grasp now. The obsessive lover in her? It was still in there, but she had been tamed and turned onto something less greedy yet perhaps a little more wanting. She wanted smoldering desire countered by a patient passion. Such wanting was intent to wait for the right man instead of Mr. Right Now.

She'd dated Miles Easton—the witch who'd tied her to the stake—for six months after the crazy notion to move to Vegas for a year, and had resigned herself to the fact most men were basic, functional and sufficient in bed. They put out no more than they expected back. And they expected to come every time they had sex, then roll over and snore. Boring.

But Ridge? As soon as the sheets were pulled away, he became a literal animal. And she wasn't as frightened by the prospect of another go-round with his werewolf as she should be. For beyond the smoldering desire, her cravings whispered of wild, spontaneous sex. Hot, no-holds-barred sex. Make-me-dream-about-it-for-days sex. Make-me-shiver-when-I-think-your-name sex. Heck, she liked it a little rough, or so she imagined she would because she'd not yet found a lover to meet her pining desire to be held under control.

Ridge recognized her need for control. He was a smart man, but then again, perhaps she was overcontrolling, and who wouldn't notice that? Ryan even rolled his eyes at her when she demanded too much from him for chores and homework.

At least she recognized her control fetish. And if the

tables turned, maybe she'd finally get a handle on it and surrender completely.

But it was foolish to feed those fantasies. The werewolf wanted a divorce, and she wanted her son, safe in her arms.

And so she had steered her course directly into the fray. The River pack, if they participated in the blood sport, would present everything she did not want to deal with. As Ridge had said, when the wolves viewed the sport, they often shifted and impromptu matches were held between their own. They became enraged and hungry for physical fight by watching two vampires go at one another to the death.

She could stand before a gang of vampires without fear, and usually walk away without giving blood. Truth was, vampires still held a healthy regard for witches even though their blood was no longer poisonous to them. And she could hold her own against any witch who possessed earth, air, water or even fire magic. She didn't mind demons, but ultimately, they were all idiots contained by their mortal shells.

But werewolves were half animal, and Abigail had a healthy respect for wild animals with big teeth. Much as her bad ole self wanted to burn magic through werewolf hides, she had to admit, she was glad to have Ridge along for the ride. He offered the instinct and strength she needed. Her magic was powerful, but facing an entire pack could overwhelm her, and then she knew she wouldn't be able to direct her magic efficiently.

Which meant she was using Ridge as a means to an end. But it was more important to her to save Ryan than to worry about using one man. Ridge was tough; he could take it.

Besides, much as she should sign those papers right now and let the man off the hook, she couldn't make it so easy to get a divorce. No, she must offer the man a challenge to prove his worth in the ending of their sham of a marriage.

You've got to stop thinking of him as a knight in shining armor, Abigail. Putting men upon a pedestal always gets you in trouble in the dating arena. Be smart.

And she would be.

"The last place I know where the River pack could possibly be holding a secret match is just ahead," Ridge said. "That building down the road."

Abigail straightened and surveyed the lights winking in the distance across the snowy field stretched before them. They'd turned onto a gravel road, which was lined with pine trees on one side and high snowbanks on the other. What she guessed were yard lights beamed across the soft blanket of snow, making it glitter as if a faerie stage. The beauty of winter offered a deceptive masquerade.

"I thought this was an old property the River pack had abandoned for digs in Wisconsin, but there are lights on everywhere. Hell," Ridge said. "Could they really?"

"They're obviously up to something," she said.

She knew it pained him to consider any from his breed could still be involved in the blood sport. His naivety was odd, coming from one who had garnered much respect from his peers through his fierce mien and honorable manner.

"Do you know this vampire? What's his name? What does he look like?"

"I, uh…" She didn't know what he looked like.

Ridge flashed her a wincing shake of his head. "How are we supposed to find the guy if you don't know what he looks like?"

"I've been told his name is Mac York. We just call out his name."

"That's your plan? If you were a vampire—any vamp—kept chained and starved by werewolves in a filthy cell, and you heard a rescue team call out a name other than your own, wouldn't you stand and plead that is your name?"

"Oh."

Ridge pulled the truck over on the side of the road and turned off the headlights.

"We can't stop—"

"We are going to think this through," he said firmly over her complaint. He cast a narrow, hard gaze at her that she could see, despite the darkness in the truck.

Abigail did not back down. Instead she lifted her shoulders and delivered an admonishing gaze right back at him. No one told her what to do.

"You can stare at me all you like, Abigail, but I can smell your fear. So just chill and let me think this through."

"If I wasn't afraid I'd be too cocky," she challenged. "Fear is necessary when facing an enemy."

"Abigail." He clasped her jaw and turned her chin to face him. Normally she'd fling magic at anyone who touched her without consent, but his domineering manner quieted that urge. "This is going to be dangerous. I know nothing will stand between you and saving your son, but let me be your shield, will you? Don't get in front of me. In fact, stay as far back as possible. Let

me stand before whatever danger presents itself, or neither of us will survive."

"But I can throw magic—"

"How far? And what kind? Are you going to geld
them all like you did me? That'll only make them
angry, and you know they'll all wolf out then. If they're
not already in werewolf form."

"I didn't geld you."

"Close."

"Whatever. I'm a master with air magic. I can toss
a man through the air, send objects flying like a car,
weapons, whatever you need me to do. I've also mastered fire."

"Is that so? Tell me how a practitioner of fire gets
herself tied to a stake with a circle of flaming fagots
laid around her feet?"

Indeed, how? Had it been because she'd been so
stupid in love—as was her frustrating mien—that she
hadn't seen it coming? "He overpowered me. I am a
woman. That means there are some men who are stronger than me, no matter what my skills."

"Exactly. So let me do the talking, right? And keep
your flaming trigger finger holstered until I say so. No
flames, Abigail. Deal?"

She nodded, but mentally crossed her fingers. She'd
walked through more than a few wars in her time. She
knew how to wield magic in battle. Real battles that
had involved men on horseback brandishing swords
and fighting for their king and country.

This witch could certainly handle a few werewolves.

Chapter 4

He had a very bad feeling about this. But he wasn't a wolf to run with his tail between his legs.

Shifting into gear, Ridge drove the pickup, headlights out, up the long drive that preceded the River pack's property. If the pack was holding a blood sport match, the grounds would be open to any wolf, even those from other packs. He'd attended a few of the games when the Northern pack had been holding them. He hadn't a choice, because that was when he would have done anything for Amandus's respect. From that experience, he knew they would be frisked and assessed before being allowed entrance into the private games.

Ridge also knew he would never be allowed entrance. Since he'd taken over the Northern pack he'd received a very clear message from the other packs that he was not welcome. He'd slain Amandus Masterson.

Strangely, many had admired the old wolf. The many who believed they could do as they pleased and participate in a vicious sport that tortured vampires. Ridge had gone so far as to denounce the blood sport. And though there were packs that had agreed not to participate after the Saint-Pierre match had proved successful, those packs would not publicly denounce it, for fear of being detested by their peers, as well.

It was a fine line to walk, yet Ridge wasn't about to cower to maintain a perceived standing of misplaced solidarity among the other packs. If they couldn't handle him open and truthful, then he didn't want to deal with them. A man was nothing without his integrity.

The only thing that bothered him was the few pack members who had left the Northern pack in search of the family he was unable to provide may have joined up with a pack involved in the sport. It hurt his heart to know the men he had once called brothers could participate in something so cruel.

Perhaps Abigail was wrong, and the River pack was merely holding some kind of party tonight, celebrating or something festive like that.

Unfortunately, intuition pricked his hackles like no full moon ever had.

Ridge exhaled, accepting what would come.

Abigail strode around the hood of the truck, fluffing the fur coat collar about her neck. The white fur framed her black hair and heart-shaped face, and for a second Ridge saw a snow goddess, pale and like porcelain, but possessed of a steely inner strength her outer appearance wanted to conceal.

A woman like her certainly did not need a man, or

a husband, to survive. Hell, with fingers such as hers wielding magic, survival was a guarantee. Too bad. He could imagine protecting her and holding her close.

The clatter of tiny ice crystals on the surface of the snow sounded like a symphony at their feet. It redirected Ridge's thoughts from holding her to eerie foreboding.

He held out a hand to keep her behind him, but when she instead clasped his hand, he sucked in a breath and tugged from her touch as if hit by her electrical magic.

"What's wrong?" she asked.

Everything. He didn't want to think about how soft and warm she was right now, even though it was her suede glove against his bare hand. How just beneath the fur rimming her neck were full, gorgeous breasts, rising and falling, tempting him to touch. He needed to stay alert and ultrasensitive to his surroundings.

"Can you stay behind?" he asked, knowing her answer before she would refuse. "If this gets tough, I won't be able to keep an eye on you."

"I'm a big girl, Ridge."

"Big enough to stand against a pack of shifted wolves?"

When she didn't reply, he almost lifted her over his shoulder to carry her back to the truck and shove her inside and lock the door. At least there he could be confident she wouldn't get in harm's way. But the scent of another warm-blooded creature distracted him.

Ridge lifted his head and closed his eyes. The icy air focused every scent, yet also kept it close to the source, making it difficult to grab distant odors. Yet it lingered, teasing his nostrils.

It came to him on a whisper. Barely there, yet traveling the atmosphere on heavy particles. Blood. And not from a small animal that may have landed in a hunter's trap in the nearby forest. It was thick, and too strong, vibrant yet with life. *Vampire*. He hated that smell.

"Something is going on," he muttered, his jaw tight. Heartbeat racing, he squeezed his hands into fists. "Follow me, and stay out of sight."

A dozen vehicles were parked in the snowplowed area before what was actually an old barn that had been reconditioned and made to look new with a fresh coat of red paint. A rooster weather vane sat still at the roof peak above the double doors.

Ridge sensed the wrongness of the place as soon as they emerged on the cleared parking area beneath a shelter of high-trimmed northern pines. The blood scent traveled his system and formed a tight knot in his gut. Aggressive male shouts from inside the barn prodded at his inner beast. No chickens or cows on this pseudo-farm.

It was difficult to maintain stealth with the ice pebbles coating the snow. It had misted fine sleet earlier in the day, and the delicate ice beads crushed like glass beneath their feet and skittered across the glossy, iced surface, no matter how carefully they stepped.

He scanned the parking area, taking in the cars and finding no one inside any of them. He saw an old farmhouse, one that had been added to over the years, as if someone glued two houses to each side and had painted each with a few tones darker paint. It was lit with a soft inner glow, but he didn't see figures moving inside behind the pale curtains.

A couple of wolves carrying blue plastic cups wandered around behind a dented SUV to take a piss. He pressed Abigail behind him where they stood in the midnight shadow of a pine tree with branches stretched out over the car in front of them.

"Shh," he said, and sensed her heart beat a rapid pace.

She'd said fear was good. That was true. But doing the right thing was also a good reason to stand tall and proud and never let them see you sweat.

Times like this, he wouldn't ask to be anywhere else. Sure, he felt it best to avoid confrontation. But if this pack were involved in the crime of blood sport, he wanted them to answer to his wrath.

Glancing to Abigail, he conveyed a warning. She nodded and pointed at the ground, studiously placed her feet together, as if to say, "I'll stay right here."

Not completely satisfied she would stay in the shadows, but unwilling to argue with an opponent who could win with a flick of her fingers, he stepped out beyond the car bumper. Here, where the tires had rolled over the packed snow, the ground crunched like Styrofoam under his boots.

One of the wolves scented him, his head lifting and breath exploding in a foggy cloud before his face. Eyes narrowed, the ski-capped wolf turned to sight the new wolf walking casually toward them.

"Chilly night, eh?" Ridge offered. "The match already begin?"

"Yeah," the one who was zipping up said, as Ski Cap approached Ridge cautiously. "Beer's inside, and on the house. Or should I say on the barn? Ha!"

"Martin, shut up," Ski Cap snapped. "Who are you?" he asked Ridge, his pale eyes narrowing. "We've closed

for the night. Full house. And I don't recall you checking in earlier at the gate."

"I'm late. And I didn't see a gate." Ridge splayed
out his hands, opening himself in an attempt to appear
as nonthreatening as possible. His fingertips tingled
though, his talons aching for the shift even as he told
himself the situation was a bad one. "I brought a roll
of cash for wagers."

The one in the back, Martin, chuckled and lifted his
cup in a toast. "Benjamins!" He was already wasted,
which was not so much a good thing as a warning.

Ridge stepped up and the one in front, taller and
slimmer than Ridge, but not lacking in bulk for his
arms arched out from his muscled form, took a step forward, as well. He wore no coat, but instead a thick, in-
sulated plaid shirt over black leather pants. He scented
the wolf's aggression, and tried not to put out his own
surging rise to anger. He must remain calm if he wanted
to gain admittance.

"What's your name?"

"Richard Addison," he answered. Few wolves knew
him by his birth name.

"What pack you with?"

Now that was the question he couldn't honestly
answer without shutting down this reconnaissance adventure faster than a speeding bullet.

"I just wanted a look at the fight," he said. "Won't
bother anyone. Come on, we're all brothers, yes?"

He saw the fist swing toward his jaw, and caught it
smartly with his open palm. The loud smack echoed in
the still winter night. A bird fluttered out from high in
a pine tree.

Martin the beer drinker wobbled, but he observed their interaction with keen eyes.

"Now that wasn't very nice," Ridge said. "I was being polite and all. Why'd you have to do that?"

"I know who you are." The capped wolf bounced in preparation to deliver another fist. "You're the one who killed the Northern pack's principal. Think you're all high and mighty now, do you? Did you come to preach to us against torturing vampires?" He swung again.

Ridge dodged the slow fist. The man's breath reeked of beer but he wasn't as inebriated as the other, who stood watching, his jaw hinged open and beer dribbling out of his tilted cup.

"I'm not a preacher by any measure of the word." Ridge lifted his fists in defense. He liked a good fist-fight. No high kicks or martial arts moves for him. Keep it simple. Nothing fancy. A well-delivered fist trumped a kick to the jaw any day. Pummel your opponent's weak spots and organs until he puked. "You know the blood sport has been outlawed."

"Yeah, yeah. Every decade or so the Council sends out a new list of stupid rules. We're wolves, man. Don't you want to live like one?"

"We don't need to kill to survive. And we certainly don't need to celebrate the deaths of others. That kind of gang mentality makes all the rest of us look bad. Why don't you think for yourself?"

"I do, and I take great joy watching vampires tear out each other's veins to get to the blood they crave."

Another swing of a fist whooshed the icy air an inch from Ridge's nose. He dodged the move easily, grabbed the man's forearm and swung him around against the side of a black SUV. "You got a vampire in there named Mac York?"

Out of the corner of his eye he saw Abigail's hair reflect the moonlight with her movement. *Not now.* He had them where he wanted them. *No magic, please.*

"I don't learn their names," Ski Cap growled. "I want to watch them tear each other apart. Like I'm going to do to you. There's a bounty on your head, you know that?"

Ridge took a gut punch, because he needed to feel the fury build. He retaliated with a hard fist to the wolf's jaw, which sent blood spattering across the packed snow and at the other's feet. "That's a lie."

"There will be if you don't get off the property right now. Martin, go get the others!"

Martin saluted them with his empty beer cup and turned, staggering yet managing to trundle along quickly toward the barn.

Slamming the wolf against the car, Ridge pounded a fist against his neck, his shoulder, and then delivered the kidney shot that doubled him and lowered him to his knees.

"You got anger issues," Ski Cap spat out in a spray of blood. "Maybe you need to go against a bloody long-tooth!"

"Ridge, watch out!"

At Abigail's shout, he turned to her—saw her gesture a hand in a manner he knew meant business—and he reactively ducked.

The wolf at his feet flew through the air and slammed into the three werewolves who charged, toppling them down like bowling pins.

"Abigail!" He growled at the witch. "That wasn't the right time for that!"

"I just saved your ass!"

"My ass didn't need saving." He glanced toward the barn, where other wolves exited in a rage. "Hell, here they come. Get safe!" He shoved her toward the dark line of pine trees and turned in time to catch a wolf still in *were* shape barreling into him.

"It's the Northern principal," the wounded wolf called to his cohorts.

"What the hell do you want?" one of them called.

"I just want to talk." Ridge shoved off the wolf and flexed his shoulders, feeling his muscles tighten and his werewolf struggle for freedom. "You know the blood sport is prohibited."

The lead wolf with curly dark hair, whom he recognized but couldn't put a name to, spat on the ground before Ridge. "We don't bother your pitiful pack—you stay away from ours. Not like he has a pack anymore, eh, guys?"

The wolves behind him chuckled tightly. One had already begun to shift, talons springing out from hands that quickly shaped into paws.

"Who is with you?" the dark one asked. "There was another. Russell, go look for the other."

"There is no other," Ridge called as the shifting wolf began to stalk off. If one of them laid a single paw on Abigail, he would be forced to retaliate. Hard.

And then he growled deep from within his chest, and lowered his head, bracing for the imminent charge.

The dark wolf collided with him, and Ridge judged the challenge would be great but not overwhelming. He could take him easily while in *were* form, but he knew this wouldn't end well if he did allow the shift. Anger and his werewolf never mixed.

Fortunately, his opponent didn't shift, either. Instead, they beat each other with fists and slammed faces against the cold, steel bodies of the parked cars. Windows were smashed out by stray fists, and safety glass flaked through the air like ice in a storm. Ridge managed to put the wolf's face through a windshield.

Gripped from behind, he was swung around, only to get clotheslined by one of the others. Quickly, three men were on him, one punching him in the ribs, another choking him from behind and the last waiting for a turn to kick him in the jaw.

Feeling his skin growing tight over his muscles, he growled and managed a few defensive punches. His werewolf clamored for release, and the shift of another of his opponents scented the air with so much bloody aggression that he couldn't see clearly for the strain to hold back his beast.

A flash of pale clothing moved beyond the parked cars. A flutter of white fur alerted him. She was heading toward the barn.

"Abigail, no!"

The wolves surrounding him turned to spy the witch. Two took off after her, one in shifted werewolf form. Not good, in too many ways to count.

Ridge charged through the half circle of wolves, feeling his beast demand release. The others were shifting, coming to werewolf form with raging howls that echoed across the countryside.

As he relented to his animal nature, his talons popped out first, which he slashed across his open coat and tore away as it was ripped beneath his growing muscles. His shirt also tore, hanging on his arms in shreds.

Behind him he heard the growls of others shifting. This was not what he'd wanted. A bloodbath wasn't necessary.

But if he wanted to protect Abigail it would be.

The witch flung a hand gesture toward the shifted wolf, who pounced, landing before her in a crouch. Magic hit the werewolf in the chest and sent his flailing body flying across the parking grounds and crashing into a pine tree.

Good play, Ridge thought, and then his mortal thoughts segued with his wolf. Fully shifted, he was more animal in mind than man. The blood scent stirred another howl. The female fear scent bewildered his beast. It was an alien scent to him, in this situation. But it drew him like no other scent did.

His paws dug into the snowy drive, sinking into the icy gravel, but as he pushed up to leap and land before the woman, he felt a slash of talons across his back.

Ridge swung about to face five werewolves, their talons flexed and teeth snarling. He could take down the one on the left who was shortest with but a smash of his paw and a slice of his razored talon. Not a smart move, though, because the others would be on him like a starving pack to a fresh kill.

A blast of magic whizzed past his shoulder. He felt it as tangible heat, an energy so strong—and familiar— that his werewolf flinched and growled snappingly at the witch.

The werewolves scattered, stunned by the bolt of magic that crackled like lightning in the air over their heads.

The witch gripped the door to the building, and when Ridge wanted to yell for her to stop, he could not because he had no mortal voice in this form.

She swung out an arm toward another approaching wolf, but this time it appeared her magic failed her. The wolf landed before her, towering two heads above the petite witch.

Ridge twisted and dug in his paws, taking a leap and landing on the back of the wolf. His talons dug into the chest, scraping ribs, and he pierced heart muscle. The wolf shook at him furiously and slammed him against the building to dislodge him.

The door flung wide and the eyes of a wolf in man shape widened.

No time to introduce themselves now. Ridge swept an arm about the female's shoulders and flung her over his shoulder. He dodged another werewolf and raced away from the parking area. Behind him, the pack howled madly and set into pursuit.

He tracked through the foot-deep snow with little difficulty because the hard, icy crust allowed him to traverse without sinking in deeply. Ice beads clung to his fur. His wolf fled the danger, yet it was distracted by the soft, scented female he carried over his shoulder.

Mine.

While instinct wanted to surrender to aggression and turn and face the challenge, he sensed he needed to get her to safety. To make her his. Gripping her tightly, he flinched when she cried out. Blood scent disturbed him, erasing the rising instinct to mate.

Arriving at the car, he set the female down on the driver's side. She clutched her thigh. From the red stain on her slacks, he reasoned a talon had dug into her there.

"I'm fine," she said.

He huffed and growled, revealing his teeth to her. She was something he recognized. His werewolf remembered her from some other time. He wanted this female.

"They're getting close!" She rushed around to the opposite side of the vehicle. "Get in!"

The door opened from the inside, and he could understand her command but kept his head up, studying the horizon. The pack was close. They wanted his blood.

Because of the female?

He could toss her to them and run off. But the remembrance that pricked his instincts nudged him in the other direction. He couldn't fit in the truck and wouldn't try. He had to lure the pack away.

Taking off across the field, he ran north, at an angle to the road.

The witch turned the vehicle around and peeled down the gravel road. Wolves in man-beast form and wolf form tracked the vehicle for half a mile or so, until the female turned onto the main road and slammed on the accelerator.

They'd given up on the truck, and though Ridge could let out a howl that would alert them to his position, he watched and waited beneath stripped birch trees. Soon the pack turned to head to the barn. They'd given up.

He trotted toward the main road, tracking the small red glow he knew would lead him to the female.

When he reached the truck, the werewolf howled and

slammed a paw against the roof of the vehicle, leaving a dent, as the shift came upon him. Bones realigned and reformed, muscles snapped like thick rubber straps and his organs crushed against one another as his veins roped them into alignment.

He howled again, suffering the brunt of the uncomfortable shift.

He was naked now, but the darkness concealed him, bent over beside the back tire. Cold swept over his sweaty flesh, icing it painfully. The plan, which hadn't really been a plan, had been fucked. And the River pack was holding blood sport. He hadn't discovered if the vampire they sought was inside, but it could still be a possibility.

Damn it all! He'd stepped into a nasty hive and stirred up the drones.

"You okay?" Abigail called out from the driver's side.

He rubbed an arm to draw heat to his skin. "Give me a minute. I've got a change of clothes in the back. Toss them out, will you?"

Chapter 5

So frenzied was the adrenaline that rushed through her system, after tossing Ridge's clothes to him, Abigail waited but a minute before sliding out of the truck cab.

He'd pulled up his jeans, put on laced-up hiking boots and sorted the sleeves of a pullover shirt, which he'd yet to put on. She could actually see steam rise from his skin as his body heat reacted to the brisk chilled air. *Bet he'd be a steaming-hot lover.*

Oh, Abigail! Not now with the distracting thoughts.

"I'm sorry, but I didn't know what to do," she said. "It's what I do. React. They were coming after you. But I did manage to take out a few wolves."

"Yes, you did," he said tightly.

He was angry with her. And he had every right to be. She'd screwed up their chances of learning what vampires, if any, were being kept inside the barn. But it was a good thing she had used her magic, or Ridge would have been taken down by the half dozen wolves who'd shifted and come after him. Go, witch!

He had been stunning in werewolf form. Two heads taller than her, all muscle and sinew, and regally pelted in dark brown fur that swept from his head, down his neck and shoulders and across his back and hips. A fully shifted werewolf was nothing to sneer at, and in fact, if you did sneer, you might walk away with talon scars somewhere on your body.

But she couldn't forget his reaction when he'd first turned to find her standing near the barn.

"Your werewolf flinched when I threw magic. Why are you so afraid of me? I don't have any reason to harm you."

"Seriously?" He tossed the shirt over a shoulder and tugged down one side of the unbuttoned jeans, exposing his torso to the thigh. Moonlight glinted on his steaming flesh. "Take a look at this, and then you tell me why I flinched."

A bright white scar cut from his abdomen down to his thigh, and so close to— "Oh."

"Oh? You nearly gelded me, witch! I'd call that a very good reason to flinch around you and your trigger-happy finger."

"Looks like an electrical burn," she noted from experience. "Electricity and I don't get along, especially if there's a leyline in the area. Pretty sure Las Vegas is situated on a healthy leyline. There's probably a major vortice stretching out from the Grand Canyon area, for sure. My earth magic reacts to the magnetic pull and... sometimes I conduct electricity through my magic."

"Is that so? This was *earth magic?* Sounds too tame,

when it felt like a million volts, let me tell you. You came this close to putting me out of commission with the ladies!"

"I'm sorry." She bent to study the scar again, but he snapped up his jeans and zipped them with a furious tug. She hadn't seen what she'd been looking for. "Is your…well, is *it* all right?"

"What? My penis? Yes, no thanks to you. This scar cuts an inch away from the poor guy."

"Ouch."

"This close, Abigail." He pinched his fingers before her. "A guy's manhood is his pride, I'll have you know."

"I'm really sorry."

"Enough of your insincere apologies. Just sign the damn divorce papers and let me out of your life."

She should do just that. He deserved an easy release now that she'd seen the result of her misdirected magic. Poor guy. Men really were touchy about damage to their manhood. For good reason, too, because a pack leader's status depended on his ability to father a pack.

But she had not damaged him beyond the emotional pain he apparently suffered. And who would be her warrior if she signed the papers? She couldn't rescue Ryan on her own. After facing the wolves at the barn she realized the big bad witch was in over her head.

Those damned witches who had her son! Who were they? And how dare they drag an innocent into the fray. When she finally met the mysterious caller, she would unleash her fire magic without regret, and this time she'd make dead sure her aim gelded.

Ridge finally tugged the shirt over his head. "Give me the damn keys."

She tossed him the keys but remained by the truck

bed, her arms crossed and her head up to prevent tears from tracing her cheeks. She didn't want him to see her like this, soft and weak. Stupid tears! Stupid emotions!

Abigail Rowan was neither soft nor weak. She was a known troublemaker, and had been called the baddest of the bad by Ridge. Which she was, thank you very much.

Had been. You're not that witch anymore. You're a mother, first and foremost.

Life had overwhelmed her of late. She was beginning to crumble, and she wasn't sure how to stand tall without some support.

"Oh, what is it?" The disgust in Ridge's voice prodded the tears pooling in the corner of her eyes and they spilled over. "Are you crying? Tough little witch like you?"

"Just stop it! So I'm not so tough. And I'm sorry for something that was an accident. And I can't make your life better right now because I'm only focused on one thing. And…" She hated him seeing her in such a state. But she couldn't stop, and the words sped out on trembling tones. "I need your help, Ridge. I can't do this myself."

She stood in his embrace before she saw him move. His arms wrapped about her like steel yet held her gently, with the reassurance that something stronger and bigger than she was close and would help. The tears didn't stop, and she didn't care because she needed to get them out.

Was this her punishment for living a wild and wicked life for centuries? Now, when she truly had someone in her life she loved—her son—would he be ripped from her arms in repayment for the cruelties she had served others?

If she could turn back time, she would erase it all. Take back all the evil, vindictive magic, the obsessive love affairs, even the wicked thoughts and actions against all breeds other than her own.

Ridge didn't say anything or offer the requisite reassurances. And she loved him for the quiet strength she could feel flowing from his body into her pores, as if he possessed a magic of his own. Clutching his shirt, she turned into him and clung to the only salvation she could find at the moment.

When he bracketed her head and lifted her face to look into her eyes, she sniffed back a tear. "You can rely on me, Abigail. I'll get your son back. No matter what is required. I promise I will do it." The conviction in his tone chimed like a clear bell.

"Why? Why do you care? A signature on a piece of paper is no reason to risk your life. We both know it doesn't matter."

He pressed her head against his neck. "I've thought of you almost every day since Vegas."

"What?" She searched his shadowed gaze, but felt his presence beam through her skin as if liquid sunshine was lighting this, her darkest moment. "What are you saying?"

"I know I was drunker than I've ever been—hell, I rarely drink—but I do remember some things. Like your giggling laughter."

"I was wasted, Ridge. That was the vodka laughing."

"I know. And your eyes. Your eyes have haunted me, Abigail. They're bluer than any sky I've ever looked at. So bright. I bought a pillow…it's the same color as your eyes. Sounds funny, but it reminds me of you every time I look at it. And your body."

She shook her head. If she agreed with him he'd know she'd been haunted by him as well, and she wasn't ready to surrender all when she'd given up the tears and had shown her weakness.

"And the flames," he whispered.

"Please, Ridge, don't—"

"Always they dance around your body in my dreams. I hate that one. It's a nightmare, not a dream. No man should treat a woman like that bastard did to you. I know he wanted you dead. You don't have to tell me why. Doesn't matter. You needed protection then. You need it now. You have it."

"Thank you for making it so easy to ask for protection." She looked aside and sighed. She owed him something for his forthright willingness to step up. And she needed to say it, to release it from the tight clutches of all that haunted her. "His name was Miles Easton and he was a fire witch like me. We'd dated for six months," she said. "He insisted I marry him because we were two alike, and when I refused because I didn't love him like he loved me, he went insane. He was a powerful witch."

"The guy was an idiot." He caressed her hair and held her so she felt the heavy pulse of his heart pounding against her breast. She liked the rhythm of him, solid, steady, deep. True. This man would never treat her so cruelly as Miles had. "I hope he's gone. He hasn't bothered you since?"

She shook her head. "Haven't heard from him. Good riddance."

And her heart sank, because, like it or not, she was forever attached to Miles. Wherever he was, she hoped he'd changed, or at the very least, had found a woman who loved him so he wouldn't use his magic in the same cruel manner as he'd used it against her.

By rights, she should have reported him to the Witches' Council for attempting to burn her alive, and they would have named him warlock and banished him from the Light, but the less contact she had with him, the better. And it had all been part of walking away from her past and looking toward a new future. Revenge and spite got a person nowhere. She knew that now.

"What are we going to do now?" she asked softly. "We don't know if the River pack has the vampire."

"Let's go back to the Northern compound. It's not far from here. I need a few hours' rest and time to think. I'm also hungry something fierce. There's a burger joint open late along the way. Mind if we stop?"

She nodded. "I could eat a little. We'll both do better with some rest. And we need to stay together."

"Yep. I gotta keep an eye on you and your twitchy finger."

At least someone cared. And that struck her hard. He cared, when he had no reason to care. Truly, she did not deserve Ridge Addison's concern, but again, she was thankful she had it.

"Does that hamburger have an egg layered in there?" Abigail asked as she sipped at an overlarge glass of iced tea.

Ridge turned the greasy burger toward her to display what he'd been treating like a prized possession for the past few minutes, as he'd lovingly caressed it and noshed away. "A fried egg. Crispy, thick, peppered bacon. Gooey cheese and crunchy onions. It's the Sin City burger."

"Seriously? You chose the Sin City burger?"

He chuckled and took another generous bite, obviously getting the implication to their lusty night in Vegas, but not caring. He tapped the paper tray of veggie fries she was picking at. "No burger?"

"I'm a vegetarian."

"No way. How long?"

"Since the early nineteenth century. I don't have a taste for meat."

"You haven't tasted twenty-first-century fast food, sweetie." He displayed the half-eaten burger to her as a game show hostess would the mystery prize in a box. "Admire the grease glistening with delicious, juicy flavors. Note how the cheese drips over the bacon in thick, oozy drops. And that egg screams for attention."

"I may be immortal, but I fear that burger will put me in the grave faster than fire ever could."

"Ah, come on." He teased the burger before her. "I dare you."

His teasing tone was welcome after a long night had gotten them no closer to results. With a forty-eight-hour deadline, they had time yet to find the vampire, and right now Abigail wanted to go home and sleep. But she did need to eat or she'd get a headache.

"Fine." She leaned forward, waiting for him to offer her a bite. "Let it not be said Abigail Rowan would ever refuse a bold dare."

"That's my girl."

She took a bite, tasting the smoky bacon and cheese and then the unique tang of egg. And somewhere in there the meat didn't offend so much as she expected it to. The juice or grease, or whatever it was, slicked a savory path across her tongue. The mix of flavors was remarkable, and a satisfied noise hummed in her throat before she took another bite.

Ridge's half smile pleased her. He was so attractive when he wasn't frowning or putting on the serious face. Hell, even his serious face was attractive. There wasn't a thing about the man she didn't like. Much like this burger.

"I do believe I've turned you into a reformed vegetarian," he said, taking another bite.

"That is the most amazing thing I've had in years," she confessed, and grabbed his wrist to get another bite. "Who would have thought? An egg on a burger. And what is that savory taste?"

"One hundred percent beef, my lady. Welcome back to the sane world. Remind me to grill some Angus steaks for you some time. The special blend of spices I use will take you to heaven."

"I don't believe in heaven," she said, leaning forward for another bite.

"I do. Not that I expect I'll be granted entrance, but it's nice to know there's a reward for those who do good and live well."

"And what of those who commit the greatest sin once a century to keep living?" she asked, unashamed of what she did to survive. The immortality ritual involved drinking the blood from a beating vampire's heart—it wasn't pretty.

"That's between you and your god, sweetie."

"Goddess," she corrected. "And when did I become your sweetie?"

"The moment this hamburger hit my palate. A man can't be angry eating this, can he?"

She waggled a fried carrot stick before him. "I'll trade a semihealthy slice of veggie for another bite of sin."

He snatched the carrot from her fingers with his teeth, and then held the burger for her to claim a big bite. Grease dribbled down her chin and she laughed as she swiped it away.

Ridge lifted a brow. "You've got some mustard on the corner of your mouth. If you're not careful I'm going to lean over there and lick it off."

Surprised at that bold statement, she put a finger to her lips but didn't wipe away the mustard.

"Did I just say that?" His face noticeably flushed.

She nodded silently.

"So I did. And I meant it."

He took another healthy bite, finishing off the burger, and Abigail couldn't determine if his smile was from having consumed such a delightful meal or his unapologetic flirtations. If he had leaned in to get the mustard, she wasn't sure what she would have done. But letting it happen sounded too good to pass up.

She swiped a napkin over her lips and took another sip of iced tea. The wolf finished off her veggie fries with intent focus, avoiding eye contact with her now.

He was a study in contrasts. From wild to soft, bold to subdued. And she had to wonder what made Ridge Addison tick. What was his motivation for being so good? And why was he so determined not to succumb to the depravities others of his breed fell to?

How had this hardened man become such a softy?

And truly, was it softness, or a shy discomfort that masked his steely core?

She hoped he wasn't steel through to the core, because she liked this quiet moment of flirtation. She'd not felt so comfortable with a man in a long time. She didn't feel as if she owed him something for sharing her time with him, no expectations, no trade-offs. Yes, he was too nice.

Could he possibly be feeling the same about her?

"What?" he suddenly said. "Now do I have something on my face?"

She realized she'd been staring at his golden-brown eyes, wondering if they could ever see beyond her crimes against him and others and into her soul. She wanted to bare her soul to him, and that didn't frighten her as much as it should.

She touched a napkin to the corner of his mouth, to fake wiping off something. "Got it."

He winked at her, and then held out his hand for her to take. "Let's get out of here."

Chapter 6

Ridge parked the pickup in his compound, slid out and rushed around to the passenger side. Abigail opened the door, but he helped her down the steps. She didn't need the help, but a man never let a lady get out of the truck by herself.

She stood in the dark of the garage, lit only by the low strip lighting, and smiled at him. "Thank you."

He brushed a thumb over her dirt-smudged cheek. His finger only smeared more dirt there. Where had he gotten dirty since the restaurant? Hell, maybe it was oil. The truck needed a good cleaning. "Sorry. I made a mess of your pretty skin."

She clasped his hand and then tilted on her toes to lean in and kiss him. A morsel, really. Just a peck, their lips barely touching. In fact, she would have missed his mouth had he not turned in to her.

She smelled like coconuts, tea and tears. And the touch shivered through him on tiny wings that awakened every part of his being. It was as if he'd never been touched before, and his very soul wakened to grasp this moment and imprint it forever.

She pulled away with surprise, and touched her mouth as if he'd burned her. "You've always been the honorable one. It makes me wonder why you haven't found a wife by now. Seems you'd be the hot catch among your breed."

"Maybe I'm biding my time until the right one comes along."

"Maybe. Are there others inside?"

"Jason lives here. We've only four remaining in the pack. Frank and Lowell live in the suburbs. The compound is sort of under construction right now. We're making some changes to the structure and by summer hope to have a plan for the grounds. That's when I hope to get the horse logging business going full force."

"Horse logging? I did know something about you being a lumberjack."

"We clear out diseased and dead trees from forests ecologically, using hand tools—and a chain saw until the new equipment arrives—and horses to move the trees about."

"Sounds like a lot of hard labor."

"It is, but I enjoy the work. Makes me feel like I'm contributing to the health of the planet. And it leaves the forest as pristine as before we arrived. You can't argue that."

"I guess not."

"You can stay in the former princess's room. She left it all girlie and bright like she is."

Blu Masterson gave colorful a new definition. The werewolf princess always wore bright wigs and dressed to seduce, yet there were no promises in her careful tease.

Ridge preferred the dark flashes of blue glinting in Abigail's hair. When lit by the lights outside the River pack's warehouse, it had glowed like flame.

He winced at the image. He shouldn't put flames and witches together in the same thought. Bad karma.

"It's late," he said, gesturing to the door. "Let's get you settled. Probably won't run into Jason until morning."

He led Abigail inside, not turning on the lights because his night vision was extremely fine. She didn't complain, though she did grab his hand, and he liked that she allowed him to lead now. He wished she had had the same consideration back at the compound when she'd felt magic the best defense.

He'd get over it.

He was already over it, because her hand in his warmed his chilled fingers and trickled heat into his dark and quiet heart.

"I think she left behind some clothing in the drawers," he said, walking her into the bedroom lit through the window by a distant yard light. "Help yourself."

"What time is it now?"

"Around two. Let's take three or four hours to sleep, and reconvene before sunrise."

"Sounds good, though I'm so keyed up I'm not sure I'll be able to sleep."

"Your brain needs the rest, Abigail, so you can come up with a plan for finding the vampire. If you've got a sleeping spell or something, use it. Good night."

He closed the door and wandered down the hallway to his room.

He should have gone for another kiss. Had she expected one? He'd not seen a hopeful look or a move closer.

Damn, he should have done it anyway. He was romantically inept, but then again, the kiss in the garage had been a reaction, he felt sure, not a play at romance.

He'd not claimed Masterson's suite yet, and he wasn't sure if he would. He didn't need the ostentatious four rooms the former principal had used for a bedroom, office and private spa. He was a simple man with simple tastes.

He liked a plain home with big and sturdy furnishings that wouldn't get stained by dirt from his clothes after a long day of work. Grilled meats and veggies for meals could keep him happy, unless there was a hamburger hot dish within smelling range. And hobbies like chopping wood, working on his truck and relaxing on the porch with a beer in hand in the summertime satisfied his rugged spirit.

He also liked to try new things once in a while, such as stepping out to a new nightclub (as long as the live band wasn't ear-blastingly loud), brewing his own beer (that hadn't been so successful), rappelling the fake mountains in the gym with friends (he'd never get tired of the adrenaline rush) and tasting new foods like sushi (he didn't need to ever eat that again) and sweet desserts (cream cheese and walnut brownies, anyone?).

Too bad the taste of another sweet treat—Abigail Rowan—had been so fleeting.

Stripping down and leaving his clothes in a trail to the bathroom, he stepped into the shower under a hot stream of water and soaped up. One thing he could imagine indulging was a massage every once in a while. After he shifted, his muscles always felt tight. As if they'd snapped from werewolf shape to regular *were* shape a bit too tightly.

A hot towel awaited him in the warmer—one of the luxuries he had moved out of Masterson's suite. Wrapping the toasty towel around his waist, he sat on the edge of his unmade bed and lay across the flannel sheets, stretching his arms high to tangle his fingers within the close-spaced iron rods fitted into the rustic cedar headboard. He breathed in the cedar tang.

Home. Here he felt most comfortable.

And yet, if this was home, why did he also hate it?

Because it wasn't really home. Well, sure, he'd grown up at the compound. His life was here. The few friends he'd claimed had been here. But the idea of home should be accompanied by family, and that was something Ridge had always struggled to find.

Sure, the pack was his family, but he'd been orphaned before he'd turned one. He'd never known his parents, and had always wondered what his life would have been like had they lived to see him grow up. Would his father have been kind to him? Would his mother have had more children, giving him siblings?

He had only known the cruel love sparingly doled out by Amandus Masterson.

"Wasn't love," he whispered in the darkness. Love wasn't supposed to hurt. Nor was it supposed to make him angry. But what he'd seen of it surely had made him very angry when he was younger.

He punched a pillow and it fell over his face. The blue pillow. The one that was the same color as her eyes.

When he'd left the compound this morning for the inner city, he'd only intended to get a signature on a piece of paper—and free himself to search for a wife and, perhaps finally, for the love he pined to have.

Now, he may have the entire River pack on his ass.

Fine bit of luck he managed to trip over every time he went near the witch. Was Abigail some kind of bad-karma magnet? She'd mentioned something about her earth magic attracting magnetism, but he hadn't followed her too well. Maybe it interacted poorly with him, as well?

Or did the two of them simply not mix? He'd wager a thousand fancy towel warmers she hadn't damaged other men as she had him. Not that he hadn't been deserving at the time. And hell, what was new about being treated poorly? Why should he expect any different from Abigail?

Then again, he had no idea how the witch treated her lovers. Maybe the wicked witch of the Midwest was a serial man mangler? Could be the reason why she was unattached. Then again, immortals who tended to live for centuries—which included most breeds—did not pair up for the very reason that having a mate for so long could prove tedious and boring. After three or four centuries with the same partner, one tended to get a little tired of the same face day in and out.

Ridge shook his head. He couldn't imagine getting tired of someone he loved. While his breed generally lived about three centuries—he was only thirty-seven—he could entirely imagine spending those few centuries with a woman he loved, and never once wishing he had someone else.

He believed in love. He'd never had it. Close, but no

real love. And perhaps that was why he subscribed to the fantasy of it.

"It'll happen," he murmured.

Finding *the one* was the trouble. No sane werewolf female would hook up with him if she found out he was damaged and couldn't produce children. Been there, done that. The females were very aware their kind was as rare as valuable jewels, and they sought to increase their numbers by having a brood.

That left mortals or other paranormals for Ridge. While he had no animosity toward vampires, he was quite sure he didn't want to get involved with any woman who needed to drink his blood to survive. And in turn, if she were to bite him, that would result in him developing a wicked hunger for blood.

No, thank you.

Faeries and werewolves had an interesting relationship. They tended to hook up for political reasons that saw the two breeds sharing entrance into their realms, for the sidhe kept Faery blocked from most in the paranormal realms. But the sidhe tended toward the delicate and proved no match for his lusty and oftentimes rough werewolf. It was his nature to mate fiercely and passionately. He couldn't worry about a torn wing because he liked to press his women against the wall and wrap their legs about his hips.

Oh, man, it had been a while since his werewolf had been satiated. The ultimate sex was when he was in his shifted werewolf form, and his mate accepted his beast. Which also ruled out skittish mortals from his list of possible mates.

He scuffed a hand over his face and closed his eyes. Enough thinking. He needed to rest and clear his head if he were going to help the witch. No matter that he wasn't sure how he felt about her now, a child was in danger, and he was no man or wolf to allow that to happen.

Abigail woke with a start in the dark bedroom. A wolf howling in the distance stirred the hairs on the back of her neck. The creature was off in the forest that surrounded the compound, she suspected. But whether natural wolf or a werewolf, she couldn't determine. Had Ridge gone for a run?

Could be the other pack member, but she couldn't recall his name.

No matter, she was awake, and though groggy, a glance at the clock proved she'd slept almost three hours. That gave her time to take a shower and brush her hair before scavenging for something to eat. She'd fallen asleep so quickly she hadn't given any thought to what the plan should now be.

First and foremost was rescuing Ryan. But to do that they needed Mac York, who could have been inside the River pack's barn. They would have learned the truth had she not been so quick to draw her magic.

Okay, new plan of attack: holster her magic and let the werewolf do the talking. No. She couldn't possibly relinquish all her control like that. Could she? The guy did have a handle on the physical confrontations. Fine. She'd let him handle the rough stuff. But if he screwed up—

"No, you can let him be the one in control. You know you need to."

But knowing something and actually doing that something were two very different things.

Blu Masterson's closet offered a few dresses in wild colors that Abigail may have cooed over a decade earlier. More of a classic-slacks-and-sweater gal after her abrupt lifestyle change, she settled on a pair of gray leather pants and a white fitted sweater with three-quarter-length sleeves trimmed with pale pink satin. She borrowed toothpaste and a brush, and then combed her hair, which she hadn't washed in the quick shower to save time.

Slipping on her ankle-high high-heeled boots, she stepped into the hallway to search for the kitchen. She didn't have to look hard. A light led her to the large room done in bleached, knotty woods and a corny mix of gingham and roosters.

"Looks like something out of a backwoods cabin," she commented when she noticed Ridge standing before the stove frying eggs.

"It's man decor," he said over his shoulder, and she could sense the tease in his voice. "Get any sleep?"

"Enough. You?"

"Same. Scrambled?"

"Sure."

"Sausage?"

"Well, since I am now a reformed vegetarian, I say if that's the delicious scent I'm picking up, then go for it. Oh, dear."

"What?"

"You're wearing plaid." He looked like a lumberjack from one of the paper towel wrappers she bought while on grocery errands.

"That's what it's called. Does it offend?"

"Uh…no," came out a little too unconvincingly.

Only recently she'd thought her perfect man would

never wear plaid. Difficult not to run into the horrid print in this neck of the woods, though. Which only meant she should stick to her guns to move back to Europe where most of the men were refined, stylish and— Hell, what was she thinking? The werewolf wore the look well, and the shirt stretched around muscles so big and hard she wanted to touch them to see if they were real.

"So what's the plan this morning?" he asked.

She poured herself a cup of coffee from a steel pot on the back burner, thankful for the rich, hot joe. The man brewed a mean cup, and she liked coffee that smacked you awake. A wobbly bar stool that looked as if a chain saw had carved it from a tree stump was much more comfortable than she expected.

"We need to get inside the River pack's compound and gain access to the vampires."

"If there are any left." He turned and set a plate heaped with fluffy scrambled eggs and four sausage links before her. The smell streamed straight to the desire center of her brain, and her mouth watered. "If they held a fight last night, one or even both of the vampires could be dead."

"Then we had best hurry," she said. "One had to have survived. He could be our man."

"Or he could not be our man, and he could instead be the dead longtooth."

"Either way, I need that vamp. The man who called me didn't specify that I bring him alive."

Ridge winced.

"Well, if you want to get technical." She shrugged and dug into the breakfast. "Oh, my goddess."

"What, too hot?"

"No, these eggs are incredible. I usually don't like eggs, having seen where they come from, but these…"

"Wait until you taste my soufflé. It'll spoil you forever."

"I may have to take you up on that challenge."

Not only was the man a warrior, but he was a darn good cook. What couldn't he do?

You know his mouth is perfect for kissing.

She'd made a mistake kissing him earlier. It had been a reaction. She'd been following instinct. But still, if he had kissed her back she would have let it happen.

You're getting soft, Abigail.

Yeah, well, girls were supposed to be soft once in a while.

She sighed and set down her fork. A new wave of tension tightened her neck muscles. "Tell me it's going to be all right. That we'll find the stupid vampire and get Ryan back."

"I don't know if it'll be all right. But we will find the vampire and we will get your son. I gave you my word. Now eat fast." He tugged a cell phone from his back pocket. "I have an informant who may be able to help."

"A wolf?"

"No, a vampire. Rev Parker. He's with the Nava tribe. Guy's probably lying down for shut-eye now, but he should take my call."

Abigail had information on most vampires in the area, but she didn't keep a running tally of them in her head. The Council kept track of everyone, but she usually paid closest attention to those of the Light. Because though the Protection Spell had long been broken, most witches over five decades old still harbored some un-spoken animosity toward the vampires.

Unless his name was Truvin Stone and she had been obsessively in love with him. Okay, so she'd learned her lesson. No need to bring that mistake back to memory right now.

She listened as Ridge explained to Rev that he was tracking a vampire who may have been taken for blood sport. She knew Rev had once been captured for the sport, and had escaped thanks to a faerie. If anyone would be willing to help, it should be him.

"Thanks, Rev. Give me a call soon as you learn any-thing." He hung up and shoveled down a few forkfuls of egg. "He's going to put out feelers and call back. Should know something within the hour."

"I don't want to wait that long."

"I figured not. Which is why I'm calling Dean Mav-erick as soon as I finish breakfast."

"The leader of the Western pack? He's so far from the cities, like a four- or five-hour drive."

"Yeah, but he knows a lot about the various packs. More so than I do because he's had wolves from packs all over the state join his pack."

The information the Council had on Dean Maverick said he was an easygoing werewolf who got along with most and never started a fight. "Isn't his wife a famil-iar?"

"Yes, a pretty little kitty cat."

Familiars were born in human form with the abil-ity to shape-shift to cat form. They served witches as conductors of demons, and tended to live nine lives. "Funny how opposites seem to attract."

"What's the opposite of a witch?"

"Not sure." She sipped her coffee. "Anyone who tries to tell us no?"

"Then that puts me on the list."

Just as they shared a smile, a man entered the kitchen dressed in sweatpants and—go figure—a plaid shirt. He slapped Ridge across the back, then noticed Abigail and swept her with a look that ultimately landed on her breasts. "Well, hello. I'm Jason."

"Ridge mentioned you." Abigail extended her hand to shake his. "I'm Abigail Rowan."

"Ah." Jason rubbed his hand down the front of his shirt, the gesture not overtly insulting, but still somewhat offensive. "The Council witch. I've heard of you. So…you two…work things out?"

"We'll talk later, Jason," Ridge said, obviously not wanting to get into the topic. He slid more eggs onto Abigail's plate. "There you go, sweetie."

"Sweetie, eh?" Jason shot his pack leader a look only two men could share when a lone woman was in the room. "So you two have a thing now."

"We don't have a thing."

With a fork, Jason snagged the last fluffy cloud of egg from the frying pan and then grabbed the carton of milk. "Whatever you say, man." He walked out of the kitchen with stolen breakfast in hand.

Ridge ate a sausage and downed his orange juice. He set the glass down with a clunk. "We don't have a thing."

"Of course not," Abigail replied quickly. "A thing would imply we like each other."

He swung a look at her, his frown slipping quickly. "You don't like me?"

That question startled her. She could feel his need

and at the same time knew he'd expected to hear differ-ent. Treading emotional territory was so difficult right now. She didn't want to divide her attention between a man and her son—but she had little choice.

"I do like you, Ridge, but not that way. You know, the like way. You're one of the finest wolves in the areas. Warrior wolf, remember. It would be hard for anyone not to like and respect you."

"After last night the River pack would have some-thing to say about that."

"They're mindless idiots. They don't count."

His easy smile relaxed her, and she realized she wasn't confessing exactly how much she liked the whole man. She did respect him. But she wasn't immune to a sexy man, either, as her straying thoughts had thus far proved. She really wished she could recall their hot-and-heavy night in Vegas, because she sus-pected he must have been an awesome lover—when he hadn't been wolfed out.

"I do the same thing every once in a while," he said.

"Do what?"

"Think about what I can't remember. Between us."

How had he...? Abigail's heart pattered. She wouldn't bring it up, because that would confirm what she'd been thinking.

"It was a wild and crazy night," Ridge said. "But sometimes I believe that I saw the fire burning half a mile off the road for a reason, and that I was meant to find you. And maybe we were meant to do the crazy Vegas-wedding thing, too."

"You have strange beliefs."

"Maybe sometimes I wanted it to work out."

"This coming from a man who insists I divorce him?"

He shrugged and tilted back on the kitchen stool. "I'm a family man. I like the idea of falling in love and making it real and forever."

"It's in your nature."

"Maybe. But you must have an idea about family. You do have a son. Why not the husband?"

"Well, I do have a husband, in case you forgot."

"Not one who has ever given a shit."

"That's not my fault."

"You're blaming me for us never giving it a go? It takes two to tango, Miss Witch, and I didn't hear you knocking on my door all these years."

"Because we both knew we'd made a mistake. So let's leave past mistakes in the past, shall we? What's important is not what we did then, but what we do now, and the intention with which we do it."

Wow, Abigail, you go with the feel-good new age stuff! Not.

"I agree." He stood and leaned over her.

She stiffened, not sure what the man intended, but sensing an oncoming kiss. Said kiss landed on her lips with firm intention. He brushed his fingers through her hair and held her to deepen the kiss.

She surrendered, her eyes fluttering shut and her hand finding his waist. Beneath the flannel shirt his hard body tensed and she felt him straighten as if unsure, or maybe it was the proud wolf claiming his right to take from her what he would. The reaction beguiled her.

"That," Ridge said as he stood back and collected

their plates, "was done with intention. Now I'll leave it to you to figure out exactly what that intention was."

He set the dishes in the sink and ran the water, his back to her. His gorgeous, broad back. She suddenly wanted to cling to it and crush her face against it to smell the faint cedar scent drifting from his body, despite the plaid.

Abigail caught her chin in hand and sighed. The wolf had some crazy, dangerous magic she wasn't capable of matching, that was for sure.

Chapter 7

"Dean Maverick is in the Cities for the weekend. I asked him to meet us at the edge of town."

Abigail sat on the passenger seat of Ridge's truck. They headed toward the meeting place. "You think he can gain access to the River pack's compound?"

"Maverick gets along with everyone. I know he's got some friends in that pack and he's got a few strayed River pack members in his own."

"You said he's the one with the familiar for a wife."

"Yep. You have a familiar?"

"I don't subscribe to using a familiar to conjure demons. But you did meet my cat."

If you call mutually growling at one another a meeting.

"He's afraid of dogs," she added.

"Hey, now."

She gave him a sideways glance. "I wasn't calling you a dog. It's the canine *and* lupus breeds that bother Swell Cat."

He wasn't much for cats. Especially the black ones like Abigail's swell beastie. Cats creeped him out. He subscribed to the "if a black cat crosses your path you get seven years of bad luck" superstition, and he was also very particular to never walk under a ladder. So he had his faults.

"Well, there you go," Ridge said. "Yet another reason why we wouldn't have lasted long as man and wife."

"I agree. A relationship would never work if you hated my cat."

The comment made him smile. The more time he spent with Abigail, the harder it became to hate her as much as he had over the years. It hadn't been hate, really, but instead a healthy fear. Dislike for what can hurt a man isn't stupid. But he was beginning to see she wasn't so tough as rumor and her own self-proclaimed legend professed her to be.

He was comfortable around her, and that was a first for Richard Addison, because he'd always been a little skittish around women. They were pretty things he needed to be careful around. Only other men got the women, while he had always been happy to stand aside, waiting for scraps.

You deserve more than scraps. You deserve real love.

But could he have it from a witch? Especially one who, admittedly, made him flinch?

And if he did ever find love, what was to say he could handle it and not end up like Amandus Masterson? The bastard had abused his wife. Ridge had never witnessed a healthy relationship, so maybe expecting he could participate in one was out of the realm of possibility.

Yeah, it was a good thing he was interested in a witch. That should cool his lust, and good.

"So you only do earth and fire magic?"

"All the elements." She tugged down the fur coat collar because the heater in the truck blasted, just how Ridge liked it. "Air, earth, fire and water. I dabbled in diabology a few decades, but learned my lesson quick."

"Diabology is summoning demons?"

"Yes. I decided to leave that for the stupid witches. Well, I shouldn't say that because someone has to do it. Dark magic is required to balance light magic, and vice versa. I know some fine witches who practice the dark arts. Thoroughly and Certainly Jones, for example."

Ridge had heard of the twin brothers who were witches. "Sounds evil to me."

"It's not if done with respect for the witch's rede, *an ye harm none.* But I prefer to hone my mastery of fire."

"Fire witches are uncommon," he stated.

"Yes, well, learning to control the one thing that can be your death is tricky. A worthy challenge I took up in the nineteenth century. I still have to be cautious when I use it. Mastery will take a lifetime."

"Ever perform magic and then regret it?" He turned the radio off since the low drone of talk radio was annoying, and he'd rather hear Abigail.

"If you're implying I should be regretful over the blast I served you, how many times do I have to apologize?"

"I wasn't implying anything. Just attempting to make conversation on this bright and shiny winter morning."

Though one more apology wouldn't hurt a thing, he thought ruefully. Even better? Remove the spell, witch.

"You're bitter about it, and I know it." She shifted to sit sideways on the seat, one leg bent under the other. "I can see it in the muscle tensing your jaw. Yep, right there. It just pulsed again. You're an open book, Ridge. But fine, I'll let you have that one since it seems to serve some kind of inner need for sympathy."

"I don't need—"

He didn't need sympathy, and he wasn't going to speak it, because that would put the word out there and then it would be as if he really did need it.

The witch wielded some kind of mental magic—he knew it. Some means to burrow inside his brain and ferret out what he was thinking and feeling.

"And since you asked," she continued, "yes, I have regretted using my magic. But there are some things a girl's gotta take with her to the grave."

"Lover's spat, eh?" Her silence answered that one well enough for Ridge to offer, "I have a few regrets."

"That surprises me. You're a young wolf. Too young to have racked up a number of enemies."

"You're not counting last night."

"I suppose. But who else? Is it from the recent events that took place after the Saint-Pierre wedding?"

"Yes and no. I don't regret slaying Amandus Masterson, but I do regret killing Blu Masterson's father, if you can understand that."

"I do. You did a brave thing by standing not only for the wolves but the vampires as well, and the Council recognizes that bravery. If you ever need anything from them, I'm sure you've only to ask."

"What does the Council do, exactly? And what

would I ask of them? They're an enigma. They're like the fictional watchers who observe and record but never interfere. And yet, they will stick their fingers into the fray every once in a while, stir things to a storm, and then deny they were ever involved. They're not a governing body, so what are they?"

"We are…" She searched for the proper description, but realized it wasn't so easy to put the Council into a neat sentence or two.

"Exactly! You don't know yourself, and you've served on the Council for how long?"

"Couple decades. We watch and enforce rules, but never make laws. The paranormal nations need guidance and government, so we do our best, but we'd never become vigilante about it. Some punishment is necessary to prove a point though."

"Sounds like a complicated job. And then they won't even help their own? That's wrong."

"I don't want them to know about this because…"

Her soft coconut scent drifted under his nose as he made a study of Abigail's pain. It was deep, and thick, perhaps deeper than he could ever know.

"Because they don't know you have a son," he guessed. "Why the secrecy? You've told me you have a private life, and I can understand that. But surely the Council doesn't have a rule against you having a family. Hell, Nikolaus Drake and Ravin serve together on the Council, and they're married and have a son."

"It's complicated."

"Man, I wish you'd trust me enough to clue me in on the complication." He rapped the steering wheel impatiently. "Is it something that could help us find your son?"

"I don't think so. Ridge, it's a touchy situation. Please, I don't want to talk about it."

"We're going to have to talk about it, sooner or later."

"No, we won't."

"I'm saying yes, we will." His knuckles turned white as he gripped the steering wheel and he cautioned his anger.

"Just because you're helping me doesn't mean you get to tell me what to do."

"Oh, I know that. Trust me, I know. You've got me by the balls, witch. One wrong move, and I expect you really will geld me."

"Don't say things like that. I don't have you by anything. I asked for your help and you agreed. I didn't force you. You're such a man." That last statement came out in a vitriolic spew, and when he expected an angry scent to rise from the witch it felt more fearful, which disturbed him.

He wasn't sure what she'd meant. *You're such a man.* Of course, he was a man. Otherwise he'd be a chick.

Women. Maybe he didn't want to figure them out.

He pulled the car to the curb at a stop sign. "Maverick's inside that café." He honked the horn, and beyond the Café Perk sign a man waved at them. "Hope he has the courtesy to bring us out some coffee."

"Do you always get your way?" she asked him, stress audible in her tight voice. "You think you can tell me what you want and I'll do it?"

"You're the one ordering me around, remember?"

She gave him a pouty lip, and it infuriated him how women could be so contrary.

"Look." He turned on the seat to face her petulant pose. "I know you're hiding something from me, and for reasons beyond my better judgment, I am willing to play along, even if it means things are going to get more dangerous than last night."

"Why would you do that?"

He turned off the engine and looked her over. All glowing blue-and-black hair and bright blue eyes he'd dreamed of too many nights to number.

The dreams were always better than reality had been. The two of them were never drunk in his dreams. And he never wolfed out, which ended up scaring her. But sometimes, she accepted him in his werewolf form, and they bonded.

Yes, his dreams went that far. Stupid wolf.

But a man didn't control his dreams, did he? It wasn't wish fulfillment, just… Hell, he didn't know how to interpret them.

Yes, he did.

So he'd say it, because he couldn't *not* say it. "I like you, Abigail."

Her lips parted. Those big, dewy eyes grew larger. Devastating.

"More than a man who has been scarred by you should like you, that's for sure. And I'd do anything you ask of me. But that's because you deserve it, and not because I'm trying to make you like me."

"I like you."

"You—" He replayed what she'd blurted out. "You…" She'd said she liked him. "You do?"

A big grin curled his mouth. He straightened it out, but it curled right back, so he had to look out the windshield or lose his cool completely.

"Don't get all excited. Like is simply the opposite of not liking. I like you as a man, as I've explained. You are exemplary. Strong and focused. Honorable. Anyone would like you."

"Unless they're from the River pack."

"They'll get over it. And if not, you didn't need their approval anyway."

"If I had it, then maybe I could convince them to stop the blood sport."

"You really do care. I marvel over that."

"Why? Because a werewolf can be concerned for vampires? It's not right that others should suffer because they don't look like us, or have different beliefs or different methods to survival."

"That's true, but most men talk a good game. They are in it for themselves. They try to live upright lives, but when it comes to proving their beliefs they let fear overwhelm them and fall from integrity." She rested her head on the car seat, her eyes going soft and dreamy. "I wish I'd known you centuries ago."

"Wasn't around then. And what difference would that make, anyway?"

"I don't know." She stroked a finger along his arm, which he wasn't about to move, because he suspected she'd stop it if he did. "Back then I wasn't so insistent on pushing the world away. I might have been more open to the idea of us. But then again, I'd be too obsessive, so nix that."

"Why do you do that? Push people away."

She shrugged. "Because it's safer. It's completely opposite of how I used to be, and when I was obsessive and needy that wasn't working so well for me, so now I'm trying this. It's what I do, okay?"

He touched her chin and stroked her petal-soft skin with his thumb. Flowers had never felt softer. "It's not okay. You're too pretty to cower from all the world has to offer."

"I never cower."

"True that. But you know it's not good to close your-self off from others. There's a difference between being safe and being compulsive. You've gone from one extreme to the other."

"You think so?"

"I'd never tell you how to act or put yourself out in the world. You gotta do what works for you. But how is it working for you, Abigail?"

She sighed, and turned away from his touch. "Swell. Just…swell."

Dean Maverick opened the back door and slid across the seat. "Buddy! How's it going? Got you some coffee." The wolf handed forward two paper cups of coffee covered with plastic lids. "Miss Rowan, nice to meet you. You like it dark?"

"Yes, thank you," she said and took the coffee without taking her eyes from Ridge's. She was thinking about what he'd said, and he could tell it disturbed her. He'd breached the walls she'd erected around herself for safety.

And that made him feel swell.

"So we're just going to wait?" Abigail paced at the back of the truck. She tugged up the fur coat collar against the brisk cold.

Under the pretense of taking a jog to explore the area, Dean had run the three miles to the River pack's compound intending to see what information he could learn, and if they would allow him entrance. The sun had begun to set; they'd needed to wait for dark.

"I feel so helpless," she said, and realized the confession was not something she would have made to anyone. How had she become such a weeping Wilma around Ridge? She was comfortable around the werewolf. And that disturbed her sense of control.

Ridge, quiet and calm, as always, leaned against the truck bed, his head bowed and eyes closed. His breaths misted from his nose in soft clouds of condensation. Not ignoring her, but rather alert and focused, he listened, taking in the surroundings, the chitter of birds scanning the snow-blanketed wheat field for a stray seed, the cars swishing by on the nearby freeway. Any unexpected noises, like a wayward werewolf out patrolling the area.

Arms crossed over her chest against the chill, she paced, marking the snow-packed gravel road with her boots, wondering why it was so easy for him to be calm at a time like this.

Well, she knew why. He didn't have a stake in this matter. As far as she knew.

Don't think about that. It can never be real.

"Abigail," he said softly.

When she didn't stop pacing, he grabbed her and wrapped her in his arms.

She didn't need a hug. How dare he always try to control her?

She started to push away, but he held her firmly. The big lug was trying to be the one in command and she wasn't about to surrender to those golden-brown eyes of his that entreated her. And then, as if struck by magic, she put her head on his shoulder and succumbed to his quiet strength.

One broad hand spread across her back, pressing

her against the hardness of his solid, sure frame. He felt real, warm and safe. Mercy, but she needed this.

"You can't push everyone away," he said.

She huffed out a breath that could have become a sob had she not already cried too many tears earlier.

"This is the best I can do for you right now," he said. His gentle strokes up and down her back soothed when she hadn't realized she'd needed a soothing touch. "I don't like not having the control, either. This standing around waiting stuff is not for me. But I trust Maverick. He'll learn what he can. We must be patient."

She nodded as he stepped away to give her the distance her rigid conscience wanted, but that her soul no longer craved. The last time she'd felt so safe and protected—it had been in the nineteenth century, surely. A time of comfort and prosperity for her, a time when she'd had ample lovers and not a care.

Why had it been so long since she'd felt that way? Shouldn't a woman *always* feel safe? She'd never thought about it before, had been so busy existing and surviving. Being a mother. Serving the Council. Practicing her magic. Keeping others at a distance. Protecting Ryan.

It wasn't working at all for her, and she wasn't near to being swell, as she'd said to him earlier. It was… frustrating. She wasn't this person.

But she was no longer the hyperneedy Abigail Rowan, either.

Who the hell was she? What did she need? And did this man want to give her what she didn't know she wanted? He'd already given her an unconditional promise to help. She could expect no more.

But you want more.

Abigail sighed and shook her head against her intrusive thoughts. *Just keep your head on straight,* she cautioned. *You can consider the whole relationship thing later. Preferably much later.*

Ridge was right; there was nothing either of them could do until Maverick returned from recon. Wrapping her arms across her chest, she hugged herself, wishing she'd the fortitude to have remained in his embrace. But then, that would have required she face the relationship thing head-on. And that way lay obsession.

A sudden spray of snow showered her head and shoulders. She spun about to find the instigator of the sneak attack with a sheepish grin on his face—and another snowball in his gloveless hand.

"Just trying to lighten things up," he said, and tossed the other snowball between his hands.

"I see that." She dusted off the snow from her shoulders. "And I didn't even flinch."

"Because you didn't see it coming. Flinch now, witch."

She dodged the incoming snowball and it missed her arm by an inch. While bent over, she managed to scoop a palmful of snow in the process. Quickly patting it into a ball, she threw it at Ridge while he was bent, claiming another weapon. It landed the center of his back, and he popped up and gave a playful moan.

"I have much better aim than you," she called, already forming another snowball. "I thought you were freaked by me throwing things at you?"

"Only the things I can't see," he said, and tossed another loose-packed snowball that, despite her ducking, landed on her arm in a splatter of cool, wet flakes.

Snow showered her face and quickly melted, leaving tiny kisses of water on her skin. It cheered her up, and she was thankful for the distraction.

Ducking behind the truck bed while Ridge was down preparing another weapon, she crept around the hood of the truck, and when she thought she had the sneak attack, he leaped around and hit her with a snowy bomb directly in the gut.

She feigned death by wobbling and clutching her gut, and then dropped backward onto the high, soft snow bordering the ditch. Winter kissed her face in a spray of snow.

"You win!" she declared. "But you had the advantage of smell."

He bent over her to offer her a hand up. "I can smell your perfume a mile away. It's kind of woody, outdoorsy in a way I like. With a weird touch of coconut. What is it?" he asked as he tugged her up and brushed the snow from her hair and shoulders.

"The coconut is my shampoo. My perfume is vetiver. It's supposed to calm tension and anxiety."

"I see." He brushed snow from his arms. "And how's that working for you?"

This time, instead of offering a lie, she punched him in the arm. "You know how it's working for me, so don't feign ignorance."

He looked off over the horizon. His razor-short hair, where snowflakes had landed and were melting, twinkled in the twilight. She loved the way he was instantly stoic and calm. His place in the world was solid and sure. Nothing could unhinge him, and it put her to awe.

"We should have tried," she said suddenly to the protective warrior wolf.

"We?" He blew out a slow breath, taking measure of the silence that followed. "You mean then? Us?"

She nodded. "It may have worked. It may not. But we'll never know now."

"We could know."

They could. But that would require she stop pushing and start pulling toward her the one thing she wanted most. Her tender and confused heart wasn't ready to surrender to that yet.

"If I let you think too long you'll talk yourself into all sorts of dark and lonely corners," he said.

Ridge tilted down his head and kissed her. His mouth was cold and slick with melted snow and he tasted like winter and everything she had never known she'd wanted. His lips teased and made her want more. His touch was tentative and unsure, but he gave her another kiss, lingering at the corner of her mouth.

An ache she'd never had before burgeoned in her belly. It was pure want, unabashed and unrelenting. She recognized it because it was something she'd often pined for when she dreamed.

Abigail rose onto her tiptoes and kissed him solidly on the mouth, tilting her head to synchronize with his opposite tilt. He tasted like coffee and his body, hard and warm against hers, felt right, so supposed-to-be, that she forgot about things troubling her and dashed her tongue under his upper lip, daring him to dance deep into her.

A growl of want from the virile wolf accompanied a shift of his hips and a slide of his hand across her back. He held her firm, his fingers brushing her breast from the side. Her coat was wool, and thick, but she did not miss the sensation of his touch. It was direct and purposeful. Commanding. She was consumed by his presence as he framed her protectively, and with an urgent hunger she agreed to answer.

He broke away from the kiss. "Don't say this is wrong."

"I wasn't going to."

"I need this from you, Abigail. More than I thought."

"Me too."

The wolf lifted her and she wrapped her legs about his hips. Crushing her breasts to his chest, she felt her nipples bead against the hardness of his form. His kiss grew harder, more demanding, and she wanted to feed his rough desire. Fingers curling about the back of his neck above his coat collar, she stroked the short hair up across his snow-moist scalp.

She imagined it had been like this then. In Vegas. As quickly as they'd made contact some kind of crazy, passionate flame had ignited, bonding them in a wicked, drunken coupling. They weren't drunk now, but she felt that same crazy passion invigorate every part of her being. This man was the flame she could never dream to completely master.

And he was the only flame she dared touch for any length of time.

Arching her back and melting her body against his, she offered herself to him. The wolf moaned at her mouth and deepened the kiss with rough enthusiasm. His hands gripped tightly, making her feel as if he owned her, and he would do with her as he wished.

"Goddess, yes," she whispered. "Own me."

"Never," he murmured. "I only want to be worthy of you."

"Oh, Ridge, I need you to take what you want, what

you deserve," spoke her heart before her mind knew it. But the confession felt right. True.

"No, this is wrong," he suddenly gasped. "I never take from women."

Damn him! He was ruining this. "You should. You deserve it. I don't mind, Ridge, please..."

"Maverick. He'll be back soon."

"He's been gone ten minutes. You'll sense when he's close. You really want to stop kissing me?"

"No, but I need you to not say those things."

She shook her head in wonder. "Not tell you what I need?"

"Not like that, I mean..."

She stroked his lips with a fingertip. So she had pushed when he hadn't been prepared for such a shove. Bad witch. "It's all right, Ridge. Just show me how desperately you need me."

She kissed him again, this time nibbling his firm lower lip and sucking it in to taste and lick and claim. He chuckled in a rumbly, sexy baritone that turned her on more, if that was possible.

"Always cold to hot with us," she said, and kissed his jaw, licking the prickly stubble. "Nothing slow and easy."

"It seems so. I like you crawling all over me like you can't get enough of me."

"You're some kind of fire," she explained. "The only kind I dare touch for any length of time."

"Your mouth is like poison, Abigail. It's something I'd love to kill myself with. You got your magic holstered?"

"Yes. Don't tell me you still worry about that?"

"Always."

"As long as you don't wolf out while I'm kissing you, we should be fine."

"I'm not that out of control. Hell." He set her down, and the lack of his mouth at hers brought her down from the cloud she'd been floating upon.

"What is it? What did I say? Can't a girl speak the truth without freaking you out?"

"This is never going to work. Not until you can trust me."

"I do trust you. It's you who needs to trust me. You won't let go, Ridge. There's a beast inside you who wants me. Why can't you let it loose?"

"I suspect you're not asking me to wolf out."

"No, not that. I'm asking you to be the man you are." She bit her lip and looked aside. This was not good. She sensed that he read her encouragement as a challenge against his manhood. She didn't, but how else to put it? Time to get back to the fun of it all. "Forget I said that. We were just kissing. Just a little flirtation."

"That's all it was to you? Nothing more than flirting?" He tugged her to him and kissed her hard and deep. His mouth bruised hers sweetly and she could not breathe, so she had to take in his breath in a gasp.

Oh, but she preferred it hard like this. He controlled her, which sent shivers up her spine. To succumb completely was out of the question, but to surrender to his strength was now as simple as sighing.

"Whatever is going on between us right now," he said, "you don't trust it to be the way you want it to be. The way I want it to be. You need control. You need to push me away because of some stupid rule you made and now you think you need to follow it."

"So do you. You need the control."

"Was that kiss I gave you controlled?"

"No, it freakin' rocked." She touched her lips, feeling they were swollen and pulsed with a lush ache. "But you're like me. You also like to keep people at a distance. I'm not the one who flinches every time he sees me wave my hand."

"As I've explained…" He tilted his head sharply.

"I know, I know! And once again, I apologize." She blew out a breath and stretched out her arms to tilt her head toward the setting sun. Then something occurred to her. "But your penis still works. You can still have sex with women, so I didn't damage you so terribly. That thing about you being unable to father a child—"

"The damned spell."

The spell she had never put on him. Seriously, she hadn't time to conjure a decent spell. It had merely been a reaction, accidental magic combined with the leylines and the hotel electricity.

She couldn't tell him that, because he didn't want to believe the truth. He wasn't ready. And she wasn't ready for her own truths, either.

What were they doing? Playing at what they didn't know they wanted?

"So you said it could be the way you wanted it to be. Does that mean you want us to be more?"

"Yes, I— He's on his way." Ridge swung around and scanned the line of trees about half a mile across the field. "He's not running full bore, so things must have gone well enough."

Her heartbeats racing with anticipation, Abigail ran around the side of the truck to wait for the wolf.

Dean Maverick's bow-legged trot took him quickly to the truck. He nodded at her, and then looked to

Ridge, who joined her side and put an arm around her shoulders. He was always showing her his gentle side. Or was it a possessive move?

If only he would possess her with his kisses again. She wanted more from him, rough and wild, and dangerous.

"Have any trouble?" Ridge asked.

Dean kicked a tire, shaking off the crusted snow from his pack boots. "None. Spoke to Don Pritchard, the principal. There's only one vampire on site, and he's not the one you're looking for."

"How do you know?" Abigail tugged from Ridge's hold and went to Dean. "You didn't use his name? I told you not to do that."

"Chill out, pretty lady. I didn't let on to anything. I casually mentioned some of my members had been asking about the sport and he offered to show me the one vamp they had in captivity. He won last night's fight. The other did not."

"He's dead?"

"Ash," Dean said.

"You're sure?" Ridge asked.

Dean nodded. "I don't think it was your vamp, Miss Rowan. In fact, it sounds like the pack is going cold turkey after this one. The principal doesn't feel the fights are as well attended as usual. And after Ridge's visit last night, sounds like he's rethinking things."

"No kidding?" Ridge nodded in satisfaction at that.

Abigail felt a thrill to know perhaps he'd been instrumental in changing the River pack over. But it was only a momentary excitement. "Now what do I do? I can't show at the meeting tomorrow without a vampire. They'll never make the trade. My son!"

Ridge grabbed her by the shoulders and made eye contact. "We'll find him, Abigail." As panic began to take hold, she maintained contact with his gentling stare. Her wobbling lip settled, and a touch of calm traced her spine.

"I don't think this is going to work." She sank against Ridge's solid form. "I want my son back!"

"I can go along too, if you need me," Dean offered. "I'll give Sunday a call and let her know I'm going to be a little late. If any pack in the area is involved in the sport, I'd suspect the one up in Ely."

"Ely is a good four-hour drive from here," Ridge noted, looking north. The small town was located in the Boundary Waters Canoe Area of Minnesota.

"I'm in it to win it, if you need me." Maverick bent before Abigail's face and offered, "Sorry. I wish he would have been in there, too," then wandered around the back of the truck.

"It's not what we hoped for," Ridge said as he rubbed her shoulders reassuringly. "But we can work with it. When's the meeting tomorrow?"

"Four in the afternoon."

"And it's six now. We've got twenty-two hours."

"I don't know if I can last that long. I've no way to contact them. I don't know if Ryan is safe, or what he's thinking. He must be so frightened. If we could get this done with…"

"All things in time," he said and led her around to the passenger door. "We're going on a road trip."

"How did they learn you had a son in the first place if you've been so protective of him?"

"I don't know." Abigail closed her eyes for a moment.

"I've been so careful over the years to keep him concealed."

"Why the big secret?" echoed from the backseat.

Ridge glanced in the rearview mirror at Maverick, who offered a shrug.

"Yes, why keep him such a big secret?" Ridge asked. "You must have enemies you fear."

"I'm on the Council. That's reason enough. Do you know how many enemies we have?"

"Everyone has enemies. Still doesn't explain why you'd fear for your son's life."

"I'm a fire witch," she said defensively. "If I were to have a child with another fire witch, do you know what the child would become?"

"No."

"He would not only have the power of fire to his arsenal, but he'd be impervious to fire. There's not been a witch like that for thousands of years."

"And someone would want to get control of him?" Maverick posited. "If he's so powerful, how could that happen?"

"He's just a kid, and he's not completed puberty yet, so I don't know…"

Ridge's jaw flexed at her abrupt silence. "You don't know? Don't know what? If he's going to come into his magic?"

"Yes and no. Most boys don't inherit their magic from the mother. But if both parents are witches that increases the chances. But if his father is not…"

"If his father is not…a witch?" Ridge asked.

She winced, and then nodded.

They drove in silence for a few miles, before Ridge

finally worked things out. "That means you're not sure who the father is."

"I'm ninety-nine percent sure."

"What? How old is Ryan anyway?"

She looked out the window. Ridge's fingers squeezed the leather steering wheel. "Abigail."

"He's twelve."

"Twelve. That means…" Ridge did the math. Thirteen years ago he'd been driving down the I-15 in Nevada, looking for a good time. Which he'd found, courtesy of Elvis, vodka and flames.

Hell. That meant— Could it possibly be?

Ridge slammed on the brakes, put the car in Park and jumped out his side, slamming the door behind him. He marched around to the passenger side and opened it. Tugging Abigail out, he pushed her against the hood.

"Am I Ryan's father?"

Chapter 8

Ridge's eyes were hard as stone. Once she'd seen golden highlights within the liquid brown, but now they were solid, cold and deadly. This was the stare other werewolves cowered from and tried to get away from. His intensity felt powerful, commanding—yet right.

And when she should have been frightened of his suspicion, Abigail grew even more eager to spill all.

To finally have it all out in the open, for good or for ill.

The werewolf slammed his palms against the hood of the pickup, pinning her between his body and the truck. The diesel engine growled as angrily as the wolf.

A car rolled by, stirring a cloud of icy snowflakes into the air, but this time they didn't immediately melt when they landed on her cheek.

She held his gaze, determined to hold her own

against whatever wild thoughts were stirring in his brain. A brain that could be half animal at times, and that made him instinctual and swift. Such instincts couldn't help him now. Or her.

It could not be possible. Much as she wished it so. How many times had she considered it over the years? Hundreds. No, surely thousands. Every moment she caught Ryan looking into her eyes, she had wondered if his were the same color as the man who had rescued her.

But, thanks to the vodka, she'd never been able to remember his eyes.

Now she narrowed her gaze on Ridge's stare. Ryan's eyes were hazel, with tiny spots of brown.

No reason to start thinking different after twelve years. She'd made peace with her actions, and could not conceive of creating a new future when it was based on ridiculous dreams. "I doubt it," Abigail finally said.

"You doubt it? But you don't know for sure? When was he conceived?"

"The doctors never really know for sure. They give you an estimate that could be off by a week or even two or three, but—"

He gripped her upper arm. The beast inside him was in control. "You know, Abigail. You know things like that. Witches are all about the calendar and seasons, and knowing themselves and the cycles of every freaking living thing. You know exactly when he was conceived. Was it in Vegas?"

What happened in Vegas...

...had gotten out of Vegas, and had been with her ever since.

"Ridge, listen to me. I had been dating Miles for

months before you and I had our silly vodka dance down the aisle. We probably had sex every day, right up until that nasty night he tried to burn me at the stake."

"An upright candidate for fatherhood, if you ask me. But you can't know for sure then, because we did it that same night."

"Drunk out of our minds. Even ask Elvis!"

"Alcohol does not prevent one from becoming pregnant. And it's ridiculous if you try to make me believe it. In fact, I'm sure it contributes to more pregnancies than most women will take credit for. The boy could be mine!"

Yes, there was the smallest, most minuscule, infinitesimal chance Ridge could be Ryan's father—if Ryan had been born late. Which he had not been.

"I did the math," she said. "Ryan would have had to be born a month late for such a thing to be true. I know I wasn't overdue. I never even got that big."

Not big enough for a month overdue.

Maybe… Ryan had been a tiny baby. Or was it hope upon hope?

No, she wasn't about to buy into desperate dreams and fantasies now. To change over a decade of thinking, in which she had convinced herself to believe Miles was the father, and that Ryan was destined for fire magic, and a life so complicated he could never wrap his mind around it all.

"He's not," she said softly. "The possibility of it being so is minuscule."

"Says who?"

"Ridge, why are you so upset about this? You wanted a divorce!"

"That was before I knew I had a family. A son and a wife!"

"Don't you dare give me that. He's not yours to claim."

The wolf reared with gaping disbelief, but kept her close, not allowing her to dash aside.

She didn't want to dash. She liked standing up to this side of the man, the angry, wanting man, determined to get what he felt he deserved.

"Family implies spending time with people," she said. "Knowing them, caring about them. Even if the minuscule possibility were in fact true, we could never be your family. The title of father is not awarded following one night of crazy drunken sex. It has to be earned. You don't know what family means."

He shoved his hand along her jaw. She felt his forceful intent and sensed that he reined in his anger. She stood defiantly, not about to show him her fear, or her need for him to be right.

"Damn it, Abigail, family is all I have ever wanted. All I have ever dreamed to have," he said through a tight jaw. "Do you think growing up in a pack without parents is like family? It's not. I had to fight for every scrap I could get. I did all the grunt work in hopes of Amandus looking favorably upon me and maybe allowing me to sleep in a bed one night instead of out in the shed on a cot. But still I tailed around behind the others, allowed them to shove me around, push me into the muck and deliver a playful but painful punch for laughs. I was a stupid wanting pup, hungry for a morsel of attention. I eagerly did as they asked for one look of kindness, of appreciation, of feeling like part of a family.

"I once thought Amandus's wife, Persia, looked upon me as a son. Fuck. Many times I put myself between her and Amandus to keep the old bastard from hitting her. Not once did she thank me. Not that I needed the thanks. Then finally, I earned Amandus's respect when I figured out that doing his dirty work was the thing. What a bastard he turned out to be. And me? I'm just like him."

He released her and turned a shoulder to her. His muscles were tight and she could feel his tension and see it in the rapid breaths huffing in the air before him. But she didn't need to see it. His words had cut through her heart and opened it to his reality. His horrible, tragic reality.

He'd protected the Northern principal's wife from beatings? How awful to have felt that he had to do that. And then, to compare himself to Masterson?

"I had no idea. You come off as confident and put together. You're so strong, Ridge. And now to know you struggled for everything and protected Persia? I am in awe. Growing up that way has made you the man you are."

"Yeah?" He huffed and punched a fist into his open palm with a smack. "Well, I don't want my son to live one more day without a father."

"He's done quite well with only a mother. Despite rumor and outward appearance, I do know how to take care of a child."

"Yeah, but you said yourself you like to push people away. Look what you've done! You've pushed the boy all the way to Switzerland."

The accusation hurt because it was true. She'd pushed everyone away in a futile attempt at changing her life around, becoming less wild and wicked and more…well, more what? Respectable? That was a label she'd never accept even if she had earned it. Responsible? Ha! She'd sent her own son away to another country under the pretense of protecting him.

How dare she use that excuse? What mother did that? Maybe she hadn't been ready for a child and single motherhood, but she'd accepted the role and loved Ryan from the tip of his head down to his pudgy little toes. She loved him so much, no man would ever have him. No man.

Abigail exhaled heavily.

No man.

That was it. She was punishing all the men who'd ever made her fall in love and then dumped her by keeping her little man away from them all, even the ones who meant well and might even love Ryan.

Like Ridge?

Her son did need a father. He often asked if she was dating someone she might bring home so he could toss around a football with the guy. She'd always looked away, and changed the topic. Easier to turn a blind eye.

Goddess, but she'd been far crueler to her son than the unseen entities she'd strived to protect him from. But the facts remained…

"Don't get your heart set on this, Ridge. I've told you, the chance you are Ryan's father is small."

"I heard you. Minuscule. But tell me this: Has he shown any signs of coming into his magic yet?"

"No, but—"

"Then until he does, my chances are fifty-fifty."

"Oh, Ridge."

"We need to move." He smacked a fist into his palm

with a loud crack. "If a gang of witches has my son, I'll tear off all their heads."

She clutched her hands against her pounding heart as Ridge stomped around to the driver's side. She expected no less a strong reaction, for Ridge to be defensive yet protective about Ryan. But he couldn't be Ryan's father. She'd never seen any signs Ryan could be part wolf.

Hell. There was only one way to know who Ryan's father was. And either way, it wouldn't go well for Ryan.

The drive up I-35 to Ely was long, and the steel-strung tension didn't dissipate until Ridge turned up the radio. When he'd gotten behind the wheel after talking to Abigail, he put on his seat belt and spun out onto the freeway, meeting Maverick's eyes in the rearview mirror. The wolf had heard it all.

Ridge wasn't in the mood to talk. Or to explain.

Thankfully, it appeared Abigail had fallen asleep, while Maverick hummed the country tunes and occupied himself with an old copy of *Car Craft* he'd found in the backseat.

Ridge maintained a firm jaw and tight grip on the steering wheel. He was possibly the boy's father. It was amazing. Impossible. Incredible. And as Abigail said, probably not true.

But the slightest chance did exist. Minuscule, as she said. And that was all he needed. He'd never been given more than a chance, and look how far he'd come.

He'd go even further if the chance named Ryan was really his.

By the time they reached Ely he was hungry, and his anger had completely fled. Ridge drove through

McDonald's and ordered a couple of McRibs, a salad, three large fries and a Coke, then turned to ask what the others wanted.

They rolled into the parking lot and ate in silence until Maverick burped, and Abigail laughed.

"Boys," she said, shaking her head and stealing another fry from Ridge's meal. "So this is the town?"

"Last pack that is considered citified," Maverick explained. "Any farther north and you get into the Boundary Waters. The packs are tight there, keep to themselves, and I suspect could care less about vampires. I gotta stretch and go take a leak. Be right back."

Ridge did not miss Maverick's wink as the lanky wolf strode inside the restaurant. He was purposely giving them a few minutes alone. The man had an impeccable feel for emotions that made Ridge marvel. Must be what having a wife did to a man. Settled him down, gentled him, made him a master of the emotional arts.

He wouldn't mind mastering a few of those himself. When he'd kissed Abigail roughly he'd felt her soften in his embrace and pull him closer. As if she'd wanted him to overpower her, and had fed off that connection. And when she'd teased him to let out his beast, she could have had no clue how close his werewolf stood. Just there. A shift away, and wanting, so wanting to claim the female he felt belonged to him.

Now you can claim your family.

If only…

"Sorry," he said, stuffing the empty wrappers into the bag. "I was harsh back at the roadside. I shouldn't have come on so strong."

"Apology accepted." She sipped the last drops of

orange juice with a loud suck. "I wouldn't have expected anything less from you. You're a good man, Ridge."

"Would you stop saying that?" He smashed the paper bag with a fist. "I am not a good man. I'm a fucked-up wolf with no more sense than to shout at women when they confuse me. I'm not so honorable as you think. So get rid of this stupid scenario about me being some warrior doing the chivalry act for you. There's a kid in trouble. I'm going to find him. Simple as that."

"Fine." She handed him her empty cup. "Not a warrior. Just a wolf. And I'm just a witch. And we're going to find Ryan."

"That's a promise I make to you. I swear it, Abigail."

She nodded, and smiled. "I know you will."

Chapter 9

"I can't do this." Ridge slammed the truck door and started marching toward the compound across the crunchy snow. Maverick had gone inside to scope out the Ely pack's grounds. "I can't stand by and let another man do this by himself."

"Ridge, no!" Abigail grabbed his arm and tugged, her boots slipping on the snowy ice, as he wouldn't slow his pace. "Stop it, you crazy man!"

He shook off her feeble attempt to restrain him and, feeling his neck muscles tighten, huffed and smacked a fist into his palm. "Why not?"

"You go in there all aggressive and baring your teeth and they'll retaliate. Let me do something."

"What can you do that won't set the grounds ablaze? No fire magic, Abigail, I absolutely forbid it."

Affronted, she slammed her hands on her hips and leaned toward him. "You forbid it?"

"Yes, I do." But he finished on a less than firm tone. "It's too flashy. We need stealth."

"But you're *forbidding* me?"

"That I am. You don't like it?"

She crossed her arms and joggled her head back and forth, considering. Her lips were tight. And he could smell her anger, but not for long. Finally she said, "Very well. But what about this?"

She swung her arm out and aimed it toward the compound. The yard light flickered out. A second later, all the lights in the compound blinked out.

"For starters," she said. "Then we can smoke them out with fire."

"Oh no." He grabbed her from behind and shackled her, his hands joining before her breasts. "No fire. You think one lone wolf is going to freak them out? Flames will drive them insane. I don't want to smoke them out. I want one vampire. Promise me, Abigail. No flames."

Wrapped within his unforgiving hold, she didn't feel the need to squirm. In fact, she relaxed and tilted her head against his shoulder. "I promise," she said on a whisper. "I'll do what you say."

And she would because something about his domineering tone plucked every needy string in her body and she was willing to see how well he could play her.

"Wait. Here comes Maverick."

He released her and jogged to meet Dean. "What did you find out?"

"He's in there," Maverick said, swiping the sweat from his brow. "Did you see that? All the lights went out. Everyone is freaking inside."

Ridge shot Abigail an admonishing glance. She nudged up a shoulder and gave an innocent shrug.

"Oh." Maverick winced. "Forgot about the witch. They have your vamp."

"Are you sure it's him?"

"Yep, I was told he was taken in a week ago. He's in a cell, sitting under UV lights. He looks bad, but still sane, from what I can determine. Not that I care about a bloody longtooth…"

"We need to get him out," Ridge said. "Before the lights go back on. Abigail, is it a fuse, or did all the current get shut off?"

"We're standing right on top of a leyline." She surveyed the snowy grounds. "It'll stay out as long as I want it to."

"All right, I think I can deal with that. But remember what you promised?"

She made a show of crossing her heart with her fingers. It was a binding gesture no witch took for granted. She would stand by her word.

Ridge slapped Dean across the back. "Maverick, you up for a little stealth work?"

"Sure, but we don't need stealth. I've got free rein inside because they know me. You're the one who needs to stay out of sight."

"Will do. So what's the layout?"

"We've got an easy path around back, which I marked. There are only four wolves inside right now; the rest are out carousing in town. Hear there's a bunch of fresh strippers at the local watering hole. We should stop on the way home."

Ridge felt Abigail's admonishing glare, though he didn't see it. He didn't need to turn around; he knew she was not delivering love Maverick's way. At least it was the other wolf receiving her disdain this time instead of him.

"You'd better do this now," she said to them, "before they return from the show."

"If the strippers are new, they'll be there until closing time," Maverick noted.

"We don't care about the strippers. Stay by the truck, Abigail," Ridge commanded. "Keep it running. We may need a quick escape."

She saluted him and climbed onto the driver's seat.

"And keep the lights off!" he yelled as they left.

Behind him the lights blinked out, but the low rumble of the diesel engine wasn't going to aid their stealth. They'd be quick. And if there were only four wolves that Maverick had noted, this would be a piece of cake.

"You like that witch?" Maverick asked as they trotted through the fresh layer of snow toward the compound.

"Depends on what you're implying."

"Well, I'd be a cad if I didn't tell you I overheard everything you two were talking about outside the truck earlier."

"We had a one-night stand."

"I got that. But what happened in Vegas obviously didn't stay there. You think the kid is yours?"

"I don't want to decide right now. If I doubt it, then my thoughts will make it so. If I believe it, and I'm disappointed, well…" He let the thought hang. Because truly, he did already believe, and he wasn't sure he was prepared to accept the disappointment. Life had given him only disappointment. Best not to go there. "You lead, since you know the layout."

"Will do. If it matters, I hope the boy is yours. Kids are cool. Wouldn't mind having a couple myself, though I'm not sure Sunday can even get pregnant by a were-wolf."

"Now that would be an interesting kid. Half feline, half wolf? Whoa."

"Yeah, I've considered that," Maverick said. "Probably best if we adopt, which Sunday seems pretty cool about. Though the pack may not approve. Not like I'm going to be principal much longer anyway."

"Why's that?"

Dean tromped over the previous tracks he'd left in the snow, his legs kicking high as his boots sank deep in the powder.

"Sunday wants to move closer to the city. She craves friendship and fancy shoes, she said. Girl stuff. You know how women are."

Not really, but Ridge did have a handle on the shoe thing thanks to Blu Masterson. That woman went nuts over a new pair.

"And I grew up close to the Twin Cities," Maverick continued, "so I'm cool with the idea. I've already got a man marked to take over as principal of the Western pack. The scion is whip-smart and, like you, he respects all breeds in the paranormal nations. Guess that'll make me a lone wolf again."

"You're welcome to join the Northern pack. I'd be honored to have you as a pack mate, man."

"Thanks. I may do that. But there are no women in your pack, buddy, so that doesn't really work for Sunday and her plan to make oodles of friends. I like that word. Oodles. She says it a lot."

"I'm working on the female part."

"I can see that. But work harder, Addison. The witch is a tough catch, but the tougher they are, the more it's worth it when they finally surrender into your arms."

"What if she wants me to be tough?"

"Like what? She likes it rough?" Dean whistled appreciatively.

"I get that distinct impression."

"All the better! It's not easy for us when we need to answer the call of the full moon and all the women flinch and run away."

"You're lucky you've found Sunday."

"You're telling me. But then, every once in a while, she conjures a demon in the middle of having sex with her. I can't tell you how that dulls the bliss, man."

Familiars were demon conduits. Witches used them to conjure demons to this realm. "She does it without a witch to summon the demon?"

"Yeah, she's on her first life. Still getting the hang of the whole demon-conducting stuff. I love her dearly, though I've smashed in more than my share of demon heads lately. The hazard of a good sex life with a familiar."

He loped over a frozen ridge of dirt plowed in the field, and landed near a barbed wire fence. Crouching, Ridge joined Maverick's side. "Up ahead. I marked the back door with my scent."

"I can smell that," he said with a sideways smirk. They walked onward, carefully tracking the darkness to the door. "You open it. I don't need to step in your piss, man. Lead on."

Once inside the cool, brick-walled building, it took a few moments for Ridge's eyes to adjust to the darkness. There were no windows, and the scent of vampire blood was so strong his bile stirred and his gut reacted with a tight clench. Many were trapped here, he guessed, gauging from the stench and the noises on the other side of the steel doors.

This end of the compound was designed like a jail with steel doors sporting tiny peek holes secured with latches. Amandus had installed similar cells in the basement of the Northern compound, but they'd had bars instead of solid walls.

"They have quite the operation here," Maverick whispered. "I think the vampire's cell was ahead. I marked it with my spit." He sniffed about, and scampered ahead to stand near a door. "Here, this one."

Ridge tested the door, which felt as if it was barred only, and did not have a padlock or digital locking device. "Just barred?"

"There's a master control that opens them up front."

"Did you happen to get the combination for this door?"

"Dude." Maverick strolled down the hallway, and Ridge couldn't see anything until the metallic creak of a door revealed tiny green LED lights that glowed across his cohort's face. Maverick punched in a few numbers that beeped with each selection.

Something in the door before him clicked, and Ridge tried the bar. It slid easily. "I knew I called the right man for this job," he said when Maverick returned to his side. "Let's do this."

"Gentlemen."

A hazy glow turned around the corner where the master box still beamed green. A man holding a flashlight stepped into view. He growled, and Ridge scented a subtle, yet controlled aggression.

"Addison and Maverick?" the wolf said with astonishment.

A flash of the light beamed across the wolf's face, and Ridge said, "Severo?"

Chapter 10

"You're the last wolf I expected to run into in a pack compound stuffed to the walls with half-crazed vampires," Ridge said to the wolf standing five feet away.

Severo was a lone wolf who occasionally served the Council and never took sides. He was married to a vampire who had once been mortal. His easy personality was mirrored in the worn leather jacket and faded cowboy boots that peeked from beneath faded blue jeans. But his expression was anything but easy.

"I could say the same of you. What are you doing here, Addison? I can guess you're not carrying an engraved invitation if you came through the back door. And Maverick?"

Dean, hands stuffed in his pockets, shoulders straight and back, looked to Ridge to handle the talking.

"We just need one vampire," Ridge said. "Then we'll leave."

Severo crossed his arms, tilting the flashlight toward the ceiling. The low light allowed them to easily see one another's faces, and he was smirking, and his aggressive scent had dissipated. Though he was the one who should submit to the two pack leaders who stood before him, he carried himself with a pride that demanded respect. "You drove four hours from the Cities to steal one vampire from another pack? What's up with that? Couldn't find any loitering in the big city?"

"It's not what you think. Someone is in trouble. I need the vamp to get her out of trouble."

"Oh, so it's about a woman?" Severo dropped the stern-enforcer look and managed a crooked smile. "It's always about a woman, isn't it?" He eyed Maverick, who chuckled uneasily, obviously respectful of the elder werewolf's standing.

"Do you support this pack's blood sport?" Ridge asked.

"Not at all. I was in the area, and thought to stop in, and—well, this is what I find. I'm appalled the packs think they can ignore the Council's ruling on the blood sport. But even more, the cruelties that thrive because of breed differences are unconscionable. I was waiting for the principal to return to discuss a means of putting an end to this without reporting him to the Council. Not that the Council would make a move to threaten anyway. They toss out regulations and rules, and then don't stand behind the threat. I suspect a more direct approach will be required with this pack. Who's the woman?"

Ridge winced. He couldn't give that information to

Severo because Abigail wanted to keep this hush-hush from the Council, but neither could he lie to one he respected.

"A witch. A friend."

"Does this friend have a name?"

"Sure, but it's not something I can reveal. We're kinda…" He rubbed his brow and looked to Maverick.

"They just started dating," Maverick offered. "Want to keep it quiet, you know."

Severo nodded. "So you are collecting a vampire for a witch? Can't she get her own source?"

"It's not for her, it's— Listen. We're not going to harm the vampire. We need to turn him over to a person who is holding something over the witch's head."

"So that person can then harm the vampire?"

"Severo. Man. Don't be a hard-ass about this. Haven't you ever done something for a woman?"

"I would walk the world for the woman I love. But is that what this is about? Love?" He narrowed his gaze on Ridge.

"Do we have to get into this? Because I am willing to stand against you if you force me to."

Severo straightened, planting his feet squarely. The wolf didn't growl, but Ridge sensed the implied growl of warning.

"Can you turn and walk the other way while we tuck the vampire under an arm and get the hell out of here?"

The werewolf eyed him carefully. The only interaction they'd had previously was when Ridge had been serving Amandus Masterson, and he knew Severo was aware of the cruel things Ridge had done under that service. Yet he also knew he had killed Masterson. But could he understand why?

"I'm partial to the safety of vampires," Severo said. "My wife being one makes me sympathetic to them."

"I am too," Ridge offered. "And I'd love to set them all free right now."

"That wouldn't be wise," Severo said. "Half of them are insane with UV sickness. They'd go after humans and cause a great scare. They…" He sighed heavily. "Some should be destroyed. It's the kindest thing to do."

Ridge stepped forward and held out his hand for Severo to shake. "Give me the vampire I came for, and I'll help you do the job."

Severo nodded and shook his hand. "Let's make this quick and efficient."

Forty-five minutes later, Ridge and Maverick said goodbye to Severo, and wiped the blood from their eyes and necks as they left the Ely compound. Severo would remain behind to face the consequences with the pack leader. It was vigilante justice at its most grisly, but it had been kindest to stake those vampires with UV sickness.

"That was tough," Maverick said as they trampled across the field.

Ridge carried Mac York, unconscious, over a shoulder, the vampire's arms banging against his back. He could taste vampire blood in his throat, though he'd been careful to keep his mouth closed. They'd staked five vampires through the heart, and most had ashed immediately. One younger vamp had not, and had instead slowly burned away. The scent of ash and burned flesh had filled his nostrils, and he felt as if he'd never erase it from his senses.

It had been a heinous job, but someone had needed

to do it, because if they'd left the vampires to the pack, they would have been forced to fight one another to the death. A few had even nodded and submitted when they'd figured out what Ridge and Severo intended to do, taking death with ease.

They'd released two who had been recent captives.

"We won't speak of this night," Ridge said. "Ever."

"Deal."

They lumbered across the field toward the waiting truck.

"I don't get it." Maverick's breath huffed in clouds as he spoke. "Why would witches want a vampire? And so desperately that they'd kidnap some other witch's kid to make it happen?"

"Abigail said something about a source. You know witches need to consume a vampire heart once every century to maintain their immortality."

"That I did not know. Yikes. So they eat it whole?"

"I'm not sure on the particulars, nor am I interested." Especially not after the slaughter he'd participated in.

"Then that means Abigail has consumed a few hearts in her days, 'cause I heard she was pretty old."

Ridge pictured the vulgar act in his mind. As much as vampires sucking blood from mortals repulsed him, the idea of a witch eating a whole heart was ten times worse. It was an animalistic act on level with the blood sport.

"Everyone does what they have to do to survive," he commented.

He was defending the witch now? It wasn't difficult to do. He'd committed acts on par with her dark deeds, so he could not judge.

They reached the truck and Abigail jumped out to

open the back door so they could shove the vampire
inside. She grabbed his arm and wiped something from
his face. He folded his fingers about her hand, and silently entreated her not to question him.

With a nod, she wiped her hands off in the snow, and
then gestured that he do the same to his hands and face
because apparently he was covered with blood. Maverick followed in stride.

It made little sense to Abigail. If they had only to
grab one vampire and run, why were both men covered
in blood? Had the vampire put up a fight against two
werewolves? It was unlikely so much blood would have
been the result. And the vampire was relatively clean,
though his shirt was torn and his long brown hair a
tangled mess. Not a drop of blood spattered him or his
clothes.

Perhaps they'd had to battle other wolves? That had
to be it. She'd read Ridge's silent plea clearly. He didn't
want to talk about it. She wouldn't question. She owed
him that much for what he'd done for her.

Maverick drove and Abigail, on the passenger seat,
turned to eye the vampire Ridge held with an arm
clamped about his neck.

"I don't think he's a flight risk," she said.

Ridge did not let up. He seemed stuck on the precipice of shifting, so tense his musculature held him, and
his eyes were narrow and fierce. If she had the scenting
skills of a wolf she felt sure she'd read anger on him.

"He's going to pass out if you hold him too tightly,"
she warned. "We need him to talk."

The werewolf shoved the vamp against the truck

door and pinned him with a hand about his neck. "You hear the lady? Talk."

"Wh-what do you want? I can't breathe. Fuck. That hurts. The vein."

"They've cut into his carotid and opened it wide," Abigail said, wincing at the cruelty the werewolves had inflicted. Then she reminded herself she had done some heinous things over the centuries. "It's scarred, but it will give him pain ever after. Ridge, let him relax. I'll keep him from escaping."

The vampire eyed her with wild, nervous eyes. He smelled of sweat and urine.

Manipulating the air in the vehicle, she coaxed the door lock next to the vamp's shoulder shut. And to make it more interesting… Blowing toward the door heated the metal. The vampire yelped and scrambled from the hot metal, but that put him right back in Ridge's clutches.

"What the hell is she?"

"The baddest witch in the Midwest," Ridge said with an interesting tone of pride.

Abigail accepted the compliment with a blush. He was the only one she'd ever abide to give her such a title. And what was wrong with that title? Someone had to be the bad witch. It was much easier than this good-girl bull crap she'd been dabbling in unsuccessfully for years.

"We need to know why you're so important to a bunch of witches," Ridge said. "They want you like a drug dealer craves his stolen dope. They kidnapped her son to make her find you."

"Really? I haven't been aligned with the Light in

over a decade. They kicked me out after they learned I was a half-breed."

"Half-breed?" Abigail peered into the vampire's hazy eyes. He returned the stare and his pupils widened as they prepared to fix onto her soul. Only another witch could fix a witch in a stare and read the other witch's soul, and he seemed capable— She abruptly stopped that nonsense by blinking. "You're half witch!"

"Born that way," the vampire said. "Both of my parents were fire witches."

"Did you come into your fire magic?" she asked hastily.

"Briefly. I was transformed to vamp, much against my will, ten years ago, about six months after puberty granted me fire magic, so I hadn't much time to use it. Spoiled my plans of world domination, let me tell you."

Ridge delivered her a confused lift of brow.

"World domination?" she questioned. "I've never heard of you until a day ago. The Council—"

"The Council?" The vampire laughed until Ridge slammed his hand under his throat, choking him into a wincing cough.

"Just talk nice to the lady, and I won't have to get rough," the werewolf warned. "Why would the witches want you?"

"If he was born of two fire witches," Abigail said, "then he must be a very powerful witch."

"Should be," the vampire corrected. "That all got fucked up when I was bitten. My magic hasn't been the same since. They have your son?"

She nodded.

"Heh." The vampire smirked, but controlled his laughter with an abrupt squeeze from Ridge's hand. "If you're a fire witch," he said to Abigail, "then where's the father? Actually, who is the father?"

Ridge gave her a scathing look. Abigail moved her hand before the vamp in a threatening manner. He got the hint and said, "If the father is a fire witch, then the son is a valuable commodity. Who wouldn't want him?"

"But they offered to make a trade," Ridge said. "The boy for you."

"That makes little sense." The vampire coughed and blood trickled over his bottom lip. "Sorry. Those damn UV lights work a number on a guy. I feel like my lungs got fried and are slowly bleeding out my mouth. Thanks for the rescue, by the way. You are going to let me go? Hell, you're not going to slaughter me like—"

Ridge squeezed the man's trachea. "Like I said, we're going to trade you for her son."

The vampire sputtered blood. His eyes bulged and Ridge reluctantly released him.

"Why would they want me instead of the fire witch? Oh, wait." He bowed his head and shook it. His eyes glittered as he looked at Abigail, and she felt the immensity of his unspoken words. "I know."

"You know what?" She spread out her hand and curled her fingers in succession toward her, coaxing his confession by tapping into his vampiric influence and turning it on him.

"No need to influence me, sweetie. I'll fess up. But this is too rich. I'm not sure why they would want to bind your son. Unless the father really is a fire witch."

"Bind him?" Her heart fluttered like a butterfly with broken wings. It sounded so wrong. And yet, she knew what it was, a process similar to shackling she'd performed on Creed Saint-Pierre last summer. Only binding hurt ten times worse, and was a permanent means to strip the magic from a witch. "He's just a boy. He hasn't even come into his magic."

She caught Ridge's gaze and couldn't find the words to plead for his help. How had this happened? Who was doing this to her and Ryan? Why would they want to harm a boy?

"Best time to bind him," the vampire said. "So he never comes into his magic. Whoever binds him ultimately controls him. I should know."

"Yeah?" Ridge tightened his grip about the vamp's neck. "And how is that?"

The vampire looked from Ridge to Abigail. "If I help you, I need assurance I get out of this safely and you won't throw me to the wolves."

"Can't do that." Ridge increased pressure under the vamp's jaw, making his face go white. "Besides, you're already in the hands of wolves."

"How can you help?" Abigail pressed. "Can you prevent them from binding my son?"

"I can," he managed, though his voice was fading as the pressure on his throat increased.

"Ridge, let him speak!"

The werewolf growled at her, and the vampire cringed from Ridge. Now was no time for the wolf to go aggressive. She needed the information the vampire was willing to give.

She waved her hand before her, twitching her fingers in a familiar gesture. Ridge flinched and released the vampire, but the angry growl he delivered her pierced her heart. She'd threatened him in front of his own, and he wasn't pleased about it.

"You don't want to hand me over to the witches," the vampire said, stroking his reddened neck.

"Why not?" Ridge growled.

"Because you'll be handing them the binding spell. That's what they need. They don't care about me."

"Do you know the binding spell?" she asked. "It's supposed to be rare, inaccessible to most of the Light."

"Know it? Not without looking in a mirror." He turned a shoulder toward the front seat. It was easy enough for him to rip down his tattered shirt.

Beneath it, tattooed on his back, read an ancient binding spell Abigail recognized was in Latin.

"I was bound a decade ago," he said. "I had begun a stint working for Himself—I was power-mad with my new fire magic, and there's a reason they call the devil the Great Tempter—until the vampires changed me and it all went wonky. Himself had no use for me after that. You want to bind a fire witch, this is the spell to do it."

"Well, I'll be," Maverick commented from the front. "Why'd you tattoo it on your back?"

"It wasn't me. Himself did that with one lick of his thorned tongue. Said it was a joke. That dude has the weirdest sense of humor."

"So if we stake you," Ridge said, "that solves our problem."

"No," Abigail said. "We need him."

"We're not going to hand him over to the vampires. They'll harm your son. My son!"

"Dude, he's your kid?" The vampire blanched. "Then he can't be a fire witch, and I haven't a clue why the witches would want him."

"He's not his father," Abigail protested. "His father is a fire witch."

"As far as you know," Ridge argued. "But there's a chance you could be wrong."

The vampire whistled. "Sounds like you two need to work a few things out."

"Silence." Abigail swept her hand before the vampire, and his next protest was muffled because he couldn't open his mouth no matter how much he struggled. "We need to keep the spell out of the witches' hands, but if Ryan comes into his magic…"

The idea of binding her son did not sit well. Hell, she wanted him to come into his magic, to grow powerful and revel in his skills. Sure, he'd drain her of her fire magic; that was what occurred when the child came into his magic. She didn't care. She'd give up all her magic for Ryan. But it could be more dangerous to him if she allowed him to come into his magic. He would never be safe. There would always be some power-mad maniac who sought to take from Ryan what he craved.

"We're here." Maverick parked the truck in the lot next to his car. "You two need me anymore? I'm willing to help."

"I think we got what we need," Ridge said, his gaze fixed to Abigail's.

A witch could fix another witch in her gaze and stare directly into her soul. A werewolf couldn't, but right now, she felt Ridge was doing just that to her. And he didn't like what he saw.

Because she denied he could possibly be Ryan's father. It didn't make sense. She had to be prepared, and to prepare for the worst. Whether or not the werewolf liked it.

Hell, it was difficult acting against him. She didn't want to hurt him. She wanted him to respect her, and yes, all she really wanted from him was to fold her in his arms again and make everything all right.

"Thanks, Dean," she said. "I owe you a big one."

"I will remember that." He shook her hand, then nodded to Ridge, and left them in the dark parking lot across from the café where he'd parked his car.

"Now what?" Ridge asked. "We've the night and then tomorrow afternoon the meeting. And we've got to figure out what to do with the longtooth."

"Let's go to my house."

Chapter 11

Abigail directed Ridge to the basement, and left him to secure the vampire. The last thing she wanted to do was turn over the vamp if he wore a tattoo of the ritual that could bind her son. But she wasn't about to let their one bargaining chip free until she had Ryan safe at home.

Whoever held Ryan must be thinking to use the binding spell against him. But why did they expect she would willingly hand over something so detrimental after she figured it all out? The logic was distorted. She must be missing some integral piece to this puzzle.

Agitated, she paced the living room above the basement, hearing a few warning growls from Ridge, and then went back into her bedroom. She wasn't tired, though it was late. Her body shook with raw energy. She knew she should sleep so she was rested for tomorrow. But how to sleep with a werewolf and a vampire in her house?

Especially, a sexy werewolf who had kissed her and held her so tenderly. It seemed impossible Ridge could be so gentle. Everything about him appeared harsh.

Everything on the outside, that is. She had gotten glimpses inside the man's soul, and frankly, she liked what she had seen. He did not react to situations with violence, as most men were wont. Careful consideration went into every move he made, and he regretted nothing.

But he hadn't tapped his gentle nature when he'd learned about Ryan and the possibility he could be his father. That was to be expected, however.

But really, she didn't need acceptance or approval from any man. She had raised Ryan well, and would continue to do so, no matter what life presented them.

But the result—if Ridge were Ryan's father—was something she was not equipped to handle. A werewolf son? How did she begin to explain a shifter's nature to Ryan? That he could be part animal whose cycles were ruled by the moon?

"Don't think about it," she murmured. "The possibilities are a long shot." She absently ran a hand over her stomach, as she'd done so many times when she had been pregnant. She'd counted the days dozens of times. Miles was the father. Ryan could not have been born a month late. "He's a witch, I know he is."

Anything is possible. You know that.

"Abigail?"

Ridge stood in the doorway to her bedroom, stretching an arm along the door frame. He looked opposite of her agitated state and was probably tired and hungry.

"You can use the shower," she offered. "I'll make you some tea. Or maybe some beer and a sandwich? I have no meat but I might surprise you with a little almond butter and green apples."

He winced at the idea of consuming the meatless fare. "Sandwich sounds fine. I'm so hungry I could eat anything. I secured Mac. He tried to bite me, but I punched him on the jaw. Knocked out a fang. I wasn't trying to hurt him." He rubbed his knuckles. "Hell. This day has been too long. You figure out what you want to do with him?"

"Not yet. I'm still running on adrenaline, and trying to come down and relax." She needed an outlet for all this frantic energy. A jog usually helped. Or some good old-fashioned vacuuming; yes, without the use of magic. "I'll come up with something. I promise. You take a shower and relax. You did good, Ridge. Thank you."

He nodded, and tugged off his shirt and turned down the hallway.

"Use the one in my room," she said. "The pipe leaks in the guest bathroom."

He balled up his shirt and the movement flexed his hard pectorals. With a shy nod, he walked past her into the bathroom. Abigail inhaled as he passed, closing her eyes to file away the scent of the most honorable man she had ever known. Fresh and woodsy, as if he belonged in the forest, a creature of nature. Wild and wolfish.

She'd asked far more of him than he had asked of her. She owed him more than he could ever know. And she would pay up.

Before heading to the kitchen, her eyes glanced upon

the digital camera sitting on her vanity. An idea occurred. She snatched the camera, and went into the kitchen to make something hearty enough to satisfy a tired, hungry werewolf.

The bathroom was the frilliest room he'd ever been in. It smelled powdery, and every step he took he brushed lace or a ruffle or a crystal bowl with funny-looking spices and dried chunks of stuff in it. Leaving his dirty clothes heaped on the fluffy pink rug seemed a crime, but he quickly got over his foul deed as the hot water poured over his scalp and shoulders.

Ridge groaned as the water massaged his aching muscles. A man needed only two things to survive. Food and hot water.

As for his wolf? A wolf also needed a visceral connection to another soul, which is why he figured he'd never quite felt complete. Whole. Not constantly exhausted by the world.

"You need her," he muttered to his pining heart. "She can give you what your wolf craves."

Connection. A warm body in his arms, slipping across his skin, healing his ache for something he couldn't quite grasp. Sex. Love. Trust. Devotion.

Family.

It always came down to family. And what a loop he'd been tossed onto this evening. He could be the boy's father. It seemed too incredible after he'd given up hope of ever fathering a child.

He twisted off the water, brushed aside the ruffled pink shower curtain and stepped onto the deep shag rug, burying his toes within the long red and pink strands. He tugged a purple towel about his waist and some thick gold fringes tickled his knees.

Surprising to discover this girlie cove buried within the stalwart witch's domain. He flicked a finger against a glass bottle and it rang like crystal. The indiscernible fruity odor in the room made him hungry, and he remembered she had offered food. Far from real-man food, but he'd consume anything with calories right now.

Glancing to his dirty jeans and shirt, he couldn't bring himself to put them back on. He'd eat then dive into bed for a few hours of shut-eye so he could be at the top of his game for the meeting tomorrow afternoon.

Checking the back of the door for a robe, and relieved there wasn't one—for surely it would be ruffled and pink—Ridge strode down the hallway wearing the towel. The laundry room was nestled next to the main bathroom. He tossed his clothes into the washer, poured in what he suspected was detergent from a glass jar, and set it to wash.

The witch was not in the kitchen. A sandwich sat on a plate, a cold beer near that. He looked about for Abigail, then sniffed, scenting a coconut trail that led toward the closed basement door. She was downstairs? The vampire was secured with leather straps he'd found in the utility room, and he was still woozy and out of it from his adventures under the UV lights, so Ridge knew he would cause Abigail little harm. Whatever she was up to, he was more concerned with his growling stomach.

The call of the wild screamed, and he grabbed half the sandwich and took a bite. Smoky gouda cheese was the first taste, followed by crisp green apple and then something the consistency of peanut butter, but milder. And did he taste honey and cinnamon? It wasn't bad. In fact, it was tasty. He gobbled the sandwich half in four crunchy bites.

Taking a bite from the other half, he wandered toward the basement stairs, and listened at the closed door. A man growled low and deep, as if biting back a lung-clearing yell.

Ridge's muscles tensed. He paused midbite. His fingers touched the knob, yet he didn't open the door. An expletive muffled behind the door had come from the vampire. He sounded angry and…afraid.

Was the witch torturing him? She couldn't possibly… He caught the scent of something burning and he turned his head away from the odor. Smelled like burned flesh.

She must have burned him with her fire magic in defense. Smart girl. But he should probably go check on her. He gripped the door handle, snarfed down the last bite of sandwich, and then caught the towel as it loosened and fell down his hips.

"Can't face the longtooth in nothing but a towel."

Before he could move, he heard footsteps on the stairs and Abigail opened the door. She touched her hair and sighed, offering him a smile.

Acting nonchalant, he nodded to the plate and beer. "Nice spread."

"Good. I'm glad I could make something you like, despite the lack of meat."

"It's filling."

"The almond butter provides protein you need."

"It's better than peanut butter. Never would have thought. So, you talk to the vamp?"

"I wanted to make him comfortable. No reason to treat him so cruelly after the Ely pack had already done so. I explained he would be free to go after I got Ryan back."

"Sounded a little less than nice to me," he said, finishing off the sandwich.

She set a digital camera on the counter. "I took a picture of the spell."

"Smart."

"Then I burned it off," she said as if casually mentioning a new sweater or purse. "He understood it had to be done."

"That explains the smell of burned flesh."

"Sorry." She opened a drawer and drew out a black candle, and with a snap of her fingers, the wick took to flame. "It's anise scented. It'll overwhelm the other smell. So I see you found the towels."

He noticed her eyes slide down his torso and stop on his abdomen. It wasn't often Ridge caught a woman admiring him. His sexual affairs were usually the get-it-done-and-get-out-of-there variety. He wasn't much for romance, because he wasn't sure how it all worked.

It felt good sitting there in her regard. Different, but satisfying. As if he was the only man in the world right now.

"You hungry too?" he asked.

"Oh yes. Er, I mean…" She shook her head and twisted an end of her hair about a finger. "I had half a sandwich when I made that one for you."

He rubbed a palm over his stomach, fully aware her

gaze had slipped to his abs again. "Wasn't food I was talking about."

"Are you implying we should get naked and do the nasty again?"

"Again? That was thirteen years ago, Abigail. Neither of us remembers if it was good or bad."

"It was good," she said, and strode past him toward her bedroom.

"It was?" Downing the beer in a quick swallow, he then rushed after her. "If you think it was, then you know there is a chance I could be Ryan's father."

"Whether or not the sex was good or bad does not provide proof of paternity."

"I suppose."

He followed her into the bedroom, and when she swung around, waving a hand through the air, he ducked.

Abigail laughed. "Think I was going to throw some magic at you?"

He straightened. "I can never be too sure with you. Just tell me you believe there's a chance, and then I'll drop it. I won't bring it up anymore."

She sat on the bed, which wasn't ruffled or even pink, and patted the mattress beside her. Ridge sat immediately. The gold fringes hung over his knees, and it felt wrong, but he puffed up his chest, going for as manly a look as he could get in the silly towel.

Head bowed, the witch remained silent for a while. He wanted to stroke his fingers through her coconut hair, but already felt the moment teetered on some precipice that felt wrong, yet oh, so right. No way could he ignore his near nakedness or the long look she had given him.

"I do believe there is a chance," she finally offered as she met his gaze with a sigh. "Good enough for you?"

He nodded. "We'll know the truth when the boy hits puberty. Which should be soon if he's twelve."

"Twelve and a half. And his voice has already begun to change. You said you wouldn't talk about it anymore if I gave you that."

"Fine." He put up his hands in defeat. "End of topic."

Though it would never be the end of it in his heart. And now, more than ever—if that were possible—he would move mountains to get back the boy.

Abigail tilted her head and scrunched up her right shoulder. "I don't want to dwell on the bad stuff tonight. There's nothing either of us can do until tomorrow afternoon."

"Exactly."

"I want to come down from this insane jittery high I'm on and try to get some sleep. My magic gets twisted into knots in my body and it builds as energy."

"So you need to release the magic somehow?"

"In a way. A good workout might help. But a jog in this weather is out of the question. I could vacuum or do some laundry. Just…something to focus my mind and energy on other things. You know?"

"Your muscles sore? Let me rub them."

He slid a hand up her back, and she squiggled to direct him higher—or maybe it was a protest. "Don't think I don't know what you're doing, werewolf."

He turned and placed both hands on her shoulders, ignoring her shrugs. "What am I doing?"

"You're sitting on my bed in nothing but a towel. And you're touching me."

"Yep, that's what I'm doing, all right. Good thing

you pointed that out. In a million years, I'd never have guessed right."

She chuckled softly, yet her body moved against his palms as he slid them down along her shoulder blades. "That does feel good. Right at the back of my neck. Oh, there, yes. How is it you're so gentle for such a big lug of a man?"

"You're a delicate thing. I wouldn't dream of hurting you. I know my hands are big and awkward, so I have to concentrate not to touch too hard."

"You're doing great. Just the right pressure. Oh… yes…"

She let her head fall forward, and the sight of her nape, the long pale column wisped with fine, dark hairs, stirred Ridge's desire. He'd not lingered on softness overmuch. Well, as he'd told her, he was too big, too clumsy with most women, so quick was the usual routine.

"You washing your clothes?" she murmured.

"You don't mind?"

"Of course not. I'm impressed, is all. Not many men know how to operate household appliances."

"Took care of myself a lot in the compound."

"Have you been in the Northern pack all your life? I don't recall hearing that your parents were in that pack."

He stopped kneading her neck, and she tilted her head. Her hair fell over his hands, like a veil of feathers fluttering over his skin. He brushed aside her hair and circled his thumb along the column of her neck.

"Ridge?"

"Never knew my parents. Earliest I can remember is playing with the other pack kids, but sleeping alone in a tiny shed at night. Never had a mother to tuck me in."

"You were an orphan."

He felt her body want to turn toward him, so he increased the pressure a little and rolled his thumbs down her spine, forcing her to sit straighter and not look at him. A tiny moan of pleasure spilled from her mouth.

"Yep, an orphan. But the pack takes care of its own."

"How did they die?"

"Not sure they are dead. No one ever told me a thing about them. Not for lack of asking on my part, either."

"I'm sorry."

"Nothing to be sorry for. I grew up. I survived. I'm now a pack principal with my own pitiful pack. End of story."

Except, he wanted to write the story differently, including a family and a happily-ever-after. Did that make him weak?

Yes, it did.

Abigail flinched and he released the tight squeeze he held on her shoulder. "Sorry. Wasn't paying attention. Why don't you lie down and let me do this right?"

She turned and eyed him, summing up his request. She was leery he was trying to get her to do something sexual. He wasn't. Well, maybe he was. It didn't have to go to full-blown sex, but some skin-on-skin contact would be the thing right now to relax them both and take their minds off the bad stuff.

"You said you needed to redirect your thoughts and energy to chill out. A little skin-on-skin might be the thing."

"It would be, you sly and clever wolf. But..."

"But you're unsure. Scared."

She tugged her sweater off over her head, beneath which she wore a thin silk camisole that revealed her peaked nipples. "I'm a big girl. And some big bad naked wolf who wants to put his hands all over me doesn't scare me."

"Is that so?" He held up his hands in offering to continue the massage. "Then lie down and let me put my hands on you."

She rolled onto her stomach and stretched out on the bed. "If I fall asleep, promise you won't stay in the room. I don't want you to hear me snore."

"I'll sleep on the couch." He knelt over her, and rubbed his palms together to warm them. "And I'll put a pillow over my ears to block out any ambient noises. Promise."

"You can sleep in Ryan's room. The bed is full size and it's comfy."

He pressed his hands to her back and eased his knuckles up and down the silk but it bunched and tugged, so he slid his hands under the camisole to massage her warm, soft skin. The pants she wore were low on her hips, so he could rock his knuckles down and work them into the dimples topping each of her buttocks.

"That feels great."

"You have a sexy back. Your obliques are nice and tight."

"I'm not sure what you said, but keep that up. It feels like you're pampering my muscles."

He kneaded along her side where the sexy obliques stretched, and then he dragged his fingertips lower, seeking the dimple of Venus cresting each buttock. She was giving him a gift, this time to explore her body,

and she would never know it. Nor had he any intention
of telling her how inexperienced he was with women.

Not inexperienced, but rather, not so skilled.

"It's going to be a quick massage," he warned.
"Unless you want to deal with the big bad wolf."

"You wouldn't wolf out from giving me a massage?"

"I sure as hell don't intend to, but parts of me are
shifting, whether I like it or not."

"I get it." She turned suddenly, and the movement
tugged the towel loose from around his waist.

Ridge grabbed the towel and started to retuck it
when her hand stopped him. "Abigail, I'm having a
hard time reading your signals. It's much easier when
I can dodge your waving hands."

"Lie by me," she said. "Hold me."

She was asking a monumental thing. But he was
no man to refuse her. He slid alongside her so they lay
face-to-face.

She traced a fingernail under his pectoral muscle,
and then put her head on his forearm and nuzzled her
face against his skin where she'd touched him. The tip
of her nose was cold against his flesh.

"I feel so safe with you," she whispered, her bright
eyes sparkling under fluttering lashes. "And the weird
thing is, I never realized I needed to feel like this until
it happened. That's so odd, coming from a witch who
has lived for centuries, and has seen pretty much everything there is to see."

"I'd like to know about the things you've seen. I bet
they were marvelous."

"And wicked."

"But some were beautiful?"

"Oh yes, and others were horrific."

"I hope you experienced kindness over the centuries."

"And cruelty."

"Gained wisdom though, I bet."

"I feel wise about some things. Other things, I feel as new to them as someone who's only had decades to learn them. Like love." She sighed. "I've already mentioned my stupidity with love. Obsess much? That's me. Abigail Rowan, the witch to avoid."

"I haven't had much practice with it myself."

"So we're both kinda stupid about love then."

He stroked her slowly, making circles across her skin. "I think I'd like to be stupid in love. Like so madly in love I'm a fool around the woman, tripping and stumbling into my blindness."

"Been there, done that."

"Did you get the T-shirt?"

"I think it was called a tunic back then."

He nuzzled his face into her hair and wished he could swallow her whole. Put her inside him and always have her close. He knew he was thinking completely opposite of how he should be thinking.

Divorce papers, remember?

But right now, this wrong felt too right. Stupid right.

"Don't stop touching me," he said on a hoarse, wanting tone. "Please?"

She obliged, trailing her fingertips across his chest in gliding strokes that traveled from his belly button to between his pecs. Back and forth, so soothing, and yet, stirring.

"Sometimes," she started slowly, "when times are tough, and you don't know what to do next, all you can do is surrender."

The heat of her mouth pressed to his stomach. The soft smack of her kiss tensed his muscles and tightened every part of him so he felt the sweet strain of desire.

"Let's do this," she whispered. "No strings. No questions. Just…surrender."

She pressed another kiss lower, beside his naval. The heat of it was insane, and Ridge felt his cock rise in expectation beneath the purple towel.

"Okay," he croaked, and slid his fingers through her silken hair. "No strings. No questions."

"Tomorrow is a new day," she said. "What happens tonight stays right here."

"We'll pretend it's Vegas," he agreed. "Without the alcohol."

"And the fire."

"And the magic."

"Deal."

He reached around and slid her up to face him. Without another word, he leaned down and kissed her parted lips. She sighed into him, and that sigh spread through him like the flames he must avoid. Her body melded against his, her breasts to his chest, her thigh nudging his erection.

He shoved up the camisole and palmed her lacy bra, liking the play of the lace against his skin. And then he found the hard peak of her nipple.

At his mouth she drank from him deeply. He wanted to taste her again, and this time remember it all.

"Is this okay?"

For some reason her big, strong werewolf seemed nervous. Not to touch her, but perhaps to take things slowly. His erection pressed hard against her thigh and she wanted to feel its power, sooner rather than after prolonged foreplay.

She slid his hand over her breast and he squeezed it softly, but not hard enough for her, so she showed him how she liked it. "Mmm, like that, Ridge."

"You like it rough?"

"I'm a big girl. I like a man who takes control."

He buried his face against her neck and his tongue dashed against her skin, tasting her. He sucked, and she squiggled against him, pressing her breasts hard against his chest. He grabbed her ass and pressed her hips against his. "Feel this, witch."

"Mmm…" Draping a leg over his hip, she studied his rigid hard-on with a slide of her hips. "So hard. Want you inside me. Now."

"Condoms?" he groaned out.

"Yes." *About thirteen years too late.*

Dismissing the thought, Abigail leaned back and pulled the drawer open by the bed. Foil crinkled and she slipped out the cool, lubed circlet. "Let me put it on you."

His drawn-out moan bellowed as she slowly slid the sheath over his shaft. He was there, waiting to meet her at the precipice, and she was ready to jump.

"Need you." He lifted her and, as he rolled to his back, settled her to straddle his hips. She wanted to slide onto his thickness and feel him part her wide, but he controlled her with both hands to her hips, allowing her only to crown the thick, hot head of him. "Christ."

He teased her by pressing into her, not deeply, just enough to make her body pulse with frenzied want, and she dug her nails into his forearms. But still, he moved her slowly. The look on his face was fierce. He looked at her, but not really at her. All focus had to be at the head of his cock. She loved that look of lost passion.

"All of you," she gasped. "Please. Let me…" She wanted the control. She needed it.

So when he flipped her and pinned her wrists to the bed, her world flipped too. He was taking control, as she'd wished, but… But what? She had no argument.

"Ridge, I— Oh…"

He slid a finger inside her and set her every nerve ending ablaze. Her core hummed and she arched her back, pressing her shoulders into the sheets. "So wet," he murmured. "My pretty little witch is ready for me."

"Yes," she said on a sigh and clutched the pillow with both hands. She wiggled her hips. "Come inside me, wolf. Please."

Ridge speared her with his hot, thick manhood, gliding in all the way until their hips hugged. The heat of him seared her so she cried out in delicious ecstasy. He filled her, and commanded her.

Grabbing her hips, he pumped quicker, moving her body back and forth upon his powerful erection. A wolfish growl startled her, and she clutched the sheets in a tight fist.

Ridge growled again, and this time it was deeper, more animal-like. She heard him gnash his teeth.

His body tremored and he gripped her tightly, his jaw tense. He cried out in ecstasy, but abruptly cut it off. He pulled out of her and punched a fist into the headboard. "Sorry."

Abigail fell from the high of near-orgasm to the light catch of the bed. "Are you going to shift?"

Gasping, he huffed out, "No. Maybe. Damn." He retreated into the bathroom and slammed the door.

She blew the tousle of hair from her lashes. What a way to end a perfectly exquisite session of lovemaking. Poor guy. Could he not control his wolf when the two of them got naked?

Chapter 12

The sun hadn't risen, but Abigail couldn't sleep any longer. She woke nuzzled against the hard, warm back of her warrior werewolf. She felt good pressed against his muscles, leeching his body heat into her own. His heartbeats were slow, as were his breaths.

At some point she had rolled over and closed her eyes, listening as Ridge had sneaked back into the bedroom and crawled into bed with her. She hadn't heard anything in the bathroom like wolf howls, so she figured he'd stopped himself from shifting.

The guy had issues if this happened every time he had sex with a woman. Or was it just her?

Reaching around over his torso, she glided her fingers along his abdomen, rigid with muscle. Probably not the reason he was called Ridge, but an apt example.

"Not sleeping?" he wondered lazily.

"I did for a bit. I got enough. I feel rested and my nervous energy leveled out. It was the great sex." She couldn't complain. No orgasm didn't necessarily mean no pleasure. And man, had he felt great inside of her.

He turned and kissed her on the forehead, then her nose, then bent to kiss each of her breasts, laving them slowly. "It was great until my werewolf wanted to come out and play. I'm sorry."

"Stop apologizing for an awesome session of sex. Instead make me understand what happens in your body while having sex with me. Is it just me? Why did you shift in Vegas? Is it so uncontrollable sometimes?"

"Not usually, but it was the full moon that night, and alcohol loosens my better judgment, and when I feel the compulsion to shift, well, I can't think to fight it when drunk."

"Yet you didn't shift earlier."

"Didn't want to freak you out. I had control because I wasn't inebriated. But man, the pull to bond mate with you was strong. It's never been like that for me."

"I thought wolves needed that kind of mating sex only before the full moon?"

"If I want to keep my werewolf at bay, I need to have sex until I'm sated the nights before and after the full moon. If not, the werewolf comes out, which I don't mind at all."

"I suppose you gotta let the guy out once in a while."

"Never around people. And only around a woman when I know she can accept it. You're the only woman who has ever called to my werewolf's desire to bond, Abigail. It startled me as much as I'm sure it did you. When we make love, my beast wants out. Wants to claim you as my mate."

"I see." It sounded dangerous, a little exciting, but also…committal.

"Don't worry, I'm not going to force myself on you. I know this was just…sex."

"Yes, it was." Mostly.

Abigail wasn't going to face the emotional truths she felt would negate that answer. Too many other worries. That was her story, and she was sticking to it.

She trailed a finger down his stomach and along the pale scar tugging at his skin. A flash of sunrise shone on it and for the first time she saw it clearly. "Wow, that scar really did cut close to your—"

He slid a hand over the scar. "Don't say cut."

"And you think it made you infertile?"

"I know it did because you put a spell on me. I didn't say anything when you asked me to wear a condom, but Abigail, it wouldn't matter. I'm serious. Thanks to that damned spell you zapped me with, I can't have kids."

He took her toying fingers away from the scar and kissed them gently. "If I ask nicely, would you please remove the spell?"

"Ridge." She didn't want to do this right now. Not after they'd shared so much, and she was feeling close to him. And yes, she had lied. It had been more than just sex.

But she hadn't any right to keep what she knew from him. By not correcting his false assumption, she was as good as a liar. And that was no way to treat the man. "Okay, fine. I have a confession to make."

She sat nestled against the pillows, and Ridge leaned on his elbows. He looked too delicious with the sheet half covering his legs and his carved-from-stone body exposed to the sunlight like some kind of god. His ass was so fine, and those powerful thighs. Mercy.

Tell him now, Abigail. He's been too kind to you to deserve your betrayal.

"I didn't put a spell on you in Vegas."

He shook his head, chuckling. "I know differently."

"Seriously, Ridge, there wasn't time to summon one. I reacted to seeing you wolf out and zapped you with an electrical charge. As I've told you, I often channel electricity when I'm afraid, and if I'm near a leyline it all goes haywire. Reactionary magic is the official term, though I usually call it accidental magic."

"Reactionary?"

"You said you were too drunk to control your werewolf. Do you think I was so sober I had the ability to cast a spell?"

"Abigail, I know you did something to me, because I can't have kids."

"Maybe it's just…trauma. From the event, you know. You were almost gelded."

"Don't say gelded," he ground through a tight jaw. "You said you would remove the spell after I helped you. I'm helping you. Show me some good faith and remove it."

"How many times do I have to say it? There was no spell."

"You specifically said you'd remove the spell when I came looking for a divorce," he growled. "There must be a spell."

She shrugged. She didn't like when he spoke to her so forcefully. And just when she was starting to fall for the big lug. Honestly though, she was to blame. She had used his belief in the spell to get him to do what she needed him to do.

He swept a hand down the scar and tugged the sheet to cover it. His somber expression hurt her heart. "You lied to me?"

"I was desperate. A knight in shining armor happened to knock on my door in a time of desperate need, and—Ridge, I needed your help!"

He got off the bed and paced before her, unmindful of his nudity, of his gorgeous, toned muscles and impossible body. Despite the damage she had done to him, his penis had taken no harm, and right now it was hard and bobbed with each step. He was marvelous to look at, even scarred and angry. Even more marvelous, for the anger tensed his muscles and gave him a fierce mien.

She couldn't have damaged him. Or had she?

Oh, what are you doing, Abigail? You lied to a wolf!

"You're not going to wolf out on me again, are you?"

"No!" he snapped. "No spell? Then why can't I have children?"

"Have you tried?"

"I've been with plenty of women."

"No birth control?"

"Not always," he said, twisting his mouth and shaking his head to negate that statement. "Usually the woman says she's on the pill, but then later she'll be like, 'I'm so relieved, I'm not pregnant,' so I have to assume she wasn't on birth control. It's never happened."

"Well, it doesn't happen every time. Are you saying you actually wanted to have a baby with some random stranger?"

"No, but I had a girlfriend for a year. A werewolf, even." His sigh spoke volumes. It was rare that male wolves hooked up with the even rarer females. "She wanted to have kids, and so did I. She broke up with me because it never happened. You know the females are particular about finding a virile mate. I just— Are you sure?"

She could but nod. The air in the room felt heavy, depleted by Ridge's disappointment. And she had been the cause of it.

"Abigail, the pack relies on me to be their leader. Part of leading is being a family man, growing the pack with my children. And, hell, I would love to be a father."

He sat on the end of the bed and hung his head.

His confession burned in her throat, yet in a good way. He would make a wonderful father; she felt it. If there were a chance he was Ryan's father, she'd choose Ridge over Miles any day. Well, she had chosen no man, so the point was moot.

His werewolf thought her his soul mate?

She knew wolves mated for life but generally preferred werewolves. Sure, they hooked up with mortals and even faeries. But a witch and a werewolf? Not too common. Although, stranger things had occurred, such as wolves and vamps pairing up. Blu Masterson and Creed Saint-Pierre being one such exemplary couple.

"I don't know what to say," she offered quietly. Stroking a finger down his back traced the heat of him, the strength of him. She wanted him again, but he was in no mood. And she'd ruined her chances by using him. But it was better than continuing the lie. "There was no spell. At least not a spell designed to make you infertile. I did zap you with some rough magic. Maybe the scar tissue goes in so deep it's affected your ability to procreate."

He swung an angry snarl at her. Either way she worked it, she was still the big bad witch to blame.

"I'm sorry. I shouldn't have led you on. Maybe we shouldn't have had sex. It was just sex—"

"It was not just sex." His fists clenched and unclenched. "Do you think so poorly of me that you assume I can have sex with anyone, whenever I please, without a care? It meant something, Abigail. Here." He smacked his chest with a fist. "And I know it meant something to you, too."

Stomping off toward the bathroom, he didn't offer another word. She heard the shower flick on.

Plopping back onto the pillow, Abigail mentally kicked herself for handling the situation so poorly. Usually it was the knight who had to win the lady's favor and prove himself in battle. So why did she feel as if the tables had been turned and it was she who needed to prove herself to Ridge?

Making love had meant something to her. And that it meant so much to him meant the world. And when had she begun to care what he thought?

Always. You were never brave enough to admit it to yourself before. You've always hoped he could be the one.

Turning to her side, she sniffed a tear. "He has to be the one," she whispered.

And yet if he were Ryan's father, her son could be in grave danger, for she'd not prepared him for life should puberty bring on his latent werewolf.

* * *

Ridge snarled at the witch when she laid a plate of scrambled eggs on the table before him. She set the carton of orange juice down, followed by a glass, and said something about checking on the vampire in the basement.

A hot shower, followed by a long cool rinse, had done nothing to chill his simmering emotions about the woman. No spell? Impossible. Though he was informed enough to know a pregnancy did not always come easily, and oftentimes couples had to spend years trying, and invest in medical means to encourage conception.

He'd never gone to a doctor to verify his infertility; it had always been something he'd felt. Instinctually, he knew he could not father a child since the witch had scarred him.

Maybe her suggestion that the scar had cut deep and damaged his insides was close to truth. It was the only thing that made sense if, indeed, no spell had been conjured.

And he could believe she hadn't had time to concoct a spell. He'd wolfed out. She'd zapped him. It had all happened within seconds.

On the other hand, Abigail Rowan had lived for centuries. Certainly she had an arsenal of spells on hand, ready to throw immediately should the situation arise.

He prodded the eggs on his plate, wishing for some sausage or bacon, any kind of meat. Vegetarians. He didn't trust them.

So he was back to not trusting the witch, not only because of her lacking interest in meat, but because he wasn't sure if she was telling the truth. But that didn't change his mind about saving the boy.

How odd would it be if the one child he had fathered had been with the woman who had rendered him sterile immediately after that conception? The mortals' God must be having a chuckle right about now.

All his life he'd gotten the short end of the stick. No reason for life to start serving him the long end any time soon. It was to be expected. He should accept his rotten fate.

Yet he'd thought life had taken an abrupt turn when he'd taken over as principal of the Northern pack and started on a new path. He wanted to make things better. And that goal hadn't changed, either.

Downing the glass of orange juice in one swallow, he shoveled in the meatless breakfast and left the counter as he heard the witch ascending the basement stairs. He wasn't ready to look at her yet, and stomped toward her bedroom.

He put on his jeans and shirt, which he'd claimed from the dryer—she must have tossed them in for him while he showered—and scavenged for a toothbrush in the bathroom closet, finding a couple of unopened ones next to the stack of soap, floss and bath oils.

He looked around for signs of a preteen boy's things, but found nothing. This was Abigail's bathroom, but it was weird he hadn't seen anything of the young male's things yet. Did she keep them all tucked away in his room? Was the boy never home? If she sent him to Switzerland for school, when did she spend time with him?

Poor kid. He was literally an orphan in a strange country. No kid should have to endure distance from his parents, or even a long-distance relationship with his mother. It wasn't right. Children thrived under their parents' guidance.

He hung the toothbrush next to Abigail's brush, and swished around a swig of mouthwash.

He knew a lot of parents did raise their kids in such a manner. Privileged yuppie sorts he could never relate to in a million years. He didn't pin Abigail as that type, but then, she was a cool number. Yet if she was sending the boy away to protect him, then he'd give her that.

If Ryan was his son, he knew one thing for sure: the kid would never set foot in Switzerland again. He'd move him into the compound and give him his own room with all the things a boy could ever want. He'd take him out to toss a football every day. Help him with his homework, teach him how to drive and how to respect others yet remain cautious of strangers. He'd teach him to chop wood and start a fire, and to fix cars and take care of the household. He'd teach him how to be a man, and not a coward. He'd proudly teach by example—an example he'd been denied growing up.

Ridge stared at his reflection. "Could he be mine?"

He wanted that more than anything. Even if Abigail still signed the divorce papers, if the kid was his, he'd be the best damned father to him.

"Ridge?"

He popped out of the bathroom. "Thanks for the breakfast. Do you have a picture of Ryan?"

"I— Oh."

He'd caught her off guard. Good. She needed to feel as unstable as he did right now. Perhaps then her truths would rise. "I have to know, Abigail."

"Sure, I understand. But like I said—"

"I know what you said, and I don't need you to keep reminding me. Just show me a picture, please?"

"I have a new one he sent me recently." She went out into the kitchen and he followed. Opening a laptop on the counter, she brought up a picture file and turned the screen toward him. "That's Ryan's school picture, taken a month ago."

Slightly put off that the woman didn't have a picture in a frame on a shelf somewhere, he peered at the computer screen. The boy had sandy-brown hair with long bangs flipped forward across his brows. He was a smiley bugger, and the smile revealed silver glints. "Braces?"

"Just got them this summer. He hates them."

"They're unnatural. I don't blame him."

His face was narrow, like Abigail's, and his eyes were pale, but he couldn't tell if they were blue or maybe brown. He looked thin, but Ridge supposed most preteens were gawky and thin.

"He looks like me," she commented.

"My hair was that color, when I was younger," he said. "And when I had more of it. He's a cute kid." But he couldn't spot a resemblance like the exact nose as his, or the same eye color. Disheartened, he sighed. "Thanks."

He shoved the laptop toward her and crossed his arms across his chest.

"He doesn't look like Miles, either," Abigail offered.

Hearing the other man's name drove a silver stake through Ridge's heart. He could feel the silver eat at his insides and needed it to stop. But it wouldn't stop until they found the boy and learned the truth.

"We should go," he said.

"The meeting isn't until four in the afternoon. It's only seven."

"I want to do a reconnaissance on the meeting place this morning. See what we're working with. I can't stand around with my hands in my pockets. I need to do something."

They had no idea what they were dealing with. He hated walking into a situation blind.

Chapter 13

"Stay here." Stern brown eyes held hers for a moment, defying her to protest his gentle command.

Surrender.

"Fine."

Abigail closed the passenger door of the truck, and remained inside, watching as Ridge stalked across the street to the restaurant where they'd been directed to bring the vampire. The abandoned Italian restaurant hadn't seen customers for years, she guessed, from the coating of grime on the front windows. The neighborhood was quiet and the storefront to the left was empty.

Ridge, instead of trying the front door, walked down the alley, apparently looking for the back entrance.

He was angry with her. She'd thought showing him a picture of Ryan would settle his curiosity. But the fact that her son resembled her, and no other man in her life, wasn't what Ridge had wanted to see. She couldn't show him what wasn't marked on her son's face, but rather his heart and soul.

When Ryan studied homework and she asked him something, he wouldn't hear her. He possessed a fierce concentration similar to Ridge when focused. And he was the kindest child, asking after the elder neighbors, and holding doors for old ladies in the supermarket, and he'd even given up his toys in the playground when other children had wanted to try them out.

Or maybe she was making up those similarities to fulfill some wanting hole in her heart. Heaven knows, Ryan had not the finest example of a mother to lead him through life, but she had done her best.

Tilting her head against the window, she sighed. Ryan was smart, too. He'd never been a problem child, never aggressive nor had he acted out. He was polite and thoughtful, much like some other man she knew.

She sat forward abruptly. Two men wielding wooden bats crossed the street and approached the restaurant. They didn't look as though they'd lost their way to the baseball game. Besides, who played baseball in January?

They could be thugs, or even hunters, in which case, they were barking up the wrong tree if they thought bats could protect them from a powerful werewolf. Or the bats could be scare tactics, with the deadlier weapons containing werewolf-wounding silver hidden away.

"He's so angry, he won't sense them coming. It's because of me. I have to do something."

She jumped out of the truck and hurried across the street.

* * *

He did not like leaving Abigail alone in the truck, but, despite the seemingly abandoned streets, the neighborhood did stir with activity, so he needed to scope out hiding spots, places where lookouts could be posted. More likely, he found it harder to walk away from the woman than usual. What was that about?

Had their making love put his brain into orbit over the witch?

Rarely did he indulge in one-night stands. He generally did not make love to a woman unless they'd been dating a few weeks and she meant something to him. Sex was not easy or free; it was a sacred thing a man must respect.

He hated that she'd so casually dismissed their tumble in the sheets as mere sex. It had been much more to him. It had been his means to speak without speaking, to open himself to her without having to explain or expect or even react. It had simply been him, open and exposed.

He respected Abigail, and hell, if she would have him, he'd be first in line to be her lover, her boyfriend—anything beyond the warrior knight she thought she needed.

Because a knight's armor could be removed, plate by plate, and beneath stood but a man. And how that man stood, how he held himself, how he walked through the world told everyone exactly who he was, and what gave him purpose. He needed to be that man for Abigail. He wanted to be that man. Someone who would protect her, and take care of her. Someone to be a father to her son, no matter the boy's paternity.

Really?

He paused in the back room of the restaurant. The haze was broken by a stream of dusty light pouring in from the storefront windows out front. Looking around, he considered his thoughts. Yes, he could entirely put his head around being a father to the boy, even if Ryan was one hundred percent witch and had no relation to him whatsoever.

You're grasping for anything you can get now. She's made you desperate with her witchy voodoo magic. Shouldn't you have higher standards?

His standards were high. And he knew a good thing when he saw it.

Something burned his shoulder. Ridge slapped a palm to it, and spun to face two men wielding baseball bats. He'd been skimmed by one of them.

"We got us a two-faced werewolf," one of them said, cracking a cocky grin.

Fellow wolves, he decided from their aggressive scent and the smell of fear dangerously entwined with cocky playfulness. He recognized one of them from the River pack. What were they doing slumming in the Cities?

"Boys," he said, putting his hands up palms out to show compliance as he sniffed the air. Only two of them. He sensed no others hiding or nearby. This would be a piece of cake. "Didn't your mother tell you it's not wise to swing a bat at another man unless you've got the legs to outrun him?"

They both chuckled, and one of them swung his bat menacingly close to Ridge's face. "You're the one who's sticking your nose into all the other packs' business. Longtooth-lover."

"You've learned poorly from your betters," Ridge

said, angered that such prejudices still existed in this day and age. "There's no reason for you to treat vampires the way you do."

"We like to watch them rip each other apart. Just like we're going to rip you apart."

"Yeah," the other snorted. "That'll teach you!"

Ridge dodged the swing of hardwood, but heard a female shout, "Oh, no you don't!"

As soon as he heard Abigail's voice, he ducked. Though angry that she'd not listened to him, he was smart enough to know she wouldn't have wandered in here without good reason.

Magic whirled through the air, lifting both *weres* and flinging them against the tiled wall. A baseball bat clattered across the cracked concrete floor, landing at Ridge's boot. He grabbed it and stood, smacking the bat in his palm sharply. Seeing Abigail gesture again, he quickly ducked.

"Let me handle this!" he yelled. "Keep your magic holstered!"

She walked to him and looked down at where he crouched. Blowing at her fingertip, she winked at him. "Just rounding them up for you, Hoss."

Holding back an admonishment over her theatrics, he shoved Abigail down behind the counter, then swung around the corner and aimed for the approaching *were*. His aggressor wielded a weapon that glinted silver. He would not be foolish enough to use a silver weapon, would he?

He slashed at him, and Ridge blocked the silver blade with the bat. "I don't want to hurt you," he warned.

"Try it, and you'll fail. Unless you sic your pet witch

on me again. Not man enough to do your own fighting, eh?"

Swinging up his leg, Ridge connected with the man's hip and sent him flying, but winced as the *shing* of metal sounded and he felt something pinch his upper thigh. He slapped a hand to his thigh. His jeans had been cut open, but he didn't feel any blood. If the silver had cut through his skin—

An electric charge of magic zipped past his ear and attacked the other wolf as he charged toward him, connecting at his chest as if jumper cables igniting a battery to life. The wolf was slammed against the wall, arms and legs shuddering, and dropped. An outlet beside him popped and sparked, hissing out smoke.

The other wolf had passed out. Ridge disarmed him, taking the blade and finding no other weapons tucked away.

The one Abigail had zapped stirred and groaned, clutching his smoking chest. Ridge limped over to him and toed his leg. "Amateurs. Get your asses out of here before I aim for your brain."

The wounded wolf dragged himself to a bent and staggering stance. His leg wasn't bleeding. Ridge had hit him in the meaty part of his thigh purposely. He kicked at his buddy. "Get up, dude!"

The twosome wobbled out, cursing and swearing revenge.

Though they had gotten the jump on him, Ridge would never admit that. His mind had been preoccupied with thoughts of that damned witch. Even when she wasn't flinging about magic, she still managed to discombobulate him but good.

He had to smirk at that. He really was falling for the baddest witch in the Midwest. Be still, his idiot heart.

"You're going to let them go?"

He reached back with his free hand and clasped Abigail's hand. "I've no fight with them."

"They were going to kill you."

"For something they can never begin to understand. They need to get smart, and no silver blade will do that for them." He flipped the blade in his hand and caught it by the wood handle.

The wounded wolf slapped a hand in the doorway and turned to flip off Ridge.

"Tell your principal I've no fight with him," Ridge called after him. "But I will continue to protect those you torture!"

Abigail touched his thigh and he flinched at the unexpected touch, but not because it hurt. "You going to be okay?"

He studied the damage through the cut blue jean material. "Didn't break the skin. Whew." He shrugged her off and tossed the silver blade under the counter. "I'm a little nervous now they might try to return during the meeting. They must have followed us here. I don't understand that."

"You think the packs are gunning for you?"

"I suspect so. I'm certainly not at the top of anyone's friend list lately."

"I'll set up wards," she said. "I can't ward the whole building, because that will prevent the ones we need to meet from entering, but I should be able to keep those two out."

He grabbed her by the waist and kissed her. It felt natural to hold her now after they'd shared so much earlier this morning. She fit into his embrace as no one ever had. "Much as I should paddle your behind for jumping in when I had things under control…"

She lifted a brow.

"Thanks for having my back."

"No problem. Someone has to keep an eye on your backside."

"I was talking about my back."

"Yeah? I was talking about your backside." She slapped his ass, and strolled by him toward the front door, where she winked, then turned to perform the warding spell.

Abigail insisted they return to her house to wait, but Ridge convinced her to stop by the burger joint along the way. Back at her house, he carried in bags of hamburgers and fries and wolfed into them without waiting for her to get settled. Halfway through his first burger, he pushed a bag toward her.

"I'm sorry," she said, and dug out a wrapped burger. "I should have let you handle that situation yourself."

"Yes, you should have. You have a spectacular knack at emasculating me every chance you get."

Ready to protest, Abigail sighed, and admitted, "I have control issues."

"No kidding." He chomped down a handful of veggie fries.

Feeling a sense of helplessness standing in his accusing stare, she couldn't stomach food, and shoved it away on the counter. "All right. It meant something to me. Are you happy?"

He huffed, and sucked down a long draw from his supersize Coke.

"The sex," she explained.

"I know what you're talking about. You're trying to make me feel better. You don't have to lie to do that. I'm a big boy. I am a master at handling rejection, trust me on that one."

"But I don't want you to feel rejected by me." She touched his arm, and he stopped eating. It was as if she'd touched a switch in him, and only now could he come down and really listen to her. So she took advantage of his attention.

"Lying in your arms. Making love with you… It did mean something to me, but I'm so stupid about trying to keep my emotions in check and not fall into the same old obsessive patterns, that I did it again. I pushed you away when all I really want to do is pull you to me and hug your big burly body, and bury myself against your quiet and kind strength. Oh, Ridge."

He dropped the burger onto the paper and drew her into his embrace, and she found her way into his strength with a sigh and a sniffle.

"It's difficult for me," she said against his chest. "I need to work it my way, and sometimes that way is wrong."

"You're doing fine, sweetie." He nuzzled into her hair and hugged her until nothing mattered but the sound of his heartbeat and hers, tapping rhythm against one another. "You're doing amazing, actually, considering what you're going through. I shouldn't ask you for anything when all your energy needs to be focused on your son."

"Two more hours," she said with a glance to the digital clock on the oven. "You should finish before the food gets cold."

"You eat, too."

"I will. I think I'll make a veggie sandwich."

It took them only moments to eat. Still one hour and fifty minutes of waiting. This would be the longest stretch of time she'd ever had to endure if she couldn't find a distraction.

"I'm impatient," she announced after washing the last plate. She wiped her wet hands on her slacks and took the towel from Ridge, who had dried the dishes at her side. "And when I get antsy I need to do something."

"Turn on the TV," he suggested. "Must be a movie or something we could watch. That should keep your mind off things."

"I don't have a TV."

He gaped. "No? That means no Monday Night Football? Hell." He scratched his head, then flashed her a confused twist of brow. "Is that because of you and the electricity thing?"

"No. I can watch TV without it blowing up. But I prefer to use magic in the house, so I keep the electrical stuff to a minimum. You haven't vacuumed until you've sat on the couch, feet up on a pillow, directing the vacuum with but a flick of your fingers."

"Think I'll pass on flicking fingers. No TV," he murmured, obviously too stunned to take that one in completely.

"I imagine you must have one of those big screens?" she asked.

"Not yet, but that's my plan. Get a big six-footer in the compound and watch the Vikings games in high-def."

She sidled up to him and gave his arm a playful

squeeze. "You would have made a great running back. Or a pitcher. Or, well, I don't know sports. I'm using the only terms I have."

"I used to row, actually. I loved rowing the boat on a quiet lake when I was a teen. Haven't done it for years."

"Interesting. I didn't think the canine breed went in for water."

"I'm lupus, not canine."

"Right. Sorry." She trailed her fingers down his chest, finding it the best distraction in the room. Moving closer to him drew his body heat to her as if a flame, and she pressed her hips to his. "Mmm, I think I can find something to waste a little time."

"Abigail," he said on a moan that told her he'd be perfectly fine with whatever trouble she got herself into.

And why not? Sex earlier had ended on a sour note, and she was determined to change that to sweet.

She undid his jeans. The scar on his abdomen started above the waistline, and she traced it, kneeling before him to examine it closely.

"I'm sorry," she said, then kissed the top of the scar. His abdomen flexed with his intake of breath. "Maybe a few kisses will make it better?"

"You can try," he groaned through a tight jaw.

Pulling open his jeans revealed brown curls and she tangled her fingers through them as she delivered another kiss, a little lower on the scar. "It's so thick."

"Uh."

The taste of his skin, the tensing of his muscles, his groans; she had him exactly where she wanted him. Her thoughts abandoned the dire—if for a moment.

She tugged down his jeans and his penis sprang up proudly, boldly, a thick shaft of steel wrapped in velvet skin. The head of him was deeply colored and she cupped her palm over it as she kissed the bottom of the scar, but inches from his heavy rod.

His fingers slid through her hair. Soft, yet seeking, wanting to direct, yet too gentle to force.

She dashed her tongue along the length of him, loving the salty sex scent of his skin, his body, his desire. Drawing her tongue along the underside, she traced the engorged vein to the plump cap that fit in her mouth nicely and elicited a gasping groan from her werewolf lover. She tightened her suction and moved over the head, drawing more wanting moans from him.

Slicking her fingers along the shaft, she decided it was angry hard and beautiful at the same time. She wanted to own it, to own him.

With a few expert tickles of her tongue along his length, and alternating taking the head into her mouth, she slowly and surely brought him to a precipice until his body shuddered, and the fingers in her hair grasped tightly as he surrendered to a tremendous climax.

She drank him and licked him and kissed him.

Ridge stumbled backward and landed on the couch. He drew her to sit on his lap and held her against him. She could feel his body shudder still, his breaths coming rapidly, and his muscles flex against her skin. She had mastered this wolf. Controlled him.

So why did she feel as if she were missing something?

"You do that so well," he muttered, sighing, and letting his head fall against the back of the couch. "I think it's high time I returned the favor."

Now that was the something she'd been missing.

Unzipping her pants and tugging them down, Abigail straddled the wolf, and let him do as he pleased.

Closing her eyes and tilting back her head she surrendered to the loss of the control she desired as his fingers entered her and slicked in and out, tracing her sensitive core, and quickly luring her to climax.

Chapter 14

Freezing rain turned the afternoon sky gray, and the restaurant at which they were supposed to meet Ryan's kidnappers had no working electricity so the only light came from the front windows. As Abigail and Ridge approached from behind the counter, she could make out five men standing before the window. Shadows concealed their faces.

Ridge, behind her with the unconscious vampire slung over a shoulder, had agreed to let her do the talking. She had no problem taking control of a situation like this. Had done it many times. Control was her thing.

Control had seemed less important the past few hours, though, when Ridge brought her to one screaming climax after another. Goddess, the man had known how to make her body sing.

As her heart pounded and her hands grew clammy, she knew this situation was different from most she had controlled. She had a stake in everything going well. And having Ridge right behind her provided support she would have never admitted to needing. And yet, she knew nothing about the opposition. That made every step dangerous.

"They're wolves," Ridge muttered so only she could hear. "Most of them."

Wolves? Her heartbeats increased. She had thought them with the Light.

"Not the one in the middle," he said. "Could be a witch, but I can't determine for sure. Be careful. This is not good."

The waiting men closed ranks, and the one in the center stepped forward. Behind her, Ridge growled low. Was it too late to let him stand in front and take control?

Yes, let him be the one in charge. You need him to be. Stop thinking you have to have a tight grasp on everything. Just surrender.

When she saw the face of the approaching man, Abigail gasped. Her heart thudded, and it wasn't a good thud. "Miles?"

Behind her another low growl shivered down her spine. Ridge must have recognized him, too.

"What is this?" she demanded, forgetting her composure. "*You* are behind kidnapping my son?"

"Is that the vampire?" Miles asked in a cold tone. Arms crossed over his chest, he gave no indication he and Abigail had ever had a relationship or even knew one another. "Bring him over here."

Now more confused than ever, Abigail nodded to

Ridge and he stepped forward and flung the vamp to the floor, before Miles's snakeskin-boot toes. She tugged Ridge behind her, and he reluctantly obeyed, but she sensed the condemning gaze he had fixed on Miles could strangle with a blink.

The entire room felt as though it had risen five or ten degrees in temperature, and she could sense the animal nature of the wolves in the prickle of the hair along her arms.

"Why the wolves?" she asked.

Miles glanced to Ridge and smirked. "You brought your wolf, I brought mine."

With a nod, one of the men flanking Miles bent to inspect the vampire.

The man she'd once fallen in love with, the witch who possessed fire magic of a level equal to hers, stared at her condemningly. His narrow face had gotten thinner, his sharp chin and cheekbones more defined. His dark eyes that had once looked at her with love, devotion even, now glittered with menace.

She'd been a fool in love. A fool who hadn't seen how desperate the man was to own her; Miles had been as obsessive as she had ever been over the years. But that had been the last time she'd gotten foolish over a man. Her eyes had opened on the night he'd proposed.

And she'd paid for it. Fire could be controlled, but never owned. When she'd most needed her fire magic to protect herself, it had failed her.

"Miles, if you don't start explaining right now—"

He put up his palm, which glowed red, threatening with fire. "Hold your magic, Rowan. You know I can match you for every spell and every lick of flame you throw at me." Asking to the side, he said, "Is he intact?"

The kneeling lackey turned the vampire over and tore away the back of his shredded shirt. "He's been burned. It's gone."

Miles sucked in his cheeks and blew out a heavy breath. The daggers in his gaze were lit with fire sparks. "Now why did you have to go and screw around with the longtooth, Rowan? This tosses a wrench in my plan."

"I've always been pretty handy with a wrench." She smirked, but her bravado wilted quickly. "It wasn't the vampire you wanted," she challenged. "It was the binding spell he had tattooed on his back."

"You don't get points for the obvious."

"What are you up to, Miles? And why involve my son? If you needed a spell, surely you could have found it on your own."

"Not this specific one, unfortunately. The grimoire that contained the original binding spell was burned. And I'm not much for a trip to Daemonia to obtain it there. Nor am I a vampire hunter, and when werewolves are involved..."

"Why not sic your own pack on them?"

One of the wolves growled, revealing his teeth.

"They are my pack, of sorts," Miles offered with a crooked smirk. "Which is why I'd never ask them to act against one of their own. I needed someone to take this vampire from the blood sport."

"Doesn't explain why you would kidnap an innocent child. Miles, what's wrong with you? I know you can be vindictive, but Ryan has never done anything—"

"The first son born of two fire witches," he stated. "Why did you hide him from me, Abigail?"

He knew. She'd never told him, but only because

she'd not once run into him since that fiery eve in Vegas.

"I did no such thing. Ryan is my son. I've raised him on my own. Whoever his father may be was merely a sperm donor."

She felt the intensity of Ridge's presence behind her, and hated herself for what she'd said. It had been meant as a blade to Miles's heart, but she'd cut Ridge in the process, surely.

"I chose to raise my son by myself. That's no one's business but my own," she stated.

"As it should be. I've never been much for kids." Miles toed the vampire. "Unfortunate thing." With a snap of his fingers, the wolf to his right tugged out a wooden stake from his jacket and lunged for the vampire.

As ash spumed in the shape of the vampire and dispersed, Abigail grabbed Ridge's forearm to hold him back. His muscles tensed in her grip and he seethed. His anger permeated her pores and she took it on as her own.

She wriggled her fingers at her side. They heated and she felt the flow of her blood increase the temperature.

"As for the sperm donor? You're not going to play that game, are you? I know I'm the boy's father," Miles said. "I can understand you keeping him a secret from me. Sorry about the stake and the fire. Your refusal to marry upset me. You know I don't like it when people say no to me, Abigail."

"You bastard!"

This time it was Ridge who caught Abigail by both arms and held her from charging the insipid witch. "Stay calm," he warned in a low voice. "Or you'll never see your son. And turn down the heat. I can feel it coursing through you."

She would not turn it down, because Miles would never relent.

"Who is this?" Miles directed toward Ridge. "Your underling?"

"You don't remember me?" Ridge asked. "I kicked your ass in Vegas."

Miles tilted his head, studying Ridge, then nodded. "Interesting. I never thought you'd slum with an animal, Abigail. Bestiality is so beneath you."

"Give me my son!" She struggled against Ridge's hold, and while she knew he had her best interests in mind, she hated that he wouldn't allow her to unleash her magic. But she didn't need his permission. "I've done what you asked. There's the damned vampire! Now hand over Ryan."

"You destroyed evidence, which negates the deal."

"Yeah? Well, you destroyed the whole damn vampire."

"I can't hand over your son."

"You never intended to hand him over," Ridge said. "What were your plans with the spell?"

"Why, to shackle the boy, of course. You know what happens when the child of two fire witches comes into his own magic? He sucks away the magic from his parents. I can't abide the loss of power. I've worked hard to master fire."

"You don't even care about him!" Abigail raged. "Let me go!"

"Abigail," Ridge warned sharply, "be smart."

"He's going to hurt Ryan." Her hands began to glow red, and Ridge released her with a hiss.

"That may be the only option now," Miles announced calmly. "If I can't bind him from coming into his magic, well then, you leave me no choice but to end his life."

"No!"

"Pity," Miles said. "Since he is my son."

"You have no proof," Abigail pleaded.

"Proof?" Miles laughed deep in his chest. "We were exclusive, Abigail. Don't tell me you were whoring around with other men—"

Shoved against the counter, Abigail caught herself against the wood, which burned and smoked under her fiery hands.

"You disrespect Abigail," Ridge said, "you're asking for pain, buddy."

"Take him out," Miles ordered his lackeys.

The werewolves attacked Ridge en masse. Two jumped him from behind, and another swung low with a two-by-four he grabbed from the floor, connecting with Ridge's knees and bringing him down.

Abigail flung out a stream of fire toward the wolves, and caught two on the hair, which burst into flames.

She shrieked as a gush of flame sent from Miles's hands pushed her over the top of the counter to land on the floor, sprawled. A quick assessment determined the fire had missed her.

Miles stepped around the counter and gripped her wrists before she could throw more magic at him.

"You want your son?" he asked. "Bring me the binding spell. I will bind him, and then return him to you. Promise."

"Binding will hurt him!"

"It's a better option than death, yes?"

On the other side of the counter the wolves growled and tossed each other about. The counter wobbled, pushed off the floor by impact.

"I'm giving you one more chance to save him," Miles said. "I'll be in contact within twenty-four hours."

Rushing around the counter, Miles pressed out a shield of fire from his palm, keeping Abigail back with a wall of flames. She ran toward it, thinking if she could step through it quick enough—

Ridge grabbed her and pulled her toward the back of the restaurant.

"No!" She struggled but the wolf had her firmly in hand. "We have to go after them! He's lying! He's going to kill Ryan!"

"Then let's go after them. Come on!"

They fled the flames out the back door and raced down the alleyway hugging the building. A black Mercedes peeled out from in front of the restaurant, and a hail of bullets impeded them from racing to the parked pickup. Caught about the waist, Abigail was flung to the ground behind the Dumpster and Ridge crouched over her as a bullet pinged the big metal garbage container.

"Don't go out there!" she yelled. "They'll hit you."

"You want me to save your son?"

She grasped for his pant leg, but he was too quick, and she watched as he dodged a bullet and ran toward the end of the alley. His shoulder hitched back—he had been hit—but that didn't slow him. He swung around the corner and disappeared from her sight.

And then he stumbled backward, his body taking another bullet to the hip, and then the arm.

Scrambling out from behind the Dumpster, she

rushed through the black smoke spewing from the restaurant and found Ridge sprawled on the sidewalk. The Mercedes squealed around a corner and disappeared.

"Ridge?" Blood spurted from his shoulder and hip. The wound on his arm had only abraded the skin. He groaned and pushed her away, trying to stand. "They're gone. We've got to get you medical attention."

"I'll heal," he growled and this time managed to shove her clear and stand. He staggered, and she caught his arm. The big lug was hurt badly, but the adrenaline rushing through his system probably blinded him to the real pain.

"I'm sorry, Abigail. I've failed you."

"You've done no such thing. Let's move." When she headed for the driver's side of the pickup, he grabbed her upper arm and swung her toward the passenger side.

"I'm driving," he growled. "I am not an invalid. Hurry. We might be able to pick up their trail."

He shifted into gear and pulled away from the curb as she was still closing the door. The man was pissed off and injured, and couldn't be thinking straight. But he was thinking the same thing she was: find those bastards.

Her son's kidnapper was Miles Easton. How? Had he watched her over the years, knowing or suspecting Ryan was his son? Why step in only now? If he'd been worried about binding Ryan's magic it could have occurred any time before puberty. Maybe. She wasn't sure about that. Probably the witch actually had to come into his or her magic before it was bindable.

All this time she'd thought she'd been so careful, so protective of Ryan. Hell, she'd thought to hide him away in Switzerland. If anyone were watching her, they'd never find her son so far away. What a joke Miles had made of her protective instincts.

"I think they went left," she directed, and Ridge swung the truck across the intersection, barely missing a turning vehicle. "Settle down, Ridge."

"I want to rip that bastard's head from his neck!"

He slammed a fist on the steering wheel, and the blood pulsing from his shoulder dripped onto the center console.

"Let me look at that while you drive." She sat on her knees and ripped the plaid sleeve from his arm. The wound was deep but when she probed it she didn't feel a bullet, and it looked as though it had bored through his skin and gone right through the back of his shoulder.

"Ouch. Leave it be! It'll heal if you stop poking in it."

It probably would heal, and quickly, as werewolves were wont. She touched his hip but couldn't see beyond the bloodied denim. He wasn't going to make it easy for her, so she sat and leaned her head against the window.

Tears gushed forth because she had been so close to getting her son back, yet so far away. And now that she knew Miles was behind it, she knew he would be ruthless and that Ryan would not be safe from this moment forward.

"Don't do that witchy pouting thing," Ridge snapped.

She turned her head but couldn't stop the tears that gushed up from her heart.

"Shit. Abigail? I'm sorry. I didn't mean to say that. Sweetie?" He touched her hair and the blood streaming down his arm spattered onto her gray pants. "We'll find him. I gotta think that bastard wants the binding spell more than he wants to harm an innocent child."

"But binding him will harm him!"

"Yeah, but the other option…"

The other option? That was death.

"Sorry," Ridge rushed out. "I shouldn't have said that. And I'm not sure where the hell I am anymore. I don't know this town. Hell, we've lost them."

The truck came to an abrupt stop somewhere in a residential neighborhood, and Ridge shifted into Park. He reached across and dragged Abigail onto his lap to hug her against his chest. He didn't say anything, didn't try to reassure her, and that felt better than a promise he couldn't make.

"Take me home," she said on a shiver. "I need to be next to the phone when he calls."

Chapter 15

Abigail crossed the threshold to her home around
6:00 p.m. It was early yet, but she was exhausted.
Meeting Miles and *not* bringing home Ryan had
stripped her of all inner strength. She trudged into
the living room, her eyes unfocused and her head spinning. With a flick of her finger, she drew the oversize
easy chair up behind her and collapsed.

She wasn't sure if he had already been in the chair,
or if he joined her later, but Ridge was there, sitting
beside her, and then holding her on his lap. They both
faced the kitchen. The green LED on the oven blinked
over to eight-thirty. No phone call.

Against his chest she lay, his arms cradling her. His
breaths were soft, his heartbeats seemed in rhythm to
the blinks of the little colon on the digital clock, separating the hour from the minutes. Silence reigned.

Even Swell Cat overlooked his distrust for the were-wolf and wandered in on quiet paws and settled on the couch opposite them to help hold vigil.

At some point she'd fallen asleep, and now she blinked and yawned as her body slowly woke and she realized she still sat in Ridge's arms, surrounded by his safety and the quiet rumble of his snores.

The oven clock blinked to five-fifteen. She'd slept through the night. Which was probably for the best. Turning on Ridge's lap, she nuzzled her cheek against his neck. He smelled like man, dried blood and sweat. His contented breathing matched Swell Cat's.

She wagered Richard Addison had never been content his entire life. Growing up in the pack and having to fight for every scrap he could get his hands on. And he probably never put up a front of false contentedness as she had done over the years. Changing her life by pushing people away? When had that been such a good idea?

She needed help. She needed people. She...needed.

"Time is it?" he asked softly. His legs shifted beneath hers, shuffling her body closer against his warm, snuggly chest.

"A little after five. We slept. I want to take a shower, but I can't risk it."

"If the phone rings I'll call you out. I promise."

She met his golden-brown eyes, dashed along one eyebrow with a smear of blood. No menace in his gaze, not a trace of cruelty. What he wore outside his soul, on the surface skin, was a means of protection for his truly kind heart. A necessary protection.

"You're the best thing that's ever happened to me,

209

Richard Addison." She traced the prickly stubble darkening his jaw. "Why can't I accept that?"

"I've never been anyone's best thing, sweetie. I think you're still swimming in dreamsleep."

"I'm completely awake. I…" She kissed him. She was doing what came naturally, like breathing. His mouth moved against hers in a lazy reply. "I need you to be my best thing, Ridge."

"I would only disappoint. As I've shown you so clearly by letting Miles and his henchwolves get away."

"We'll get Ryan back. And you've shown me you are the warrior I guessed you to be. I am the one who wants to deserve you."

Again, she kissed him, and moved to straddle his hips with her knees. How easy it was to fall into his quiet strength, to surrender. To release control.

He winced as her hand skimmed the bullet wound on his shoulder. It was healed over and scarred, crusted with blood. "You can take the first shower," she told him. "You need it. I'll feed Swell Cat and get the photo of the binding spell while I wait."

"You could join me."

"Then who will listen for the phone to ring?"

"Right. Got it. Dragging up my aching bones and walking to the shower. What I wouldn't give for some clean clothes," he muttered as he strode down the hallway. "I might have some in the back of the truck. Usually I carry along a couple changes of clothing because we wolves, well, you know."

"I'll run out and check."

He winked and disappeared down the hallway.

There was indeed a duffel packed with clothing in the bed of the pickup truck. The whole thing was cold so she tossed his jeans and plaid shirt into the dryer to warm them while he showered.

The phone rang and Abigail dashed toward the kitchen, leaped over Swell Cat and performed a sliding landing across the linoleum floor to snatch the receiver.

"Hello!"

A woman spoke, and Abigail almost screamed at her and hung up, but she recognized Ravin Crosse's voice and slumped against the refrigerator and listened.

"Sorry to call so early, Abigail, but I'm still on European time. Just got back in town a few hours ago. I wanted to give you a heads-up. There are stirrings that the newest principal for the Northern pack has been butting heads with other packs. They're all growling for his dismissal and some complaints have been lodged with the Council."

Ravin, a fellow witch who had walked this earth since the Middle Ages, served on the Council alongside her vampire husband, Nikolaus Drake. She was one tough witch, known to cruise a street chopper through the streets of Minneapolis, and she and Abigail often rubbed each other the wrong way for their strong personalities.

"And why do I need to know about that?" Abigail said, wincing at the snide tone she couldn't stop. "Why doesn't Severo look into it?"

Ridge had told her they'd run into Severo inside the Ely compound. If the elder wolf had been the one to complain, she'd serve him some bad magic.

"I don't know where that werewolf is right now, and yours was the first name to come up when we needed someone to investigate. You do normally handle these sorts of inquiries. Unless…"

"Ravin, spit out whatever you're trying to say. I'm in no mood to beat about the bush."

"Reports link you to Ridge Addison. That you were along with him when he tried to stop the blood sport at the River pack's compound."

"And you have a problem with what, exactly? That Ridge was trying to stop the violence against vampires? Really, Ravin, I don't understand you. Aren't you married to a vampire?"

"You're avoiding the question. Were you with him? And why?"

"Did you find any clothes?"

At the sound of Ridge's voice, Abigail turned to see him enter the kitchen, his hips draped in a towel. She signaled him to check the dryer.

"Is that them?" he asked. She shooed him out of the room.

"I guess that answers my question," Ravin said. "You're with him, and I can make one guess at why."

"Oh, really? What reason is that?" Again, she shooed the wondering werewolf away because she couldn't manage the distraction of his muscles displayed in nothing but a towel while Ravin chattered in her ear.

"The guy's hot," Ravin said. "Have you counted the ridges on his abdomen? Because I know I have, and there's a hell of a lot more there than a six-pack."

If the situation weren't so dire, Abigail could almost break down into girlfriend chatter over her boyfriend's sexy attributes.

She glanced down the hallway. Ridge, still in a

towel, stood in the doorway to the laundry room, staring at her, one foot hooked at the wall. Boyfriend?

More like husband, her conscience snickered with an admonishing giggle.

"We're not involved," she said hastily, yet directed her did-you-get-that? stare toward the werewolf. "He's…helping me with something, and we got sidetracked. He's adamant about stopping the blood sport, and why should the Council point a finger at him for trying to do some good?"

"We're not pointing fingers, we're investigating the complaints. It helps to hear your perspective on it. That is a professional opinion, yes?"

"Yes."

"Good. I hadn't imagined Addison would be doing anything wrong. But we're going to need to chill the wolf out for a while, so the steam brewing in the River pack can settle."

"You want me to tell him to stop? I won't do that. We should be thankful someone is taking matters into his own hands and not sitting back and watching like we do."

"You and I have very different opinions of what the Council does and doesn't do."

"I've been on the Council a lot longer than you, Ravin. They're not innocent by any standards."

And to get into that would open up a can of worms Abigail had not the patience to sort through.

"Listen, I have to get off the phone. I'm waiting for an important call. We can go at it next Council meeting."

"Which is in two days."

"Seriously? I didn't get the memo. I don't know if I can make it."

"You'd better, Rowan, or we'll become suspicious of your involvement with the wolf."

The phone clicked off, leaving Abigail furious enough to want to throw the receiver across the room, but instead she slammed it in the carriage and turned into the werewolf's arms.

He was right there. Again. Always when she needed him, he was there. But she didn't question his weird sense for her emotions, and let him lead her down the hall toward the bathroom.

"I guess that was Council business," he said as he lifted her shirt and pulled it over her head. He bent to plant a kiss atop each breast, delivering a scintillating shiver with each. "Shower, and you'll feel better. I'll keep one hand on the phone until you get out."

She nodded. "You're a good man, Ridge."

"And you are an amazing mother who will see her son very soon."

"Thank you," she whispered, and she ducked into the bathroom and closed the door before the first teardrop fell.

"Didn't ring," Ridge offered as Abigail stepped into the bedroom, a fluffy pink towel wrapped around her torso. He sat on the bed, head resting against the elaborate gold filigree headboard. He'd put on his jeans, but the plaid shirt lay at the bottom of the bed. He wasn't ready to get completely dressed. "Hot water feels great, doesn't it?"

"I don't know. I took a cold shower to wake up."

She slid next to him, tilting her head onto his shoulder. "What do you want for breakfast?"

"You," he said and pulled her to sit on his lap. She offered no protest when he kissed her, and tugged open the towel to slide his hands over her breasts. "You taste good."

"Cherry toothpaste. You taste the same." She glanced out the open bedroom door.

"If it rings we will hear," he said, and nuzzled his nose against her neck where her skin was still wet. He licked the water droplets and she squirmed against him in a welcoming motion. "I was thinking about what you said about me being your best thing."

"And?"

"I want to be that best thing for you. If you'll let me."

"That would mean a lot to me. But can it wait until my son is safe?"

He nodded. Right. He was getting ahead of himself. Rushing toward the light when he'd never been able to get too close to it before without the door getting slammed in his face and leaving him in the shadows. Who was being obsessive now?

"Just touch me," she whispered at his ear. "Touch me like a wolf who wants his mate."

"Abigail, you don't know what you're asking."

"I'm not giving you permission to wolf out."

"I know that, and I won't. I promise." But it would take all his effort not to. "But…I can get a little rough. I like it…frenzied. Powerful. Hard."

"I'm a big girl, Ridge. I want to feel your strength." She sat up straight, straddling his legs and lifting her breasts before his appreciative gaze. A tease of tongue slipped over her bottom lip. "I want you to claim me."

His hands clasped about her waist and lifted her to the side as if she were a doll. "You don't know what you're asking."

"Oh please." She trailed her fingers down his chest and toward the dark hairs above his waistline. "I think you're afraid to go one-on-one with the baddest witch in the Midwest."

"Not at all."

She cupped her breasts and stroked her fingers over her nipples, tilting back her head with a moan. A pinch to both ruched the flesh up tightly. Ridge's mouth dropped open. His cock instantly hardened.

"Abigail. You're teasing."

"Would you prefer I had my mind on other things? Dire things?"

No, he wanted her mind occupied, not thinking about her son. And with his hard-on growing, who was he to argue her amorous mood?

He moved over the top of her, coaxing her to lie back on the bed. She unzipped his jeans and pressed his hard-on against her thigh. Boldness flashed in her eyes. His skin hungered for her touch.

She slid her foot along his jeans, inching the pant legs down his thighs, and he bent to her breasts and suckled at them, softly at first, and then he tugged wantonly and clasped firm fingers about them. The nipple grew hard and tight. Delicious moans filled the room. Her pleasure hummed in his heart. He loved making her squirm like this.

He managed to kick off his jeans and he knelt over her, his cock thrust out above her mons, which displayed dark hair. So that really was her natural color. She clasped his shaft and Ridge forgot about the color of her hair. His pectoral muscles tightened, as did his abs. His entire body wanted, needed to be fulfilled.

"I want you inside me right now," she said. "This gorgeous, thick cock of yours. I need it, Ridge."

"Then we're doing it my way this time."

"That's the way I want it."

He held himself up with one hand and with his other hand, lifted her under her waist and turned her over. He clasped her body tight up against his until she knelt on all fours.

He kissed the nape of her neck where it was hot and soft and smelled of coconuts. Sweet mercy, she smelled so good. And her lithe body arched up against his to fit perfectly. One of his hands found her folds and slid between them, testing her wetness and delivering a satisfied growl when he learned she was hot and moist.

"Spread your legs more," he ordered with a tightness to his voice. Foreplay was going to be quick. He needed. Now. He clasped her hair and wrapped it about his hand. "Is this okay?"

She wiggled her hips and rubbed against his hard weapon. "Oh, yeah."

His thickness nudged between her thighs and butted against her folds. He slicked over her wetness, up and down, wetting himself and tugging at her clitoris as he did so. He felt too swollen to get inside her, but in the expectation of it she let out a peal of delight.

Reaching down she guided the full head of him toward the goal. He grasped both her hips and allowed her to guide him inside. Together, they cried out at the pure delight in the hot connection. He filled her slowly, creeping deeper by measured caution. And then, he rammed her hard and quick. She had to grip the bed covering to not slide off onto the floor.

She moaned at his wicked claiming, his forceful thrusts marking her as his, sheathing him deeply, and then almost pulling out, but not quite.

And then he grabbed her hair again and twisted. He used it to hang on but not pull her about. He pistoned inside her, racing the insistent pull of climax. So hot. She hugged him tightly. Gave him all he wanted. Needed.

Ridge cried out and clasped a hand around her body and over her breasts as he pumped inside her forcefully until he answered the incredible call of orgasm.

"My goddess," Abigail said on a gasp. "You're so powerful. Ridge, I… Let's do it again."

He chuckled and fell down beside her, pulling her on top of him, and kissed her cheek, her eyelids, her nose, her mouth.

And then the phone rang.

Chapter 16

Abigail hung up the phone and turned to Ridge. He didn't like the look on her face. This powerful witch had been beaten and pushed to the ground. That bastard Miles was going to pay for the harm he'd caused both Abigail and Ryan.

"He said..." Her hands shook. The silk robe she'd hastily pulled on fell from one shoulder. Behind her the chrome toaster on the counter sparked, and she jumped. It had reacted to her nervous magic.

"He wants you to go alone," Ridge guessed.

She nodded, and then grabbed the photo from the counter. He slammed his palm over the paper before she could claim it. "You're not going anywhere without me. He was able to get the better of you once before, he'll do it again. Think, Abigail."

"I know, I know. And I'm not at the top of my game

right now, so I'm worried I'll fail or my magic will freak out." The lighted buttons on the oven flashed to red and the microwave began to beep. "But he said if he saw you he'd kill Ryan."

"He's not going to see me," Ridge said. He lured her out of the kitchen to the relative safety of the living room, where her magic could affect only the outlets. "But you'll know I'm there. If that bastard makes a wrong move, if he so much as looks at you crooked, I'll be there to put an end to this stupid game of his."

"Think only of Ryan," she cautioned, grabbing his forearms and looking directly into his eyes. "Above all, his safety is most important. I can handle myself."

Ridge winced. Sounded like something Persia Masterson had once said to him after she'd taken a brutal beating from Amandus. *You can't protect me all the time. Protect yourself.*

He hadn't thought of her for years. The memory hurt his soul.

He wasn't about to fail another woman.

He folded the photo and handed it to Abigail, then kissed the corner of her mouth, a bittersweet connection. "Let's go."

They found the meeting place using the GPS coordinates Miles had given her. The area was forested, with patches of open field here and there, and houses were spaced miles apart from one another.

Ridge stopped the truck a quarter mile from the destination and Abigail got out to walk. The midafternoon was gray, darkened by clouds. The chirp of a hawk disturbed her.

Her hands warmed inside her gloves and she tugged

them off and shoved them in her pockets. Her magic was reacting to her nerves. She had to calm down before reaching Miles.

Confident Ridge would track her from the cover of the forest, she wandered down the gravel country road, her boots crunching packed snow as she held a stern countenance. If Ryan saw her coming, she wanted him to know his mother meant business.

Ryan was not visible when she arrived before Miles and his henchwolves. Her peripheral vision took in no place where they could be hiding the boy. A house was half a mile off near a wooded area. Shoving her hands in her pockets to remind herself that she had to maintain control, she approached Miles.

"Where is it?" he asked.

"Where is Ryan?"

"The binding spell first."

She hated this loss of control. But she knew Miles was as determined as she, and he was the one who always reacted to the extreme when things didn't go his way.

"What happened to us?" she asked, hoping to get into the man's brain and subtly influence him to calm before he unleashed his fire. "Will you tell me?"

Miles cast a wink over his shoulder that Abigail could not see from where she stood. Every muscle strapping Ridge's body tightened and instinct reacted. "That bastard isn't going to let the boy go."

Abigail had said she could take care of herself. But the boy? He was an innocent trapped in a sinking ship. And Ridge could think of only one sure way to get close to the boy to help him escape. He had to act now.

Abigail would look upon it as betrayal, after asking him to remain out of sight. He'd have to trust she would forgive him later. If they both lived to have a later.

Sighting in the wolf flanking the witch, Ridge determined once he knocked that one out, the other two would be on him like hounds. He could take out at least one more before the other three pounced. Abigail would have to run for his plan to work.

Racing across the field, keeping behind the line of trees, he stealthily gained upon them. One of the wolves lifted his chin, his nose scenting the air. He'd been marked.

Ridge pounced on the first wolf, and wrenched his neck. Not enough to break it or kill him, but it put him out. Another wolf slammed onto his back and jerked Ridge's head under the chin. His throat muscles stretched and burned. Dropping backward and crushing his attacker into the snowy ground, he kicked high to fend off another who jumped on him. The wolf landed in the snow, but would be up in no time.

"Abigail, run!" he yelled.

"You tricky witch!" he heard Miles shout. "You'll never see the boy now."

The crackle of flame ignited in the air. Ridge could feel the heat suck away the winter chill.

Abigail's shriek was the last thing he heard. A meaty fist clocked him on the temple and the world went black.

Abigail fled to the truck while she had the opportunity. She hated running away from Ridge and Ryan, but if she was taken then no one would be in any position to help anyone.

The exchange had been a disaster, but she should have expected as much from the werewolf who couldn't stand to let things play out without raising a ruckus.

"Stupid wolf!" She slammed a fist against the steering wheel. "Why couldn't you have stayed out of sight?"

Now she'd never see Ryan or Ridge again.

But that didn't mean she would ever give up. She started the truck, but had no intention of driving away. She'd watch and follow Miles and his band of werewolves as they drove away. If her warrior wolf couldn't get the job done, then she'd have to take matters into her own hands.

Hands throwing flames. So much flame, Miles would swallow fire and eat her wrath.

Don't jump into things like this. Just think. Take a deep breath. Do not react.

Emotionally, she was a wreck. She could not charge into the fray and expect a successful outcome until she got control of herself and calmed down.

Though his actions had been foolish, Ridge had fought valiantly. And yet, something bothered her about that quick exchange between the werewolves.

Ridge had given up too easily.

Sure, he'd been bleeding and outnumbered, but she'd seen him in action before; he could have taken those wolves. None of them had shifted. They'd all been equals, yet when judging brawn and strength, she would have put Ridge far above them all.

Why had he given up on the fight? It made little sense.

Pressing her forehead to the steering wheel, she closed her eyes. "Damn him! Now I've two to worry about. How dare he do that to me?"

Just when she had begun to accept him into her heart. To begin to think they could really be a they, and that after this was all through, they might start dating, and continue to share what they'd shared these past few days.

He'd touched her heart, and made her realize she did need someone. That there was no possible way she could push him away, because if she tried, he'd push back. And he would win.

And she wanted him to win—her heart.

Scanning the horizon of snow, she sighted no one who may have followed her, nor did she see another vehicle. They couldn't have walked out to the meeting spot. There must be a building close by where they'd taken Ridge. Perhaps where they kept Ryan?

She was unsure what her next move was, and feeling as if Ridge had abandoned her to handle this all by herself.

No. That wasn't like him.

Something didn't feel right about her assessment of Ridge's actions during the fight. He would never surrender if that meant leaving her alone. He always put the woman first. *Always protect the female.* He'd risked his own life to protect Persia Masterson.

The only thing that would see him abandoning his fierce stance had to call to his even stronger protective nature.

"He did it to get close to Ryan," she said on a whisper. If Miles held Ryan anywhere nearby, they would likely take Ridge to the same place. Tears flooded her eyes. "By the goddess, I think I love that werewolf."

Chapter 17

His boots thumped and his hips hit hard as he was dragged down the concrete stairs into a basement lit by lighting strips along the floor where it met the wall. Ridge could walk, but he wanted to give the illusion that he was injured and too tired to fight back. The less damage he took from the rowdy wolves the better he'd be able to function. And plot an escape.

He was shoved inside a cell and caught his forearms against a mattress on the floor. It reminded him of the basement in the Northern pack's compound, and stirred a sickening roil in his belly. It was the first thing he'd demolished and stripped clean after taking on the role of principal. The Northern pack would never again hold anyone captive, or use vampires in the sickening blood sport.

The cell door clanged shut, and his captors wandered

to the next cell. "Sleeping?" one of them said as he observed the person inside the cell. Ridge didn't look, but instead remained facedown on the mattress.

"Leave him alone," the other said. "Did you remember to bring him dinner?"

"He's not my kid."

The acrid scent of fear reached Ridge's nose. It came from the prisoner in the next cell. Stay strong, he wanted to whisper.

The wolves clattered up the stairs, and he heard the door slam.

Ridge shot over to the bars separating his cell from the other. A boy lay on another mattress, his body curled forward as he clutched his stomach. His eyelids were shut tightly, and Ridge sensed he was not asleep but rather faking it as he just had.

"Are you Ryan?"

The boy's eyes shot open. They were bloodshot, and Ridge could smell the salty tears that stained his cheeks.

"My name is Richard Addison," he said. "You can call me Ridge."

"Go away." The kid curled in tighter on himself and his entire face winced.

"Are you in pain? Did they hurt you? I'm here to help."

"No one can help me," he said weakly. "I hate stupid wolves."

That wasn't going to help enamor him to the boy. But he wasn't about to lie and create more distrust. "I'm werewolf, but I'm not allied with those creeps, or the witch Miles."

"Miles shoves me around," the boy said. "I hate him, too. And I hate you, you ugly wolf!"

The kid had every right to fearful anger, and Ridge wasn't about to try to convince him otherwise. He knew what it was like to be pushed around and treated poorly. All the boy must imagine right now was getting some retaliation, and then…freedom.

"You shouldn't trust me," he offered. "That's smart. Never trust a stranger. I won't hurt you, though. I'd never hurt a kid. You look like you're in pain. Please, tell me if they've hurt you. Have they been feeding you?"

The boy sat up on an elbow and eyed Ridge through his shaggy bangs. "Cold pizza."

That he'd offered a bit of information meant a lot. He could win the boy's trust if he revealed…

"I'm your…" He couldn't say he was his father. He didn't know that. And if he was, it was likely Abigail had never told her son about the possibility that a werewolf could have fathered him. "I'm a friend of your mother's. We were both outside to make the exchange. I knew Miles would try to trick Abigail, though. He never intended to hand you over."

"My mom was here? Where is she?" He sat straight, but with a sharp grimace, his shoulders wrenched forward, and he clutched his gut. "She came to save me?" he managed through a gritted jaw.

"We both did. And we will get you out of here."

"Dude, you're behind bars. Way to go with the save."

At least he could find some humor. "If they've been starving you…"

"They feed me all the time. Pizza every night. I love

pizza. Even the cold stuff. You know you can't get Little Caesar's in Switzerland?" He moaned again.

"Ryan, tell me what's wrong." He sensed the boy was hiding some pain. Hell, he wasn't doing a very good job of hiding it, bent over and moaning. "Come over here. Can you do that? I promise I won't hurt you."

"No. You're a wolf."

"Helping your mother, remember?"

Ryan met his eyes, and strained against the pain. "It hurts in my gut. All over sometimes. Like in my spine."

"How long have you been in pain?"

"Since this morning."

"Did one of those thugs hurt you?"

"No, it's nothing like that. I must be sick. But I've never felt like this before when I've gotten a cold. It's in my arms, too." His voice cracked on that last sentence and the deep tone leaped an octave.

His voice was changing. Which meant…

"Did your mother tell you what would happen when you hit puberty, Ryan?"

He nodded, and tucked his head down. "Yeah, my voice has been wonky for months. It's embarrassing. Mom said I'd come into my magic when I became a man. But I don't remember her saying it would hurt."

Ridge didn't suspect a witch coming into his magic should experience pain and body aches like the boy endured. Hell, he had no clue how it was for a witch. The closest thing he could relate it to was his own puberty. Now that had been an eye-opener, even growing up in the pack. It hadn't hurt, but his wolf had come on strong and ready to greet the world with a howl.

He gripped the cell bars. Could Ryan be nearing his first shift? That would mean he really was his son. He had no proof, and he should not jump to conclusions. The boy could have a bug or the flu, because that was usually accompanied by muscle aches. Hell, gaining magic could be as uncomfortable as a shift, for all he knew.

"Ryan, does your skin feel prickly sometimes?"

The boy's head shot up and his eyes met Ridge's. Just like his mother's eyes. Maybe a little darker? Almost… brown? "Yeah. How did you know?"

"How long has it been feeling that way?"

"Just today. Oh, here comes another one. It hurts so bad I have to squeeze my legs…" He flopped forward, grasping his bent legs tight to his chest.

It hurt Ridge to see the boy struggling against the pain, but he was so brave. He didn't want to cry out, when any normal kid would surrender to the mysterious agony and yowl.

Deep inside, he felt pride for the boy's bravery. And he knew why, but he wouldn't think it. Not yet. Not until he was sure. But if he was on the right track, then they didn't have much time. The shift—if it was the shift—would come upon the boy as soon as the moon was high in the sky. Didn't need a full moon, either. Just moonlight.

That gave them about…three hours.

He checked the bars separating the cells. They were secured in the floor, but it looked as if they'd been drilled down into the concrete, and in fact, with a little jiggling, he was able to twist one of the bars.

Ryan lifted his head and he watched in wonder as Ridge bent the bar inward toward him and the bottom of it popped free.

"I thought you were hurt when they brought you in,"

the boy said. "You're strong. Stronger than those other nasty werewolves."

"Be quiet, boy. We don't want any of them coming down to check up on us."

"Pizza should be coming soon."

"Then we'd better work quickly. I'm going to need your help. You stand lookout, will you? Can you do that? If you're hurting…"

"No, I can do it." He crept to the bars by the door where Ridge had noticed the outer bars were secured with bolts to the concrete. He wouldn't be able to bend and break those as easily. What he needed was the key.

"The skinny one with the leather wristband is the one with the key," Ryan offered with a painful wince.

"Good boy." Ridge was able to slip into the boy's cell through the space he'd made in the bars. Ryan stiffened as he approached, so he stopped and put up his palms in placation. "Is it okay if I touch your forehead? Feel for fever? I promise, I'm not like the other wolves."

"You know my mom?"

"Yes. I've been helping her the past two days, trying to get to you."

The boy nodded. "Go ahead. You're big." The kid stretched his gaze up to Ridge's. "Are you in a pack?"

He pressed the back of his hand to the boy's forehead as he'd once seen Persia Masterson do when he was a young pup in the pack. "I'm the leader of the Northern pack."

"Cool. Do you know those nasty wolves?"

"Nope, but if they're working for a witch, I'd say they are unaligned with a pack, and that puts them on my list of bad guys."

"Mine too. How do you know my mom?"

"We…go back a long way. Before you were born."

"Do you like her?"

Not answering, he gave the boy an assessing look. No fever. But he could feel him shiver and his hands were chilled. "Are you cold?"

"A little. It's the pricklies again. It feels like sharp hairs are trying to poke through my bones."

"The pricklies, eh." He knew that sensation. Too well.

"You didn't say if you liked my mom."

"I do like her. She's beautiful, and kind."

"And a witch. You know she's a witch, right? And so am I. Or I'm supposed to be soon enough. Do you think this is it? Do you think I'm coming into my magic? I never thought it would hurt so much. Or maybe it doesn't hurt so much as it's just freaking me out."

At the sound of footsteps overhead, he shushed the boy with a finger to his lips. Ridge rushed into his cell. He'd never be able to fit the bent-out bar back in place, so he hoped they'd notice the missing bar later rather than immediately. The basement door opened.

He picked up the bar and turned his back to the cell doors, concealing the bar along his body. "Tell me when he's right at your door," he whispered.

From the corner of his eye he saw Ryan nod. He clutched his gut and his face muscles tightened, but he did not cry out. Good boy.

"Now," Ryan hissed.

Ridge shoved the bar through the other bars and connected with the jaw of the werewolf holding a pizza box. He slammed the bar and the wolf's head against the cement wall. The wolf went down, crushing the pizza box under him and sprawling out cold.

Ryan gave him a thumbs-up as Ridge slipped through the bars again. He reached out for the keys dangling from the wolf's jeans pocket, but couldn't quite make the distance.

"Use the bar," Ryan directed. "Oh, man, it feels like my skin is moving over my bones."

Yet another familiar feeling. Ridge glanced down the dark hallway, but spied thin light at the end near the stairs. Moonlight?

He jerked the bar and the keys slid closer so he could grasp them. They hadn't much time if the moon was already shining across the snow-covered fields.

Abigail had driven to the edge of town, but hadn't wanted to get too far away from the meeting sight. The short drive had given her time to breathe deeply and settle her nerves. She was ready now. She could approach Miles and maintain calm, yet watch for the perfect time to use her magic against the witch, who was a master over fire.

They were equals when it came to fire magic. And she could defeat the bastard if she focused her anger inward and streamed it out concisely.

Shifting into gear, she turned in time to see the headlights flash from the side of the truck. Before she could react, the oncoming vehicle collided into her door and the impact pushed the truck bed around. Her spine compressing and head snapping to the right, Abigail clutched the wheel and screamed.

Chapter 18

Ridge, with Ryan's hand in his, raced from the building and out into the forest. The chill air bruised his cheeks and mouth and he realized neither of them had a coat, so he had to find shelter quickly.

He didn't run full speed. The boy was slowing, more so with every second that passed. He wanted to get to the other side of the wooded area, where he heard distant traffic. They could flag down a car and catch a ride into town. He knew wherever she was, Abigail could take care of herself, so he focused on the boy right now.

But when Ryan dropped to the ground, he knew his worst expectations would come true. Worst, and yet, also beyond his hopes.

"I can't," Ryan said, gasping and huffing more than he should be. He clutched his chest and wriggled his shoulders as if trying to fight off some unseeable beast.

Ridge knew the beast would soon be visible.

"It hurts!"

He knelt before Ryan and rubbed his palms down the child's trembling shoulders and arms, but the boy did not feel cold, rather hot, actually. Another telling sign. Ridge lifted his chin to force him to meet his eyes. "Ryan, I know what's wrong with you."

"What? This is awful. I feel like I want to crawl out of my skin. And it's freezing out here, but I'm burning up!"

"Crawling out of your skin is sort of what is happening. Hell. What I have to tell you is going to freak you out."

"Why?" His narrow shoulders twitched and he jerked his head back, fighting what he should be embracing. "What do I have?"

"It's not what you have, it's what you are."

"A…w-witch." His body twitched and his head shook as he tensed against the weird sensations Ridge was all too familiar with. "Like…my mother. Th-this… sucks!"

"She was wrong. Your father wasn't a witch. You're not coming into magic, Ryan. Your father was a— Hell. How do I say this?"

"What?"

"Judging by the symptoms I've observed in you, I'm pretty sure your father was a werewolf. Your body wants to embrace your inner beast, Ryan. You're coming into your first shift as a werewolf."

"That's c-crazy." He clutched Ridge's forearm and gritted his jaw. Abigail's determined eyes stared up at him. He was a brave young man, and it made Ridge proud.

"Just relax, Ryan. Don't fight it. You have to let
it happen. It's going to feel weird and stretchy, but
I promise, it won't be painful. You'll shift to wolf
shape the first time, and then possibly werewolf
form."

"No!"

"I promise you it won't hurt if you just relax into it.
I wish I had more time to explain, but our bodies are
controlled by the lunar cycles, and the moon will have
her due. Now. I'll shift with you. Just stay close to me,
no matter what."

"H-how do you know this? About my father? Oh!"

He slammed his head against the forest floor, dig-
ging his fingers into the snow. His chest arched upward
and his arms jutted out, groping the air. It looked more
painful than it felt, Ridge knew. And since the boy had
not been prepared for this, he was doing well by not totally freaking out.

Ridge tore off his shirt and began to prepare for
his own shift by loosening his jeans. The last place he
wanted this to happen was out here, so close to danger,
and yet, that it was happening when he was with Ryan
was optimal. Had the boy been alone and in the cell,
there was no telling what he would have thought was
happening to him. Or what the wolves would have done
had they found him shifted.

"Do you trust me, Ryan?"

"I…" He shook his head erratically, not positive or
negative. "H-help me—yes!" His right shoulder popped
forward and in reaction he jerked back his head. "Trust
you. Can't stop this!"

"Then release. Close your eyes, and don't think
about fighting it. Let the wolf come over you. It knows

what to do. You follow its lead. I'm going to shift now, so you can see it doesn't hurt me, and it will happen quickly. Okay?"

Gritting his teeth, Ryan nodded.

Kneeling beside the writhing boy, Ridge closed his eyes and called upon his wolf, which was close as always during the moonlight. It was his nature, as much a part of him as the human form. His bones hummed and his muscles twanged as they moved and shifted. His fingers curled inward and his wrist bones clicked. Fur prickled along his skin—the pricklies, as Ryan had described earlier. His *were* mind gave over to his animal mind, and he no longer assessed each body part as it changed and became wolf.

In less than thirty seconds, he stood on four paws before the boy, his panting breath forming clouds in the air.

When in his wolf form, he had a vague grasp on his humanity, yet he could think partially as a human. He knew this human boy was very important to his *were* shape.

With his front paws he dug playfully at the snow before him, then lifted it with his nose to scatter it over the boy's arm.

"Wow," the boy said. And then he nodded at Ridge's wolf, as if agreeing. "I think I can do this. I don't have much choice."

With a cry to the heavens, the boy gave way to humanity and surrendered to his destiny. Clothing tore, braces popped off his teeth and the shift wriggled his body into the shape of a sleek, brown-furred wolf. With a yip, the new wolf came to his paws.

Ridge howled, crying out in joy and announcing to the world his happiness. The wolves took off, prancing through the forest.

After a run as wolves, they'd not shifted to werewolf form, and for that, Ridge was thankful. It was difficult enough adjusting after your first shift, let alone not knowing to even expect it.

Keeping his pup close to him, they'd tracked through the forest, and ran north, away from the danger, until Ridge's wolf had scented the truck that had brought the *were*-shaped wolves to the area. They were searching—he could scent their human pheromones—so he directed the pup to circle around.

He had led them back to the place where they'd initially shifted, and communicating to the panting pup that now was time to pay attention, Ridge shifted to *were* shape, twisting and gyrating on the snow until his human form was complete.

Ryan followed suit, impressing Ridge with his easy shift. It had always been easier when he was younger. His muscles had been loose and elastic and he'd taken joy in the shift as it massaged his organs and delivered him back to human shape, renewed and energized.

He tossed Ryan's clothes to him. His jeans were intact, and his shirt only a little torn, so that helped ease some of the embarrassment of being caught out naked after shifting back to human form.

Ridge's shirt was always a loss, but he wore his jeans loose for a reason. After kicking aside the snow, he settled onto the loamy moss coating a tree root, and waited for Ryan to speak first.

The boy paced a while, his bare feet tracking in

the snow, but he didn't seem to mind the cold. Their human flesh could withstand much more than that of mere mortals. Ridge knew it was from all the energy his body was trying to grasp and make sense of. From this moment forth his life would never be the same. He hoped the boy didn't hold it against Abigail for not having told him there was a chance he'd grow fur instead of shoot fire from his hands. Quite a different result after he'd been groomed to expect the latter.

Suddenly Ryan stopped before Ridge and squatted, his fingers touching the snow lightly for balance. His brown hair was tousled and Ridge noted now his jaw was square—like his.

"That," Ryan began, his hands shaping the air before him in an attempt to grasp the event, "was awesome!"

And like that, Ridge's anxiety fled.

"I'm a werewolf," Ryan said to Ridge. "How cool is that? That is so much better than being a stupid witch."

"Hey now, your mother is a witch, and she's not stupid."

"Yeah, but Miles is stupid."

"I'll give you that. How do you feel?"

"Amazing. And when we were running through the forest? I never felt so good in my entire life!"

"It is freeing to take off in wolf form and lope across the land. I always feel my best then, too."

"Dude, my braces popped off. Yes! When will I learn to shift to werewolf form? Will I be like a big ugly monster with talons and kill people?"

"Whoa, boy. Where did you hear something like that?"

Ryan shrugged. "That's what they do in the movies."

"We are not in a movie. Our werewolf shape is our

ultimate form. It combines man and wolf. We are not monsters, but we do have talons."

"Cool."

"And we do not kill people. The last thing we want is trouble with the mortals. We don't need them, but we have learned to exist among them. That's your first lesson, boy, and don't forget it. Be kind to others, and accept all breeds. No man or woman is lesser or better than you."

"Even vampires?"

"Even vampires. The paranormal breeds are like the mortal races. We're all the same beneath our outer costume. Some of us may be nasty and evil, like certain mortals. But we're all trying to live together on this one small planet. So respect the world and respect others. And most of all?"

"Yeah?"

"Respect your mother," he said, wishing he could have made that *parents*. But if anyone were going to reveal the complete truth to Ryan, it would have to be Abigail. It was her right, much as it killed him not to tell it.

"Where is my mom? I have to tell her. Why didn't she know about this? She thought I was going to be a witch."

"I'll leave that for your mother to explain. But whatever she says to you, don't judge her, and don't think she's ever lied to you, because she has not. She's done the best she could for you over the years."

"I know. She sent me to Switzerland because she thought I'd be safer there. That was a joke. They picked me up in Detroit and escorted me to a flight to Minneapolis. Told me my mom sent an escort. I didn't figure it out until they'd driven me to that nasty place. Did we get away from the bad guys? I hate that Miles dude. He was always looking at me like I was a piece of garbage he wanted to kick out of his way. When can I shift again? We didn't shift to werewolf form. Can we try that now?"

Ridge glanced toward the half-moon waxing in the sky. "Only a few hours of night left. I think we should take things slow. Let you get comfortable with this shift first, then by the time this moon turns full, you'll be ready for the big shift."

"So if I'm not a monster, and I don't kill people, what do I do in werewolf form?"

"Whoa, boy. Sit down, and I'll tell you a few things."

Ryan sat next to Ridge on the moss, clasping his skinny arms about his knees. He had not stopped smiling, and he sat close, obviously needing Ridge's body heat. It felt awesome to have his son sitting so close.

"The killing thing is a myth. We might only kill small animals that cross our paths when we're in wolf form."

"Eww."

"It's in our nature, and it won't bother you when you're out on a run, trust me. The beast needs meat. But mostly, you shift to werewolf form because…" He had no intention of keeping the kid in the dark, and sensed Abigail would never have the words to explain, but he must be careful how he chose his words. "Well, it's a mating thing. Our werewolves seek sexual satisfaction."

"Seriously? I'm just a kid. Sex freaks me out."

"Don't worry, boy, you won't be having sex for a good while. But once your werewolf matures it'll seek a mate to bond with and make a family. And, once your werewolf is older, it'll need sex during the full moon. The only way to keep from shifting to werewolf shape is to have lots of sex the day preceding the full moon."

Ryan flashed him a wonky look. "Again, yuck. I think I like the running through the forest part better."

Ridge tousled his hair and slapped him across the back. "You don't have to worry about that for a while. You getting cold? We should find the road and catch a ride to town."

"I am getting cold, but not as freezing as I think I should be."

"That's your wolf nature. You can manage extreme temperatures better than the average mortal."

"So that means I'm not a mortal now?"

"You are a wolf shifter, but you are not immortal. The werewolf's average life span is about three hundred years."

"So I will live long enough to see the future, like traveling in spaceships and robot dogs? Cool! Thanks for getting me out of that cell, Ridge. And for being there when I shifted."

"I'm glad you're taking this well. Especially since it was quite a surprise."

"Yeah. I'm going to have to talk to Mom about that. Does that mean she thought the guy who was my father really wasn't?"

"I think I'll let you talk to your mom about that. But remember, she has never lied to you. Sometimes adults don't know everything, and they do the best they can. So give her a huge break. Deal?"

Ryan slapped Ridge's palm. "Deal. Even more than being cold? I'm hungry. I could eat three Big Macs. Maybe four."

"I'll take you straight to McDonald's. We're not out of the clear yet. You have to tell me everything you can about the men who held you. And, as soon as we get into town, I have to call your mom."

"Where are we anyway?"

"I have no idea. Let's walk."

Chapter 19

Words could not describe how great Ridge felt as he
helped Ryan into the rental car and handed him the vanilla shake he'd wanted after sucking down a chocolate shake and two Big Macs and an order of large fries
inside the store.

This boy was his son. There was no other man in the
world who could be his father. He had a son!

And the kid had his appetite.

Sliding behind the wheel and turning on the ignition, Ridge wished he'd had the truck where he kept
extra clothes packed away. They'd been lucky to walk
by the rental shop, and that it was still open, or else he
would have resorted to hitchhiking back into town.

"I can't wait to get home and tell Mom about this.
She's going to be so surprised."

"I can imagine the look on her face right now,"

Ridge said as he pulled onto the main street. And he'd be sure to protect his privates in case she decided to get jiggy with her magic after hearing the news.

She should be relieved Ryan was not a witch. That meant Miles had no reason to harm the boy, and the sick bastard could hop on his broomstick and fly out of Dodge. Things would be fine as soon as they worked out the new family dynamics.

Because no way was Ridge going to hand off Ryan to Abigail and turn around and walk away. Absolutely not. He'd already been denied twelve years of the boy's life. Not another minute would pass without him sharing that time with his son.

"So what do they teach you in that fancy school you go to?" he asked, as he navigated the roads. It was around six in the morning, and the streets were empty. "Do you speak Swiss?"

"It's a Swiss German they teach, and I'm not very good at it. I'm supposed to learn it, but I've been cheating on my homework."

"Hey, now, that's no way to do things. If you need help, you should ask for it."

"Yeah, I do, but it's a lot more fun skiing. They have a killer slope like a half a mile from my dorm. It's distracting!"

Ridge laughed, loving that his son was like any other kid. Playing sports and ditching schoolwork. He'd probably start ditching school for the girls soon enough. "So is it one of those all-boy schools?"

"Yes. It's such a drag. The only time I ever get to see anything wearing pink is on the weekends when we go to town for a movie or fast food. Not that I'm looking," Ryan said with a wry tone. "But once in a while a pretty girl will look at me and smile real big. I don't understand why. It's so weird."

"Because you're a handsome fellow. Soon you'll have to chase all the girls off with a stick. Oh hell, what's this?"

Ridge pulled the car over behind a tow truck hooking up a black Ford 350 pickup. The driver's side had been smashed in, and the front windshield was shattered.

"That's my truck!" He jumped out and told Ryan to stay inside. The boy, unaware who had been driving the truck, nodded and agreed to stay put.

The tow truck driver hadn't any good information, other than that the accident had occurred hours ago, and they hadn't found the driver behind the wheel or in the area. Nor was there any other vehicle, one that could have collided with the truck. When Ridge showed him his vehicle registration, the driver gave him a receipt and told him where he could claim the truck.

Ridge walked the street where the tow driver had yet to sweep the broken glass, looking for signs that Abigail had gotten out and walked away from the scene of the accident. He wished he had a cell phone to call her and check in, let her know everything was all right. The rental shop had been closing and the cranky manager had refused his request to make a quick call.

His heart stuttered and he couldn't stop clenching and unclenching his fists.

The last thing she'd seen was him being taken captive. She must have figured out by now he'd done that on purpose. Or had she? Did she believe that both her son and he were captives?

And why the crash? Had she been sitting here at

the intersection thinking about what had gone on and hadn't seen an oncoming car? Had the distraction caused her to pull out into the lane without seeing the car? Didn't make sense. The witch was sharp as a tack.

The truck had been facing north, which meant she had been driving toward the scene of the meeting. Had she decided to take matters into her own hands and use her magic to rescue them both?

He had to get hold of Abigail.

Climbing into the car, he met Ryan's wondering gaze. His heart sinking, he couldn't offer the boy a lie. That was no way to start their relationship. But the truth would hurt.

"That's my truck," he said. "Your mother was driving it."

"Where is she? Did she get in an accident? Did they take her to the hospital?"

"No. She wasn't in the vehicle when the police arrived, so I have to believe she walked away. She's probably at home right now. It's not far from here."

He pulled away and leaned over to put a hand on Ryan's shoulder and give it a squeeze. The boy met his gaze with watery eyes, as he sucked on the vanilla shake.

"Everything will be all right, Ryan. I promise."

They pulled into the driveway of Abigail's house and Ryan did not wait for the car to stop. He jumped out and ran to the dark house. Ridge rushed up behind him, but the boy hadn't tried to open the front door. Instead he stood there with his palms flat to the cold wood door.

A little metal lockbox sat beside the doorknob to

keep an extra key inside. "Do you know the combination?"

Ryan nodded. "But it doesn't matter. She's not in there."

"You haven't gone inside to look."

"I don't have to. I've always been able to tell when my mother is near. I can sort of feel her presence. Always thought it was a witch thing."

"I get that. We wolves are extraperceptive of family. Let's go inside anyway. Get you some warmer clothes, and take stock. Maybe she left a note."

He crossed his fingers she had indeed been home. Because the other option did not sit well in his gut. If she had been hurt in the accident, how could she have possibly walked away?

Ryan punched in the combination and entered the house. Swell Cat, who sat on the back of the pink couch, took one look at the approaching boy, hissed and skedaddled out of the room.

"I wasn't gone five months," Ryan called after the spooked cat.

"He senses your nature now," Ridge offered. "Cats and wolves. They don't get along all that well."

"I didn't think of that. Weird. I really liked that cat."

"Give him a chance to figure you out." Ridge strolled into the kitchen. "He'll come around."

The counter was bare; no notes. He eyed the fridge, where the whiteboard hung. It was clean. The burned outlet sat like a silent warning that things were not right in Kansas.

Now he was worried. Abigail should have gone directly home if she'd had any sense. But why he thought that was anyone's guess. She was a fierce witch who took matters into her own hands and protected her own. She wouldn't sit around waiting for the world to right itself. She'd take action.

Unless someone had gotten to her first. Whoever had slammed into the truck had done so purposefully, Ridge decided. And the reason Abigail hadn't been found behind the steering wheel was because whoever had hit her had then taken her from the scene.

The scenario hurt his heart to imagine, but it was the only thing he could come up with. And he didn't have to guess who had taken her.

"Miles." He slammed a fist on the kitchen counter.

Ryan wandered into the kitchen, hands shoved in his jeans pockets. "Did you figure out where she is?"

"I think Miles may have taken her after he crashed into the truck she was driving. It's a guess."

"If that nasty witch took my mom—" Ryan kicked the counter baseboard.

"Exactly," Ridge said. "I've got to go back to where they held us."

"I'm going with you."

"No, you're going to stay here—" He couldn't leave the boy alone. Not so Miles or his henchwolves could show up and snatch him again. "Change of plan. You are going along with me."

"Yes!" Ryan pumped a fist at his side.

"Until I can find someone to watch you. I'll have to give Maverick a call and see if he's still in town."

"Who's that?"

"Another wolf. He's a good guy. You'll like him. You run and get some clean, warm clothes on, and grab a jacket."

"What about you? You're in tatters."

Ridge looked over his torn shirt. The counter clerks in McDonald's had given him a long, strange once-over. He didn't have time to run home and change. "This'll do."

It would just get torn again when his werewolf got near that witch Miles Easton.

Chapter 20

Abigail surfaced from a bruised muddle of darkness and winced as various parts of her body screamed with dull pain. Her feet were on the ground, and she leaned against something. Her head hung forward, and the first thing she saw when she opened her eyes were her boots and the torn leg of the borrowed gray leather pants.

Upright, then. She was standing, but not on her own. Weakness encompassed her muscles and she felt like a ragdoll harnessed to a mast.

"Hell's bells," she muttered, as realization flooded her foggy senses.

Trying to twist her hands resulted in no movement because her hands were bound behind her back, palms flat together and wrists tightly encircled with some kind of soft ribbon of flat rope. A leather strap crossed above her breasts, binding her back against a flat surface that with a bit of wiggling she decided was a square pole, like a support beam. Her hips were secured with more rope, but her legs were free.

Not that she could walk away from the situation.

She remembered wondering why Ridge had been stupid enough to get captured. And then she'd known he'd done it on purpose to save Ryan. And then—impact.

Now she smelled blood and tasted it on her lip. Her skin tugged above her left eye and she guessed she'd been cut by windshield glass upon impact. Nothing else on her seemed to scream for immediate medical attention, save for a general overall ache.

"Good morning, sunshine."

The deep voice put bile in her throat. She lifted her head and eyed the man who stood not five feet away, his arms crossed high over his chest and the devious smile she'd once thought sexy aimed like a laser at her.

"Where's my son?" she gasped, startled her voice was dry and barely there. She may have taken more damage to her body than she could assess. Didn't matter. She simply had to stay conscious. And try to work her fingers apart. "Damn it, where's Ryan?"

"He's gone missing, thanks to your pet hound."

"Ridge and Ryan escaped?" She didn't try to hide her joy over that news. "So now what? You need to take your anger out on someone? Why don't you release me and make it a fair fight?"

Miles's low chuckle tugged the thin skin on his face, shadowing his skull to a gaunt mask. What she'd ever seen in him was beyond her.

He was like you. You both shared common magic. And he had, initially, been kind to you.

That was it. It had been more admiration and mutual teaching than an actual heated sexual affair. They'd been intimate, but never more so than when they'd been using their magic together.

"If Ridge has Ryan," she said, "you'll never lay your hands on him again. You know that."

"I don't know that. The boy is mine. I'll fight the werewolf, and anything else you put in my way to get him."

"You don't love him. You want to cripple him so you remain strong. You're such a bastard."

The stroke of his fingers along her cheek sent a chill up her neck. She wanted to spit in his face, but her throat was dry. "A bastard you once loved. We shared everything, Abigail. More than everything. When we conjured magic together it was better than sex. You deny it?"

She shook her head. "That was the only thing I could tolerate about you."

"You're lying. I know because you can never look me in the face when you fashion a sweet little mistruth. It's something I adore about you."

"Let me go. Let's end this once and for all."

"You think so? You don't think the werewolf will consider handing over one insignificant man-child in exchange for the woman he loves?"

"He doesn't love me."

"I think differently. You always were blind to emotions. I think that was because you're such a raging tornado of emotions you cannot see beyond your own storm. The wolf adores you. Poor guy."

"He has a heart, unlike you."

"Oh, I've a heart. Recently ate a vampire heart, too. Tasty."

"You—? You took a source when we were seeing each other. That was thirteen years ago. You only need to do that once a century."

His cadaver grin cracked. "I do it as often as I'm able. No reason why I shouldn't build up superimmortality, eh?"

"I don't think it works that way." And how sickening he could engage in the ritual so frequently. Consuming a beating vampire heart was not for the squeamish, but it was a necessity if a witch wanted to retain immortality. A necessity required only once a century. "Thought you said you weren't a vampire hunter?"

"That's why I have my wolf pack."

"You're twisted, Miles. What do you want to let me go? Information about Ridge?"

He shook his head. "The wolf is too easy. I suspect he's gone to your house with the boy. I've sent my pack after them."

"How did you ever get those wolves to work for you?"

"They're bewitched, of course. Dumber than logs, but nothing a little magical instruction can't correct."

"That was always the one thing you said you'd never do."

"Control others with magic? Yes, it is grounds for banishment from the Light."

"You're a warlock, Miles. You've committed heinous crimes against the Light."

"This, coming from little Miss Never Does Wrong? You've centuries of indiscretions racked against you,

Abigail. Wouldn't the Council love to know your connection to The Order of the Stake?"

"They know." They didn't know she had been instrumental in forming the order of mortals that hunted vampires, but she wasn't about to give him the upper hand. The Council overlooked most of her indiscretions in exchange for her service. "I promise I won't allow Ryan to use his fire magic."

"Not good enough. You know when the boy comes into his magic it will be innate. He won't have to study. It'll just be—" he flipped out a hand dramatically "—to hand."

She closed her eyes. Without her hands free, she was helpless to direct her magic. And if werewolves had gone to her home, then Ridge and Ryan could again be in trouble.

She scanned the room. The dirt floor and support beams hinted that it was a basement. Nothing sat on the floor. Not a single box or piece of furniture she could send at Miles in an attempt to knock him out.

"So, while I have you here…" He dug out a piece of paper from his shirt pocket and unfolded it. She recognized the binding spell photo taken from the vampire's back. He must have taken it from her after the crash. "Let's make sure I've no competition from you should you find a way to wiggle from those restraints."

"No, Miles, don't do this. It's not going to change anything."

"Of course not. The only thing that'll make me happy is binding the boy. You don't think I enjoy consuming vampire hearts, do you? I want to protect all my hard work."

He flicked the paper dramatically, and began to read the spell.

Something on the level above them toppled and hit the floor with a thud. Abigail searched the ceiling, hearing footsteps. "He's here."

Miles glanced upward, and then resumed the spell. Faster.

Chapter 21

He could smell the witch's presence. Coconut, overlaid with an acrid fear. He didn't like that. Charging the burly wolf who blocked the door, Ridge guessed behind that door, he'd find Abigail.

He collided with solid muscle and bone. The wolf didn't move a step upon impact. He lifted Ridge by the neck until his feet left the ground, and then flung him with seeming little effort across the room. He landed at the convex corner of two walls, the sharp edge like a blade to his spine.

Dropping, Ridge blinked at the blackness threatening to knock him out cold. He breathed in deeply and growled. It kept him conscious. And now he was angry.

Talons clicked on the hardwood floor. He stretched his neck and twisted as it lengthened and thickened and fur grew from his pores.

The wolf who'd tossed him let out a howl, and stomped toward him, in werewolf shape. And across the room, two more fully shifted werewolves entered.

Abigail shouted at the noise of a scuffle overhead. It distracted Miles but momentarily. He refocused and studied the photo he held. It was a clear photograph of the binding spell, but the words were tiny, and blurred a bit by the old tattoo. He spoke the next Latin word, and Abigail felt a tingle scurry through her veins.

The binding was beginning to enter her on the growling tones of Miles's recitation. He was halfway through. She screamed again, and twisted her body forward, feeling the leather strap above her breasts loosen, but her hands remained clamped together as if glued.

The female's screams echoed from below as Ridge's face met the floor and his nose crunched. Blood spilled down the back of his throat. His canine teeth grazed the floor and his tongue lolled. But he sensed the next attack, and swung out his paw, talons extended, catching the wolf across the chest and dragging deep wounds through his rib cage.

The wolf gave a howl tangled with a whimper and rolled away, clutching his chest.

Dragged upward by the scruff at the back of his neck, Ridge was smashed against the wall. Teeth tore through his shoulder and ripped his skin. He kicked backward, dislodging the attacker, and leaped toward the one who stood by the door. With a swing of his arm, his talons cut through flesh and bone and took the were-wolf's head from his shoulders.

* * *

Abigail tried a movement spell on the beam she was bound to. The wood rattled, but the nails held it securely, and she guessed it was probably cemented into the floor as most support beams were.

Frustrated, she struggled and continued to scream, hoping to throw Miles out of his concentration, but the witch maintained the spell by speaking it slowly and with fierce intent.

Now he held his palm up to focus his magic upon her, and though he stood four feet away, she could feel the heat of his power. His determination melted her resolve and she stopped struggling.

The door above smashed open and wood shards clattered down the concrete stairs.

Miles shouted the next word, and then…he waited.

A werewolf trampled down the stairs, stood its full seven feet tall, and scanned the scene, chest heaving and arms flexed. Its maw revealed bloodied teeth and its talons were dripping with blood.

But the golden eyes softened at sight of her.

"Ridge, wait!"

The werewolf clenched its talons.

Miles hissed, "What the hell? Where's the last word?"

The werewolf stalked up behind Miles, though the witch was unaware of the wolf's proximity, so stymied he was by the missing word.

"I burned it off the vampire before I took the picture," Abigail said, triumph lifting her head. "I win, Miles. You'll never bind me or my son."

Behind him, the werewolf raised a paw, prepared to slice off the witch's head.

"Ridge, no!"

Miles spun about and blasted the wolf with a stream of fire. It hit the beast directly in the gut. The witch scrambled for the stairs, clambering over the fallen wolf.

"Help me, Ridge," Abigail yelled. "Get me loose!"

The werewolf's fur smoked and he shook his head miserably at the sudden blast. Finally he stomped over to Abigail and, chest heaving and jaw open to reveal deadly weapons, looked her over.

She knew he was now equally in his animal mind as he was his human mind, so he must recognize her. He had before.

"My hands," she said. "Please. And then we can go after Miles. Where's Ryan?" She knew he couldn't communicate with her. "Stay shifted. We can't let Miles get away. But I need you to free me first. Please, Ridge, my hands."

The wolf drew a talon down her arm, carefully, not cutting, until he moved around behind her. She felt the sharp, solid heat of a talon slice between her palms and winced as her skin took a cut. But her hands were free, followed by her arms and hips.

She stumbled forward, and the wolf hooked her under her breasts with one arm, holding her up. This was no time for a reunion hug or celebratory cheer. He was in predatory mode, and she didn't want to spoil that.

"Now we go after him," she said. "Lead the way."

The werewolf bounded up the stairs and she followed, using the handrail because she still felt weak from the accident.

Above, three werewolves lay sprawled on the floor.

One began to shift as she walked by, and her gaze was drawn to the detached human head that began to shed fur.

Ridge's werewolf grabbed her upper arm and tugged her away from the scene. He kicked open the front door—and was put back by a blast of fire.

The werewolf swung his arms but flames quickly encompassed him, igniting his fur. He stumbled backward and Abigail tried to push him down to help snuff out the flame.

"Shift quickly," she directed, knowing if he could do so, then he might have a chance at smothering the flames.

The werewolf howled and slapped the floor with a paw, which shifted into a human hand.

At the door, the wood frame ignited. Miles was throwing fire at them. They couldn't stay inside, but Ridge was in no condition to do anything but try to defeat the flames right now.

He transformed completely to *were* shape, and his skin smoked but there were no flames. His shoulder revealed a gaping wound and he lifted his head, stunned by the shift and the fire.

Abigail knelt by him. "Miles is outside. The house is on fire, but the door is right behind you. Can you manage?"

He nodded, and dropped his head.

"I have to go after him."

Ridge grabbed her hand and tugged her close to his face. "Give him flame, Abigail. Give him flame."

Oh, she would give that bastard flame.

Dodging a lash of crackling red fire, Abigail slapped

her hands together and rubbed them fiercely. Chanting a summons that drew up the earth's energy, she combined it with her fire in a wicked roil of flame. Beneath her feet, the earth rumbled and shuddered with a static electricity of motion. The leyline fixed to her power, and the truck Miles ran toward suddenly burst into flame, sending the hood flying into the air.

Miles turned and thrust a rolling wave of fire toward her. She couldn't dodge that large ball, but she was able to send out her own flames in a wall before her that defeated Miles's magic by dispersing it, and scattering millions of fire sprites to the snow, where they sizzled and smoked out.

"You'll never win!" Miles called. "Give it up, Abigail!"

Drawing in a deep breath, she focused on the man who had harmed her son, and her lover. "Eat my flame," she said calmly, and then thrust out her arms, fingers spread, to open herself wide to the fire and earth magic.

A roaring wave of fire charged toward Miles, catching his flailing limbs and slamming him against the blackened hood of the vehicle, pinning him there and moving over his flesh. He couldn't fight the enormous flames, and in seconds they consumed him.

Dropping her arms, Abigail lifted her head but couldn't witness the death of one of her own. He'd been a warlock, deserving of the punishment she'd served him. If she had not ended his life, he may have harmed many more.

"An ye harm none," she recited softly as the flames incinerated her ex-lover in her peripheral vision. It was the beginning of the witch's rede that

insisted on karmic way. "Unless you harm my own."
Screw the rede.

Stalking to the house, she called on her water magic
to lift the snow banked along the front porch and fling
it toward the burning threshold. It took three large
waves of snow to put out the flames. In its wake, the
charred wood dripped with water and steamed as if hell
had opened wide.

She ran inside and found Ridge huddled against the
wall, clutching his burned gut. The wound was red and
angry, yet he smiled weakly at her before falling to the
floor and passing out.

"No, not this. You're not going to succumb to Miles's
flame."

Plunging to his side, she touched his face. His skin
was too hot, but he hadn't been burned there. His body
reacted to the damage by bringing up a fever. Even with
his healing capabilities, he'd never defeat the burns.

"I'm not going to lose you now. You mean too much
to me, you big lug."

Pressing her hands over the angry flesh on his stomach she closed her eyes and began to chant. She called
on the ancient powers that had been instilled in her
bloodline throughout the ages. Her mother had been
a powerful witch, master of all elements, as had her
grandmother. The power to heal was simply about connecting to the body and mastering it.

Murmuring the Latin incantation that would open
her to Ridge's suffering, Abigail's muscles tensed as
she took on his pain. The flames had begun to course
through his system. She just needed to cleanse him of
the fire.

With a command to the elements, she called upon

her water magic. Snow blew in through the window and, clouding above their heads, turned to rain to douse her smoking werewolf. It startled him awake and he clutched her wrist, but she kept her hands firmly on his body. She could feel the cooling waters loosen in her belly, and knew it was doing the same to him.

"Abi—"

Squaring her palms over his abdomen, she began to hum rhythmically, which enhanced her magic and focused her concentration. Ridge's body jerked. His hand grasped for her, but clutched only air.

"Let my spirit heal you," she said. "Take my magic into your soul, Richard Addison."

She felt the burn soften beneath her palms, and pulled them away to watch the skin revert from an angry red welt to pale flesh. The scar she'd given him in Vegas remained. He must wear it as her mark.

"So mote it be," she said. "I love you, Ridge."

Chapter 22

From the three vehicles parked in front of the property, Abigail selected the Mustang because it was the only one that hadn't been reduced to a crispy critter. Before she got behind the driver's seat, she pulled out the keys and opened the trunk.

She was on his wavelength, Ridge realized, as she pulled out a duffel and tossed it at him. He caught it and found inside a change of clothing that belonged to one of the wolves who had attacked him. He quickly dressed in the frigid air, pulling on dark jeans that fit and a heavy blue wool sweater, wondering all the while how the hell Miles had managed to get the wolves to do his dirty work.

"Can a witch control a werewolf?" he asked as he tossed the duffel and took the keys from Abigail. He was in better shape to drive than she.

"Miles bewitched them. It's another spell." She shivered and scampered around to the passenger side and got in the car. She wasn't wearing a coat and her pants were torn up to the thigh and one sleeve torn off the shoulder.

Ridge pulled her into a hug and rubbed his hand up her arms and back. "I think you saved my life in there."

"It was a little burn. You would have been fine. I just helped you heal faster."

Maybe. But he'd felt the burn all the way to his insides. Much like the burn he'd taken in Vegas, only more insistent. He had been close enough to the pearly gates to consider knocking.

"Witches and their magic always seem to go for my gut," he muttered, rubbing his belly.

"I knew you'd come for me," she said and hugged him tightly.

"I only wish I could have protected you."

"You protected what was most important to me. Where is Ryan?"

"Safe with Maverick at the compound. I'll take you there right now to get him."

They'd driven in silence for a few minutes before Ridge could no longer stop himself from slamming his fist into the dashboard. The plastic cracked and the radio stopped playing.

"What?" Abigail asked, rousing from a near sleep.

"I failed you," he said. "I wasn't there to protect you."

"What are you saying? You saved me."

"Not until the last minute. If I had been a few minutes slower…"

"It wasn't like with Persia, Ridge."

She hit him directly in the heart with that statement. The witch's aim was always spot-on. "Miles was this close to doing you damage."

"He didn't have the complete spell. He would have never succeeded."

"And if I hadn't been there he may have killed you instead."

"Exactly. But you were there." She stroked his arm, but the soft touch only illuminated their differences. He was too rough, too wrong, too not right for her. How dare he think he had a right into her life?

"We'll talk about it later," she said on a sigh. "I want to hold Ryan in my arms."

"About Ryan," he said, as he pulled down the road leading to the compound. The winter sun flashed off the rearview mirror and made him wince. "Miles is not his father."

"Please, let's not start this again."

"Abigail, five minutes after I got Ryan out of the cell Miles had been keeping him in, he shifted."

She shot him an open-mouthed gape.

Ridge pulled the car into the drive before the compound, and before he could explain further, Ryan came running out to meet them.

"He's mine," Ridge said, bowing his head and closing his eyes. "The boy is mine."

Abigail's head spun with the revelation Ridge had laid upon her, but she hadn't time to react before Ryan opened the car door and she got out to catch her son in a hug. He felt taller, and his hair was long and hung in his eyes, and she realized it felt like years since she'd held him like this.

Tears streamed from her face when Ryan's eyes met hers. "Mom, I missed you."

Out of the corner of her eye she saw Ridge stride by, gripping his wounded shoulder. His eyes followed hers, and they weren't happy, but almost condemning. *He's mine.*

It had been a relief to learn the truth, yet at the same time, mentally, it brought her to her knees. She'd deprived Ridge of his son for twelve years. Probably he could never forgive her for that.

"Mom! You'll never guess what happened to me."

"Can we talk about it at home, sweetie? I'm so tired. I want to take you home and hold you until you tell me to stop it."

"Oh sure, but I have to say it. I'm a werewolf!"

"Ridge told me."

"I can't believe it. It's so freakin' cool!"

"I'm sorry, Ryan, I didn't know. Well, I knew there was the smallest chance."

Ryan caught her as she stumbled. "It's okay, Mom. I know sometimes we don't know everything. You're right, we have a lot to talk about. Let's get you home. You don't look so good."

Had her twelve-year-old boy just said that? He'd grown up so much.

She dusted the hair from his eyes. "Are you okay? What with everything that's happened?"

"I'm fine, Mom. Thanks to Ridge." Ryan turned and looked for the man he'd mentioned.

Ridge stood at the compound door alongside Dean Maverick. Battered and bruised, the noble warrior had sacrificed much tonight. He looked like hell. He also looked as though he'd like to write the two of them out of his memory forever.

"We both owe him more than he can ever imagine," Abigail said, threading her hand through Ryan's. "Can we talk tomorrow?" she called out to Ridge. "I want to get Ryan home and, well, we both might need some distance."

The stoic wolf merely nodded.

"I'll drive you home," Maverick offered. "All three of you have been through heck."

Chapter 23

Two days later

Ridge pulled the repaired truck in front of Abigail's house and put it in Park, letting it idle. He fingered the divorce papers lying on the seat beside him. After what she'd said about needing some distance from him, his hopes had been vanquished. He had stayed at the compound for two days, pacing, staring at the telephone, wondering if he should call her.

She hadn't called him.

It wasn't meant to be. Sure, they were his family. Ryan was his flesh and blood. But Abigail was tied to him only because of some flimsy piece of paper. He wouldn't do that to her. Wouldn't use a tired old convention to argue his point. She was a woman who needed her freedom.

He wanted—needed—a woman who could embrace togetherness.

He didn't want to walk up the sidewalk and climb the steps to knock on the door. He didn't want to look into her gorgeous blue eyes one more time, knowing he'd have to turn and walk away. The papers signed. His life cut loose from any ties to Abigail Rowan.

Maybe she'd change her mind?

He shook his head and banged it against the back of the seat. He wasn't stupid. A woman like her didn't need a man. She'd made that clear.

Opening the door and grabbing the papers, he also snatched a pen he kept propped in the empty cigarette lighter.

It was a beautiful day. The sun shone across the snow, giving the yards a diamond twinkle. The temperature neared the thirties, and he'd driven past a local park boasting a hill crowded with sledders bundled in bright snowsuits.

He wondered if Ryan liked to sled down hills in the wintertime, and then couldn't decide if the boy was too old for that. A guy should never be too old for having fun. Would Abigail let him take Ryan on the weekends so he could get to know him better?

He needed that. The boy needed to be with others of his breed, to learn and grow into the strong werewolf he was meant to be.

No regrets, Addison. Chin up, and get on with it.

Before he mounted the shoveled steps, the front door opened, and Abigail propped a shoulder against the door frame. "Nice day, isn't it?"

"That it is." Her tone was light, which gave him

some hope. But then she had reason for a good mood now that Ryan was safe.

Dressed all in soft pink from the cashmere sweater that emphasized her full breasts to the soft pink suede pants—even to her pink toenails—the woman was a dream Ridge could taste on his tongue. But this tough old wolf wasn't meant to realize his dreams.

The papers in his hand crinkled, reminding him he'd come with a purpose. He thrust them toward her, extending the pen, as well.

She took them without comment and began to sign.

Ridge's heart stopped beating. His mouth went dry. She was signing the papers. Just like that.

No argument.

No discussion.

No nothing.

She handed him the papers and pen.

He reluctantly took them, and when he gave her the wonky eye, she said, "It's what you wanted."

He nodded, not daring to speak because if he did his voice would falter and he'd probably go down on his knees before her to beg she give him one more chance.

"About Ryan," she said.

"We could discuss it over the phone, if you'd prefer."

"Oh. Yes. Sure. I've every intention of letting you see him as much as you like. He hasn't stopped talking about you since we got home."

"Thank you." His heart cracked open and his chest tightened. He wanted more now. He wanted them both. He wanted…things that could never be his. But he wasn't deserving.

"Thank you," she said. "I owe you so much, Ridge. You're a fine man."

Enough with the platitudes. He stepped up and wrapped an arm around Abigail's waist, drawing her body against his. He kissed her even as she began to speak. He wouldn't allow protest. If he had to turn and walk away from the woman he loved, the very least he was owed was this kiss.

She beat a fist against his chest, and it felt as though she were pounding a silver stake through his soul. She didn't want him. She didn't want this kiss.

"Oh, Ridge." And then she was grasping his coat and pulling him to her and kissing him deeply.

And he didn't know how to read this moment, so he stopped trying. Just a kiss. That's all it was.

A goodbye kiss.

He parted from her mouth, memorizing the shape of her lips, small against his, and soft and pink like her sweater. "Yeah, I suppose I should get going."

She traced her lip with a finger and looked aside. "I need time, Ridge."

He nodded, but words abandoned him.

He kissed her cheek and stepped back. He didn't look over his shoulder as he turned to march down the sidewalk to his pickup truck that waited, idling, huffing out clouds of exhaust into the atmosphere.

Abigail sighed into the cold air but nothing about her felt cold as hot tears streamed down her cheeks, slipped into her mouth and down her chin. She'd done the right thing.

Right?

If they were really meant to be they would come together. When the time was right. But when would the time ever be right? Who was she to even know?

All her life any relationship she'd had had been crazy, obsessive and wrong. This one felt different. It had been different. It didn't feel wrong. But she didn't know what right felt like, either.

Hell, it had only been a few days. She couldn't even call it a relationship. That way lay obsession.

The cold air bruised her lips and her arms where Ridge had touched her, icing them more quickly than any other part of her body. A cruel reminder of all she did not deserve.

"Mom?"

She sniffled, realizing Ryan stood behind her in the doorway. With a diesel rumble, the truck pulled away. Ridge did not look toward the house or wave.

"What, sweetie?"

"I can't believe you're letting a guy like that walk out of our lives."

She smirked and wiped the tears from her face. "Me too." She had yet to tell him Ridge was his father. Where to begin with that one?

"Then why?"

"Ryan, sometimes you have to do things you don't want to do. And maybe…" What was she saying? She sounded like a bitter, old woman. Maybe she was. She'd lived so long. Did she even know what was right anymore? "I don't know. I think this is the right thing to do."

"Yeah? I think you're wrong." Ryan touched her hand where tears wet the skin. "I didn't think doing the right thing was supposed to make a person cry. If something is right, shouldn't it make you happy?"

"It should." It did. The past few days she'd spent with Ridge she had been desperate to find Ryan, and yet so calm and yes, even happy because being with Ridge had changed her heart. She had truly become the woman she needed to be, thanks to him. "But it's over now. He's gone."

"You love him."

"Ryan, you don't know—"

"Listen, Mom, I don't know what love is between a guy and a girl, but I know how it feels for a son to be loved by his mother. It feels great. Right here." He pressed a hand over his chest. "I want you to be happy, Mom. I want you to feel this, too."

"I am happy, now that you're home and safe."

"Go after him, Mom," he insisted. "Ridge is a cool guy."

"Oh, Ryan." She closed the door and Ryan raced off into the kitchen.

He had grown up this winter. He'd become a smart, respectful young man. *He'd become a werewolf.* And she had no intention of ever sending him away again. It was time they began living their lives, and stopped running away or hiding.

Oh really? And yet, you let the best thing that ever happened to you walk away.

Yes, but that hadn't been her running away, instead it was— No, the argument was stupid. Ridge Addison really was her best thing.

She wandered into the kitchen. "Ryan, what are you—"

"Mom." He dangled the car keys between them. "Ridge Addison is the best thing that ever happened to the both of us."

He used the same words she'd just been thinking. And Ridge had not been able to comprehend being anyone's best thing. How could she let him continue to think such a thing when it was true?

"The both of us," she whispered, her eyes fixed on the dangling keys. They flashed in the sunlight and she felt as if her son had touched her with a much-needed magic, which blossomed and began to glow in her heart.

"Yes," she said slowly.

Why was she being so selfish? There were two of them in this little family. And as Ryan had said, they'd both been touched by Ridge.

She met her son's blue eyes, speckled with little spots of brown—from his father. His smile grew and he nodded encouragingly toward the keys.

"Yes!" She grabbed the car keys and hooked an arm through Ryan's arm. "Let's go. He's headed toward the county courthouse to file divorce papers."

"Divorce papers?"

"It's a long story, Ryan. I'll explain it all on the way. Hurry!"

They lost the black pickup truck that should have been easy to follow because it was so big and audacious. Ryan directed Abigail right down a city street lined with light poles painted an old-fashioned red.

She'd spent the past ten minutes rambling through the whole story, that fateful night in Las Vegas, the marriage by Elvis and the reasons she never believed Ridge could be his father. So Ryan really had been born late. Better late than never was so good.

"Can you forgive me?" she asked, spinning the steering wheel and taking a right. "I never told you because I wasn't sure."

"I kinda figured it out already. I look a little like him, don't you think?"

"You do. You have his strong nose and you'll grow tall and powerful like he is. But you have more hair."

He chuckled. "But I had no idea you two were married. And by Elvis? That's so cool."

"Yes, well, it won't be cool for much longer."

"Then drive faster, Mom. There! That's the place!"

She pulled into a parking lot across the street from the county courthouse and scanned it for the big black truck.

"Out front!" Ryan pointed out Ridge's truck, parked in front of the building. "Go! I'll wait outside. Run, Mom!"

Leaning over to kiss Ryan on the head, she hugged him. "I love you, and your father."

"Same from me, Mom. Go!"

She dashed off across the street and ran up the steps and right past the reception desk.

"Wait! You need to sign in!" cried the receptionist.

Abigail ran to the desk and grabbed the pen the woman handed her. The receptionist tapped a page in an open register with the tip of her bright red fingernail.

"Did you see a big lug of a guy with short hair and an angry scowl come in?"

The woman's extremely tweezed brow quirked. "Kind of sexy fierce?"

"That would be him."

"A few minutes ago. And let me tell you, that was the finest look I've had in days."

"Where did he go?" She scribbled her name on the register, but her fingers shook.

"To the legal office down the hall, but you can't go in there. He has an appointment. You do not."

"It's okay." She scampered down the hallway. "This is an emergency!"

Abigail threw open the door to the office, which was actually a small legal room with rows of people sitting in chairs, and another row of standing people queued up to a registrar's desk.

Ridge stood at the front of the line, talking to a woman wearing black-rimmed glasses behind the desk. He handed her some papers.

"No!"

The broad-shouldered werewolf turned and gaped at her—as did the entire room. Abigail pushed aside the people standing in line to make her way to the startled wolf.

"You can't do this," she said to the woman behind the desk.

"Abigail, what are you doing here?" Ridge asked her.

"Who are you?" the woman asked, her high-magnification lenses enlarging her eyes as she stamped the papers under her hands.

"Are those the divorce papers?" Abigail asked Ridge. "Tell me they're not the divorce papers."

"Signed, sealed and delivered," he said. "For good or for ill. Much as I would have preferred it remain good. Why are you here? I thought… Well, I thought we were—"

"We're not. We never will be. We can't be. What I mean is, we have to be. We really can be. For us. You. Me. Ryan."

"Ma'am, who are you?" the woman behind the desk insisted.

Abigail eyed the papers, and then an idea stirred a little flame in her thoughts. She never used magic when there were mortal witnesses, but in this instance…

She swept her finger to the right and the electrical cord attached to the automatic stapler sparked. The woman behind the desk jumped and shrieked as the papers she held ignited. Hot, swift flames consumed the papers within five seconds.

Ridge cast a wary eye at her, but she sensed the levity tickling his mouth. She threaded her arm through his, and leaned over the desk toward the woman. "You want to know who I am? I'm his wife."

The crowd behind them tittered, and she realized they had an audience.

Ignoring everything but her heart, Abigail looked into Ridge's soft brown eyes. "That is, if he'll have me."

"You mean it? You want to give us a try?"

"Us includes Ryan," she noted. "Is that something you're willing to try?"

"Try? You don't have to ask, Abigail." Ridge slipped his hands through her hair and tilted her head to kiss her.

The crowd began to cheer. Abigail wrapped her arms around her husband's neck and he lifted her from the ground to make their connection deeper, lasting and loving.

He looked aside to the secretary. "Are those papers completely burned?"

"They're ash. I'm so sorry. We must have had an electrical malfunction. I'll get you some new ones to fill out."

"Nope. Not interested. Me and the wife have a family to take care of."

They clasped hands and walked outside. Sitting on the bed of Ridge's truck was Ryan. He saw them standing on the steps, hand in hand, and let out a hoot and gave them a thumbs-up.

"He's a smart kid," Ridge said.

"Just like his father. He's going to be a handful too, like his father."

"I'll teach him to be a man, Abigail."

"I know you will. He won't have a better role model than you."

"Thank you for letting this happen. Does this mean you'll be my wife and we can do the family thing, and you'll move in with me?"

"Hell, yes. But I want a real wedding first. Nothing fancy, just some flowers and—"

"And a ring. Girl's gotta have a ring."

"And about your werewolf…"

"What about it?"

"Don't you need to bond with your wife, or something like that?"

"I do. You know what that involves. Knowing that, do you still want to be my wife?"

"Bring on your werewolf, lover boy."

Epilogue

Ryan insisted on finishing out the school year in Switzerland, much to both Ridge and Abigail's disappointment. He had friends there, and much as Ryan was eager to move back to Minnesota and spend time with his new family, he had wanted a chance to say goodbye to his friends. And he'd winked as he'd implied leaving his parents alone for a while might be okay with them.

Indeed, the boy had grown up.

Spring designed the full moon in gorgeous silver against a pale midnight sky. May was unseasonably warm, and Abigail didn't have to tug a sweater over her arms as she walked out back behind the compound.

She liked living in the compound. There were three other pack members living there now, including Dean Maverick and his wife, Sunday, who had moved in last month. The familiar was a bit of a tomboy—she'd fixed

Ridge's truck after the accident—yet when Abigail suggested they drive into the city to shop at Macy's, Sunday had eagerly agreed, mentioning shoes and silk scarves in one excited burst.

Abigail and Ridge had used this time with Ryan away to reignite the flame that had never died down, and it had only grown brighter and stronger each day. The Council was aware they were married, and made no comment, but she felt their approval. It was always a good thing when those from the paranormal nations married into different breeds, for acceptance was never a bad thing.

She was the werewolf's wife. And she loved it. She loved him, every part of him, both wild and reserved.

And tonight, she intended to welcome his werewolf into her arms. She'd seen Ridge in his werewolf shape many times, and each time, though she knew his human mind shared space with his animal mind, he knew and respected her as no other being in this world had or would.

The grass was soggy from rain earlier in the day. She'd decided to pad out through the forest barefoot because it felt great to squish nature under her toes and let her hair down and surrender to it all. Ridge did not mind her penchant for skyclad while vacuuming one bit.

Witches were a part of nature; their magic relied heavily on the seasons, the earth elements and the tides of the moon. She'd let that close connection to nature slip away over the decades, and Ridge had brought her back with a new respect for all things wild and free. They couldn't be more compatible.

The place she sought was a quiet cove set hundreds

of yards into the birch forest Ridge had cleared of dead-wood over the winter. She climbed over a rocky out-crop, and the glint of flame caught her eye. Candles?

Ahead sat the cove, which was covered in moss. To-night, the rocks and ground glittered with candlelight as if a faerie fete. Ridge had lit dozens of candles.

"Romantic lug," she muttered, and quickened her steps.

Blankets lay on the ground before a massive old oak they often sat beneath holding hands. Sometimes they more than held hands. Most of the time naked, yes, even in the winter. This was their lover's retreat away from the world. It was protected by a spell she had placed in a fifty-yard perimeter. Others who wandered into the woods would be diverted without knowing they had been.

She stepped onto the blanket and heard a branch snap.

Tilting her head, she closed her eyes to listen. Soft breathy huffs accompanied the sure footsteps of her husband. He walked up behind her. She stroked her fingers across the fur on his arm, drawing them to his paw.

The werewolf pressed his tall length along her back. Hot breaths panted against her neck. His fur was so soft. She tangled her fingers into it and clung. A talon tickled down her back, cutting open her dress until she felt his soft fur against her bare back and thighs.

He would take her in his werewolf form, and they would bond for the rest of their lives. And with luck, maybe tonight she would conceive his second child. She wanted to have half a dozen children with her husband;

their own pack. The witch and the werewolf belonged together.

"I love you," whispered the werewolf's wife.

* * * * *

PARANORMAL

Dark and sensual paranormal romance stories
that stretch the boundaries of conflict and desire, life and death.

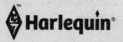

Harlequin®

nocturne™

COMING NEXT MONTH
AVAILABLE APRIL 24, 2012

#135 A WOLF'S HEART
Vivi Anna

#136 THE WITCH THIEF
Lori Devoti

HNCNM0412

REQUEST YOUR FREE BOOKS!

2 FREE NOVELS FROM THE PARANORMAL ROMANCE COLLECTION PLUS 2 FREE GIFTS!

YES! Please send me 2 FREE novels from the Paranormal Romance Collection and my 2 FREE gifts (gifts are worth about $10). After receiving them, if I don't wish to receive any more books, I can return the shipping statement marked "cancel." If I don't cancel, I will receive 4 brand-new novels every month and be billed just $21.42 in the U.S. or $23.46 in Canada. That's a saving of at least 21% off the cover price of all 4 books. It's quite a bargain! Shipping and handling is just 50¢ per book in the U.S. and 75¢ per book in Canada.* I understand that accepting the 2 free books and gifts places me under no obligation to buy anything. I can always return a shipment and cancel at any time. Even if I never buy another book, the two free books and gifts are mine to keep forever.

237/337 HDN FEL2

Name _____ (PLEASE PRINT)

Address _____ Apt. #

City _____ State/Prov. _____ Zip/Postal Code

Signature (if under 18, a parent or guardian must sign)

Mail to the **Reader Service:**
IN U.S.A.: P.O. Box 1867, Buffalo, NY 14240-1867
IN CANADA: P.O. Box 609, Fort Erie, Ontario L2A 5X3

Not valid for current subscribers to the Paranormal Romance Collection or Harlequin® Nocturne™ books.

Want to try two free books from another line?
Call 1-800-873-8635 or visit www.ReaderService.com.

* Terms and prices subject to change without notice. Prices do not include applicable taxes. Sales tax applicable in N.Y. Canadian residents will be charged applicable taxes. Offer not valid in Quebec. This offer is limited to one order per household. All orders subject to credit approval. Credit or debit balances in a customer's account(s) may be offset by any other outstanding balance owed by or to the customer. Please allow 4 to 6 weeks for delivery. Offer available while quantities last.

Your Privacy—The Reader Service is committed to protecting your privacy. Our Privacy Policy is available online at www.ReaderService.com or upon request from the Reader Service.

We make a portion of our mailing list available to reputable third parties that offer products we believe may interest you. If you prefer that we not exchange your name with third parties, or if you wish to clarify or modify your communication preferences, please visit us at www.ReaderService.com/consumerchoice or write to us at Reader Service Preference Service, P.O. Box 9062, Buffalo, NY 14269. Include your complete name and address.

PARA11

*Colby Investigator Lyle McCaleb is on the case.
But can he protect Sadie Gilmore from her haunting past?*

*Harlequin Intrigue® presents a new installment
in Debra Webb's miniseries,* COLBY, TX.

Enjoy a sneak peek of COLBY LAW.

With the shotgun hanging at her side, she made it as far as
the porch steps, when the driver's side door opened. Sadie
knew the deputies in Coryell County. Her visitor wasn't any
of them. A boot hit the ground, stirring the dust. Something deep inside her braced for a new kind of trouble.
As the driver emerged, Sadie's gaze moved upward, over
the gleaming black door and the tinted window to a black
Stetson and dark sunglasses. She couldn't quite make out
the details of the man's face but some extra sense that had
nothing to do with what she could see set her on edge.

Another boot hit the ground and the door closed. Her
visual inspection swept over long legs cinched in comfort-
ably worn denim, a lean waist and broad shoulders testing
the seams of a shirt that hadn't come off the rack at any
store where she shopped, finally zeroing in on the man's
face just as he removed the dark glasses.

The weapon almost slipped from her grasp. Her heart
bucked hard twice, then skidded to a near halt.

Lyle McCaleb.

"What the…devil?" whispered past her lips.

Unable to move a muscle, she watched in morbid fasci-
nation as he hooked the sunglasses on to his hip pocket and
strode toward the house—toward her. Sadie wouldn't have
been able to summon a warning that he was trespassing had
her life depended on it.

HIEXP0512

Lyle glanced at the shotgun as he reached up and removed his hat. "Expecting company?"

As if her heart had suddenly started to pump once more, kicking her brain into gear, fury blasted through her frozen muscles. "What do you want, Lyle McCaleb?"

"Seeing as you didn't know I was coming, that couldn't be for me." He gave a nod toward her shotgun.

This could not be happening. Seven years he'd been gone. This was…this was… "I have nothing to say to you." She turned her back to him and walked away. Who did he think he was, showing up here like this after all this time? It was crazy. He was crazy!

"I know I'm the last person on this earth you want to see."

Her feet stopped when she wanted to keep going. To get inside the house and slam the door and dead bolt it.

"We need to talk."

The stakes are high as Lyle fights for the woman he loves. But can he solve the case in time to save an innocent life?

*Find out in COLBY LAW
Available May 2012 from Harlequin Intrigue®
wherever books are sold.*

Harlequin® *Desire*

ALWAYS POWERFUL, PASSIONATE AND PROVOCATIVE.

ALL IT TAKES IS ONE PASSIONATE NIGHT....

NEW YORK TIMES **AND** *USA TODAY*
BESTSELLING AUTHOR

MAYA BANKS

CONCLUDES HER IRRESISTIBLE MINISERIES

PREGNANCY & PASSION

Pippa Laingley has one man on her mind: hard-driving Cameron Hollingsworth. So when Cam proposes one commitment-free night of passion, Pippa jumps at the chance. But an unexpected pregnancy turns no-strings-attached into a tangled web of emotion. Will Cam feel trapped into reliving the painful losses of his past or will irrepressible Pippa break down the walls around his heart and lay claim to him…once and for all?

UNDONE BY HER TENDER TOUCH

Find out what the heart wants this May!

HD73168

Royalty has never been so scandalous!

When Crown Prince Alessandro of Santina proposes
to paparazzi favorite Allegra Jackson it promises
to be *the* social event of the decade!

Harlequin Presents® invites you to step into the decadent
playground of the world's rich and famous and rub shoulders
with royalty, sheikhs and glamorous socialites.

**Collect all 8 passionate tales written by *USA TODAY*
bestselling authors, beginning May 2012!**